Life in Continuous Present

A Novel

~∞~

ISBN: 978- 1514162446

To my parents, for always believing in me.
To Judy, for introducing me to Emily.
To Wilbur, for sharing Manchester with me.
and
To Ralph, without whom I could never have written
a single word.

Thank you.

A book is made from a tree. It is an assemblage of flat, flexible parts imprinted with dark pigmented squiggles. One glance at it and you hear the voice of another person, perhaps someone dead for thousands of years. Across the millennia, the author is speaking, clearly and silently, inside your head, directly to you. Writing is perhaps the greatest of human inventions, binding together people, citizens of distant epochs, who never knew one another. Books break the shackles of time — proof that humans can work magic.

~ Carl Sagan

It's like everyone tells a story about themselves inside their own head. Always. All the time. That story makes you what you are. We build ourselves out of that story.

~ Patrick Rothfuss

Prologue

~∞~

Life-changing moments are seldom revealed in advance—they are understood only as we view our lives from some "end." You don't wake up one morning, walk down the same-old street, then without thought turn a brand-new corner, without something, some little thing—or a series of little things—

leading you to *that* morning...

that walk...

that corner.

It's those little things, piling up grain by grain like sand, until one day the direction of your life, like the course of a river, is changed forever.

I know, because it happened to me.

When I was a child, my mother used to tell me a story, again and again, describing the chain of events leading to the day she first met my dad. One late September afternoon—after both had been students on the same college campus for two years—they sat next to each other in a classroom, and were nearly inseparable from that moment on. But before their meeting could happen, my Iowa-born father and Connecticut-raised mother had to move thousands of miles across the country to Washington State. My mother broke up with her then-fiancé and made a last-minute decision which landed her at a community college where she took a 19th century British literature class, rather than planning her wedding. She enjoyed it so much she later decided to transfer to the University of Washington, in hopes of becoming a high school English teacher someday. My father, likewise, chose a class in Shakespearean Tragedies rather than the American Lit he preferred, simply because the class was full and he needed to fill a humanities requirement. If all those little things had not happened, they would likely never have met. Their story would not exist.

And neither would I.

Whenever I had a decision to make, I would remember her story. I've thought of it every time I came to a crossroads in my life. Moments matter, and the ones we are least aware of can often matter the most. Those unconscious moments are the building blocks of our lives—and our stories.

My story.

In many ways, I believe this story has been waiting for me all my life, but I am certain its origins lay well before the day I discovered a dusty trunk in the corner of Uncle Dean's attic. It may have been born the day I got a call from my accountant about a buyer for the farm or when my agent called for an update on the book I'd promised to write, or even when my uncle left his old Iowa farmhouse to me. It might have been conceived the day I claimed my mother's old steamer trunk from the rafters of my grandparent's garage, hoping to discover some great treasure inside—yet finding it empty of all save the musty tang of memory which left me with a longing to recover a past I had never actually lived. It may have even found its genesis the day the daughter of a 19th century farmer placed her mother's diary in a wooden trunk shoved into the deepest recesses of what would one day, not too many years later, become my uncle's attic.

A hundred little moments, like grains of sand, piled up.

They all led to *that* trunk...

that diary...

and the book in *your* hands today.

If you're always looking back at what you've lost, you'll never discover the treasure that lies just up ahead.

~ J.E.B. Spredemann

Chapter One

~∞~

In a way, I recognized it even before I saw it—as if time somehow paused in its passage. Past, present and future warped into a single strand, its ephemeral fibers shivering down my spine.

Releasing its bonds with hesitant fingers, I lifted the lid. Inside lay a muddle of loose papers, envelopes bound with ribbon, and several timeworn volumes. Almost without thinking, I reached for one, removed it from its shelter, and pressed open its yellowed pages. Written in a distinctive feminine hand, it began with a date—March 29, 1858.

My breath caught in my throat.

Setting the first aside, I took up another of the books, then another. Dates begin to diverge: August, 1861. January, 1882. May, 1868. Despite the disparity in years the handwriting appeared much the same.

1858... more than a century before I was born.

Regardless of its absurdity, a single thought crossed my mind—

You've been waiting ... all this time.

***

June 20th - *One small step...*

In spite of the heat shimmering outside the tiny aircraft window, I couldn't help but feel a little like Neil Armstrong on his descent toward the lunar surface. Circling Des Moines and contemplating the I-80 below—a freeway spanning the state of Iowa from the Missouri to Mississippi Rivers—we cruised over countryside so flat you could see for miles in every direction. Its contrast with the mountain-ringed Puget Sound view of my Seattle home could not have been greater.

Yet, alien though it might seem, the landscape around me—like the face of the moon—was nothing if not spectacular.

Less than an hour later, I had collected my luggage from the carousel, picked up my summer-leased car, and headed due east down the same freeway I scanned not long before. With the fiddle of "Boot Scootin' Boogie" wrestling road noise for my attention, I slid my gaze across the sun-washed farmland lining the highway and pushed my sunglasses higher on my nose. Several years before, I had visited Ireland on my way home from a writer's conference in London, convinced there was never a landscape so luxurious. The scene surrounding me now, sprinkled with farms and carpeted by cornfields, paraded past me like a fresh and dazzling younger sister to Ireland's lush primordial prospect.

My father often told me stories about Iowa, the flat green land of his childhood home. A family farm with acres of corn so tall you could lose yourself in it. He and my Uncle Dean spent late summer afternoons playing hide & seek in the fields, one trying to find the other with no hint of their whereabouts save their shrieks of childish laughter amidst rustling cornstalks. Later their summers filled with farm chores—making hay and stacking the bales in the barn before jumping from the overhead beams into the deep piles of straw yet unbundled, over and over until their mother would call them in for supper. Set alight with his tales of fireflies—lightning bugs, he called them—I listened in awe as Dad described their dance like drunken fairies flickering across the lawn as he tried to catch them up in jars. To me, the farm sounded idyllic. It was my favorite place to visit—at least until Mom died.

Mom...

Stopped at a railroad crossing on southbound Highway 6, I waited as a freight train hurtled past, blasting its horn. Memories of road trips rose with the sound—my little sister Charlie and I counting the cars as they hurried by, while our baby brother Will slumped in his car seat fast asleep. In an attempt at keeping hot and sweaty little girls occupied, Mom made a game of guessing which states the train might pass through before arriving at its destination while we shouted out their capitals. Dad, antsy to get moving, would grouse, "This one is so long I'll bet it's in two cities at once."

Even as a child I adored trains, caught up in a romantic longing to one day traverse the country on one. I imagined the thrill of watching prairies fly past my window as I sat curled up in a private compartment, cheek pressed against the glass, visualizing a grand adventure. But two and a half years ago, the crash of a commuter train with my husband Jack aboard, wrenched it all away from me. My life-long dream warped into a nightmare of loss from which I'd yet to fully awaken.

My grief lingered in a more tangible form, as well—I had lost my ability to write. Since Jack's death, I felt incapable of committing to paper anything more complex than a grocery list. As someone who always sheltered my identity in writing, there could be little more shattering. And in spite of my plans for starting a new book this summer, I hadn't an inkling how to even begin.

At the direction of the digital voice of the GPS, I turned off the highway down a dirt road, driving due west toward the gingered sun now suspended above the tree line. Inching along to avoid kicking up too much dust, I squinted at house numbers in an effort to find the B&B I booked, wondering how much farther I had to go down this long, straight-as-an-arrow lane. As I was starting to wonder whether I'd been led astray by a machine, she announced "arriving at destination—on left." About thirty feet ahead, I spied the farmhouse from the website—as well as a plain black buggy, its two-horse team clip-clopping in my direction. A grin spread across my face.

My Grampy had been chockfull of stories about his Amish neighbors around Manchester who still lived as if the Industrial Revolution never happened, farming in little pockets across the state, and driving their black, horse-drawn buggies down the road alongside automobiles and tractors. On Sunday morning they'd dress in their best and drive to the home of one of their neighbors, hold their church meetings, share a community meal, and head back home as the sun set--only to repeat it again the next week.

"They were good farmers," Grampy told me. "And good neighbors—always ready to lend a hand when needed." I hoped for a chance to meet some of them here in Kalona.

For the moment, though, all I wanted was a hot bath and a soft bed.

***

After calling my daughters—Daisy, doing a summer internship at a New York publishing house; and Alice, freshly settled in Canberra for a semester study abroad in Australia—to assure them of my safe arrival, I headed outside to stretch my legs and take a look around. The last light of the day was fading fast as I strolled the dirt road and crossed the bridge straddling a creek which curled around the house. A cacophony of croaks and chirps circulated amidst the laughter of my host's children as they chased fireflies with open jars. I stopped for a moment, an overwhelming sense of déjà vu washing over me...

Charlie and I huddle over a washed-out mayonnaise jar with a hole-punched lid, mesmerized by the tiny fairy light now pirouetting inside, watching in wonder as the night around us comes alive with a myriad more...

Alerted by the crunch of gravel behind me, I turned and faced my shadow. As if he'd been dropped into the road by a tornado, a scruffy little cairn terrier—the mirror image of Oz' Toto—padded up beside me, his button-black eyes intent and curious about the stranger trundling through his territory.

"Well, hello there fella! Where did you come from?" A giggle bubbled my throat as I leaned down and scratched him behind the ears. Looking him square in the eye, I couldn't help but ask, "Hey, did you know you're not in Kansas anymore?"

With my Gramma Zizzie, I'd reveled in Baum's description of Toto as "a little black dog, with long, silky hair and small black eyes that twinkled merrily on either side of his funny, wee nose." Months later, seeing 'The Wizard of Oz' for the first time, I found myself disappointed when the movie's Toto looked so unlike his literary counterpart.

The next afternoon, I wrote my first story—all about the Scarecrow dyeing Toto's hair so the wicked witch wouldn't recognize him. I recall little else about the tale, however, I do remember Toto was not happy with the results. It had been such fun watching the scene play out inside my head and writing it down to read to my sister. From the moment I saw the smile on her face, knowing she could see what I saw, I was determined to become a writer.

With one last ruffle of the pup's wiry coat, I stood and asked, "So, little guy, did you get a bad dye job, too?"

Since I was little, I've habitually lived in my head, imagining interactions and conversations with the people I met in books. ("She's talking to herself again," Charlie would all-too-often whine). But the significance of those spoken words was never clearer to me than through my Zizzie's example. She read to us regularly, her lighthearted renditions bringing stories to life, filling my mind with images which kept me awake for hours afterward. I would envision going to the ball with Cinderella, imagine pushing through rows of coats in the wardrobe with Lucy Pevensie—or even conjuring up ways to explain away the wrong color dog.

In writing my own stories, those imaginings continued, but now with the characters I created. Sometimes I argued with them over the things they said or did—things I never expected, in spite of the fact I was the one telling the story. It might have been silly, but the cast and crew of my imagination seemed so alive—even if only in my thoughts.

Yet when Jack died, my muses fell silent. There were no more conversations, no arguments. What replaced them were worries. Fear over my daughters' futures. Nameless anxieties which haunted my

13

nights and undermined my best intentions. Making this trip across the country was the gutsiest thing I'd done in over two years.

I'd traveled to Iowa for two reasons: to see the farm again, and to begin a new book. Somehow I knew, even then, the first was the key to the second.

***

Between the shift in time zones and my usual anxiety in unfamiliar surroundings, I woke for the day well before I wished to. From the window, I could see the rapidly lightening sky and decided I might as well greet the day face-to-face. I threw on some shorts, snatched up a notebook, and tiptoed down a staircase lined with cross-stitched samplers and out into the first breath of a brand-new day.

If I was going to write this summer, journaling seemed a good way to start. Tucking sleep-crumpled hair behind my ears, I picked up the pen, and—watching and listening intently—said a little prayer the words would come.

June 21st- *Everything is still—just a few tiny breaths of air stirring the leaves above my head. They quiver and then quiet, like a baby beginning to wake. I wonder—does the breeze always arrive with the dawn, or is it here just for today? The sound so familiar—like uncooked pasta shells sheeting into a bowl... Not exactly poetic. Still, I am writing. A week ago I wouldn't have thought it possible...*

Sitting beneath the trees until the sun was fully risen, I scribbled down every word bubbling through my thoughts. Little of what ended up on the page could be called prose, but I had actually written something.

I knew this trip would be good for me.

***

For the rest of the day, I played tourist around Kalona. Driving into the heart of the town was almost like traveling back in time. The area itself was a peculiar mix of old and new. Sparkling new sidewalks—inset with colored-concrete quilt-like designs—vied with storefronts that screamed vintage 1940s, yet were bordered by homes

14

built near the turn of the last century. Kalona was nothing if not quaint, but surely its greatest appeal was the Amish presence.

I paused several times, watching Amish families circulate amongst tourists and townspeople. Children walking single-file like ducklings following Mother—who dutifully shadowed Father. Wives, their little white prayer caps perched atop their heads, shopped at the bakery, and prayed over meals in the diner. Buggies drove the main streets, horses tethered beside parked cars.

I spoke with an Amish woman who greeted me with a smile before pointing out the crumbling chimney of the building across the street. She wondered if it might need rebuilding after being struck by lightning a few days earlier. Sharing her concerns in that brief moment allowed me to observe her closely and consider her life. In many ways, the Amish held themselves apart from the world, but they were still quick to offer a smile and "good day" as they passed. I saw such a sense of serenity on the face of my newfound acquaintance and admitted to a bit of envy—though I wasn't sure how I would handle her lack of twenty-first century technology. She, however, seemed to be doing fine without it. What I saw as her desire to linger within the security of a bygone era somehow echoed my own.

Once I'd exhausted the supply of shops in town, I drove out to *The Cheese Factory* to sample some of their celebrated curds and ponder the purchase of a handmade quilt.

After months spent sharing the splendors of Shakespearean prose with cynical high school students, I felt more at peace than I had in a long time.

On the drive back to the B&B, I toyed with the idea of making my next book about the Amish. Was there perhaps some heroic woman who assisted slaves during the Civil War, or offered some other daring story to tell? A shopkeeper spun a quite a resourceful yarn for me about quilt patterns directing escapees along the underground railroad—assuring me of its veracity in spite of the fact there were no...facts.

"Is that true?" I asked. "I've never heard anything like that before."

With a conspiratorial smile, she leaned toward me whispering, "Well, there's no proof, if that's what you mean. But there are stories, you know—and those always come from somewhere...don't they?"

Her expression was so earnest, I didn't dare laugh—though I was tempted at first. I understood, though, about searching for direction. For safety. In some ways that was why I came back to Iowa. From the moment I heard about a possible buyer for the farm, I felt compelled to return. To see it again—and remember. Even the buggy I passed as I arrived felt like a sign.

Maybe there was something for me to discover here.

Memory is a living thing—it too is in transit. But during its moment all that is remembered joins, and lives—the old and the young, the past and the present, the living and the dead.

~Eudora Welty

Chapter Two
~∞~

June 22nd- *I can't wait to tell Amy how wrong she was. I'm sure I'll be able to work here...*

"Iowa in the summer? Liz, are you sure? It's hot and humid, not to mention tornados—and the bugs! What about all the bugs?"

Amy, my literary agent, called a few weeks ago asking about my progress on a new book. Before I knew quite what came over me, I told her I was headed to my uncle's farm as soon as school was out for the summer—all with a plan to start writing.

"The farm will be a perfect place to write without distraction."

"What distractions? You don't have any distractions now!" She fell silent for a moment, but her disapproval radiated through the phone. "And what on earth will you do there? Iowa is nothing but corn and cattle."

"But that's why it's so perfect," I said, surging ahead before she came up with any other reasons why Iowa was a bad idea.

"I haven't been there since I was nine, so it's practically an unknown. The trip will also give me a chance to reconnect with half my heritage—my dad was born there, you know. So was his dad. Maybe I can find a story about some amazing woman who pioneered the Oregon Trail, or something...something I can base the book on. I've never written an American story before..."

But as I spoke, my heart sank. I could tell she wasn't keen on the idea. Kylie, the publisher's rep, mentioned more than once that Avalon hoped for another book like my last—*The White Heart of the*

17

Rose—based on the life of Elizabeth of York, wife of King Henry VII. British historical fiction always sold like hotcakes, so Avalon was not likely to be happy with something else.

Particularly a story I haven't even started yet...

***

By ten a.m., I was on the last leg of my journey to Manchester. Unlike the brilliant colors of yesterday's dawn, today's sky was veiled in a flutter of clouds, alternately exposing and concealing the blue. I slept through an overnight thunderstorm, but the grass glistened and several large puddles dotted the still-damp road in front of the B&B. Insignificant though it might have been, my pleasure in yesterday's writing still sang in my veins. Headed for the farm I remembered with such joy from my childhood visits, I knew I made the right choice about coming back.

Just north of Cedar Rapids, a scan of my rear view mirror revealed a darkening sky boiling up behind me. A hot wind kicked up and the previous patches of blue began to evaporate, dissolving my earlier optimism with it. In the face of escalating anxiety, I peered at the blackening sky and considered the possibility of tornados, wondering what they looked like before they fell from the sky.

Were there storm warnings in the weather report I'd switched off this morning?

I tried to push away the spiral of negativity that seemed to drop out of nowhere and forced my focus toward a strange thumping noise coming from somewhere underneath my car. Sure, at first, what I heard was tires bumping over sections of concrete roadway, I ignored it—until I realized I was having trouble steering.

I pulled off onto the shoulder, getting as far over as possible, turned on the flashers and shut off the engine. I closed my eyes for a moment and took a deep breath, assuring myself all would be well.

"It's fine Liz. Everything will be just fine."

Yet somehow, the sound of my own voice was less reassuring than usual.

I had my AAA card. There was nothing to worry about—this would all be taken care of with one phone call. Still, I was the one stuck on the side of the freeway just before noon on an increasingly turbulent day.

I got out of the car to assess the situation. Moist and heavy, the wind whipped across my face, my uneasiness rising with every gust. Pushing the negative thoughts aside, I circled the car searching for the source of the noise—a flat rear tire with a large nail visible in the tread. A few drops fell around me, almost sizzling as they hit the pavement. I popped the trunk and rummaged around, only to discover that although there was a spare tire, there was no jack.

No Jack...

Out of nowhere, a sob heaved my throat. Rapidly-multiplying raindrops splashed hard around my feet and a pop of lightning flashed the sky. As the rain began to fall in earnest, the dam holding back all my fears gave way.

I wept. Wildly. It didn't matter that there was no jack in the trunk—I had no idea how to change a tire anyway. What was lacking in that moment was *my* Jack. Not just because he would have handled the whole thing (although he would definitely have been the first to point out I needed to learn how to change my own tires), but because I missed his companionship, his bad jokes...the sound of his voice. There on a freeway in Iowa, I grieved—yet again—the loss of my husband and the life I so carefully built. A life now gone forever.

Somehow, I managed to drag myself back into the car.

While the storm raged outside, inside I sobbed as I hadn't in months—as if the accident which stole Jack away from me was happening all over again. In the origins of my grief, I'd held myself together during the day, allowing myself the luxury of tears only at night, hoping my daughters wouldn't hear. There were occasions though, without warning, when my anguish would crash like surf on the shore. As the months passed, those waves came less often and with less intensity, yet occasionally, the pain would still arise at odd moments and refuse to be denied.

Finally spent, the tempest inside began to calm. I dropped my head to the steering wheel, my hair sheeting around me as if veiling me from the world outside. Drawing shaky breaths in an effort to regain control of ragged emotions, I considered once more the life left in the wake of Jack's death. Once the initial shock passed, I pulled myself together enough to handle the details of our lives—my life—to be a passable mother and to do what needed to be done. But without him, I found myself unable to write. The thing which always brought me so much joy seemed to have left me—forever, I feared—just as he had.

And now, here I was, wailing like an overwrought toddler on the side of an Iowa freeway. The promise I made to write a new book roared from my pocket, and the only writing I'd been able to do in over two years was scribbled in a notebook now resting uneasily in the back seat of the car. I was so encouraged yesterday as a joy of it surged through me. Yet not one day later, I was terrified by the very existence of those pages.

Afraid I'd never write another book, I was also worried even if I somehow did manage to do it, it would be awful. That without Jack's support I'd never be able to stick to the work long enough to accomplish my goal. But I also faced another fear—that I'd be betraying him if I could find a way to write without him. The force of that realization hit me—hard—threatening another round of tears.

"You won't be, you know...betraying me." The voice was soft inside my ear—but it was there.

Jack.

I squeezed my eyes shut, and listened with everything in me. If I didn't move, maybe—for just a little while—I could believe he was actually there.

After a few heartbeats, I heard it again. Jack's voice—raw— filled with the same ache I carried deep inside.

"This kind of life isn't what I wanted for you. Fear of failing. Fear of succeeding. If I were here, I'd..."

"But you're not here, are you?" I interrupted. Drawing a shuddering breath, I asked the question it seemed I'd been asking all my life. "Why did you have to go?"

My question seemed to swell, filling the space around me.

"You know the answer."

I did know—or at least, I thought I did. For over two years it haunted me. Was it my fault jack had been killed on that train? He might not have even been in LA if not for me. If I had gotten a real job, rather than holding tightly to my dream of writing—a dream requiring so much of my time yet offering such capricious rewards—I might have helped more with the family finances. Jack might not be dead if it wasn't for my dream.

Is that true? Or am I indulging a misguided sense of guilt as way to avoid living my life?

A professor of Asian history and culture, Jack was in great demand as a consultant for private corporations and military contractors. With two daughters in college, tuition was a huge expense—even for an occasionally-successful author, and a college professor. The honorarium from the Southern California conference where Jack was speaking when he died would almost cover a semester's tuition for one of the girls, allowing me to stay home and write, thus perpetuating my image as a "professional" writer as opposed to a high school English teacher who wrote historical romance novels in her spare time. He took on the position because he believed in me and my abilities, but occasionally I wondered if my fierce determination to be a "real" writer forced his hand.

But a writer is all I ever wanted to be—crafting living personas from the dusty pages of history and my own vivid imaginings. Decanted into a draft, I fashioned identities for characters who never truly existed outside my own invention. I offered my readers a vision of heroism and strength in women who simply lived their lives as the rest of us wished we could, facing things as they came and trying to make the best of their circumstances. Heroism is often more accidental than anything, Jack reminded me more than once—sometimes it is just being available to do what needs to be done. Although the strength of character I created in my protagonists was lovely, it was all part of an illusion—an identity fashioned with words.

Jack once asked me whether I tried to do the same, using my words—even those spoken by the people in my books—to create an image of myself and my life, showing the world what I wanted them to see. Rewriting history as I thought it should have been, not necessarily as it was.

"But isn't that what writers do?" I asked him. "Don't we create the worlds our characters live in? The worlds we want to live in?"

But it's not just writers. Every day, in every conversation, don't we all create images of ourselves we want the world to see—all through the stories we tell?

So what kind of story am I telling myself now? If it's grounded in guilt, then being unable to live my life is simply the punishment I deserve.

Pulling myself back from the internal interrogation, I could hear the gentle irony in Jack's voice as he spoke again.

"I went because it was time to go."

"That's not what I mean, and you know it." I was a little irritated at the direction this conversation seemed to be taking.

"You want to know why I died? You're asking the wrong guy if you want the answer to that one, love...but *why* isn't really your question, is it?"

He was right. I had screamed those 'whys' into a soundless void so many times before—beginning with my mother's passing over forty years ago, and through so many others I had loved and lost. With Jack's death, 'why' was still a question I had no answer for—at least none which satisfied me. But he was right. I no longer asked why, but how?

How do I move on with my life? How do I act as if your death hasn't changed everything—including my own identity? If I can live without you, what does that say about me—and our relationship?

22

How do I escape my fears?

"You know how," he said. "You start by letting go of them—and me. Don't use me as an excuse anymore. Not for not writing. Not for not living. The only way can you betray me is by refusing to move on."

I took a moment to consider his words, recalling lines Joan Didion penned in *The Year of Magical Thinking*, as she neared the end of her first year as a widow. Lines which tore at my heart when I first read them nearly two years ago—"if we are to continue to live ourselves, we must relinquish the dead, let them go, keep them dead." We must—*I must*—let them go.

Let you go.

She was—*you were*—right, I knew. I had been avoiding my own life. Jack was so much a part of me just continuing to exist without him seemed a betrayal of his importance to my life.

For a split second, I could almost feel his fingers ruffling the hair on the back of my neck, his breath tickling my ear. See his crooked grin. Sighing deeply, I leaned into the rush of memory before the feeling faded. Outside, the wind and rain began to abate. The world around me hushed, giving me the time I needed.

Jack was right. I had been using him as an excuse. Afraid to let go, I simply stood in place—unwilling to move forward with my life.

"Let me go, Lizzie," he said at last. "Pick up your pen. It's time to write for someone else. To find another audience."

I had tried. At Charlie's suggestion, I tried writing about Jack, and our life together. I even scribbled lines of poetry, attempting to give voice to my grief—but I couldn't write a thing worth reading. The harder I tried, the worse it seemed. The words simply refused to come.

"I don't think I can."

"You can, love. I know you can. The story you've been waiting for is just down the road...waiting for you. It's time to go and find it."

It's time.

I sat for a few minutes, eyes still closed, breathing in the stillness. Whether the imaginings of my own mind or not, Jack's words were true. It was time to find my own story. I lifted my head from the steering wheel, peering through foggy windows to see patches of blue starting to burn through the clouds. I rubbed now-sticky tears from my cheeks, blew my nose, and picked up my phone.

It's time.

After speaking with roadside assistance, I was assured help was on the way. The car rental office promised there would be a replacement spare and jack waiting for me—along with their profuse apologies. Within what seemed mere minutes a tow truck arrived, the driver changed the tire quickly and efficiently, and waved me off toward Waterloo, with the directions programmed into my GPS.

I was supposed to be in Manchester by three to pick up the keys.

There is still time.

A story is not like a road to follow ... it's more like a house. You go inside and stay there for a while, wandering back and forth... You can go back again and again, and the house, the story, always contains more than you saw the last time. It also has a sturdy sense of itself of being built out of its own necessity, not just to shelter or beguile you.

~ Alice Munro

Chapter Three

~∞~

June 23ʳᵈ - *How is it possible this house—a place I haven't seen since I was 10 years old—feels so much like home to me? Why does it seem to call my name?*

The farmhouse looked like I remembered it—double hung windows and white clapboard siding. Tall oaks surrounding the house. A widow's walk—"kind of pretentious for an Iowa farmhouse," my mother once said—circled the roofline. Maybe a bit more rundown. Was it my imagination or was the front porch listing a bit?

What did I expect from a house built at least 150 years ago?

Climbing the front steps, I turned on the porch and surveyed the scene around me. All hints of the earlier thunderstorm were gone—there was truly not a cloud in the searing blue sky. Just as I remembered, the fields surrounding the house and barn rippled with the verdant leaves of knee-high corn plants. I could almost hear cattle mooing in the yard, my Grampy and Uncle shouting at them to "git."

I'm not sure how long I stood there, sodden with memory, before the crunch of tires on the gravel roadway caught my attention. A red truck turned down the drive, its gray-haired owner smiling and shielding his eyes with one hand as he called from his open window.

"Hello there. You wouldn't be Dean Platt's niece, would you? I heard you'd be coming sometime soon." His pleasant face and wide-open grin offered a soothing welcome which mirrored the countryside around me.

"I am." I wasn't sure who he was, or how he knew who I was, but he seemed harmless enough. "I'm here for the summer. Getting the place ready to sell, I think."

"Now that's too bad. Platts have owned this place for a long time, ever since..." His voice dropped off, as if far away. "But I'm forgetting my manners. I'm Alex... Alex Hikler. I live just up the road—next farm over."

Approaching the truck, I held out my hand.

"Good to meet you, Alex. I'm Liz Benton."

For a few minutes, he talked about his family and the neighborhood, even sharing a few stories about my dad and uncle. When I mentioned my tentative plans for the summer, he seemed eager to hear more.

"That's right, you're a writer, aren't you? Your uncle was pretty proud of you, you know?" Squinting at me from under his hand, he asked, "Are you planning to write about someone from Iowa this time?"

I told him I was considering a story about the Amish, but didn't have anything definite planned yet.

"Well, we've got plenty of Amish around here. They're good woodworkers. A couple of Amish boys helped me rebuild one of my barns last summer. I've got some great stories, if you're interested..."

I assured Alex I'd love to hear them, and told him to drop by anytime. With a promise to look in on me in a few days, "to see how you're doing," he gave me his phone number, "just in case." Thanking him for his thoughtfulness, I waved as he drove off down the road. I stood a moment, basking in the warm welcome Manchester offered so far. Alex had known my family since childhood, and seemed eager to share what he knew of our history, as well as offering to help me settle in any way he could. I don't think any of my neighbors in Seattle would be so considerate.

In that moment, I decided I liked Iowa.

A lot.

Walking back up to the porch, I fished the key from my pocket and pressed it into the lock, my heart beating wildly with anticipation. I couldn't wait to get inside the house.

I'm not sure what I expected as I walked through the front door, but what faced me were spare furnishings, bare floors and stark white walls. Yes, the layout of the front room was pretty much as I remembered it, but all my Great-Gramma's homey touches—the gleaming wood of her dining table and sideboard, the Victorian-style settee and chairs, and the prized mantle clock passed down from her grandmother—were now replaced by a few pieces of standard rental furniture. It was silly to expect it to look as I remembered, but I couldn't help feeling a little disillusioned.

Setting aside my disappointment for the moment, I took stock of the house. Aside from the furnishings the property manager left for me, the fragrance of still-curing paint filled the air, mingled with the citrusy scent of wood polish and just a hint of bleach. Wood floors, though worn in spots, gleamed in the sunlight pouring through the blinds. It was nearly as warm inside as out, so I opened a few windows to let in some fresh air. With the ceiling fan in the dining room going, I figured it shouldn't take too long to get some air circulating.

I meandered the downstairs rooms, running my hand along the satiny wood of doorframes and mantle before entering the kitchen, a sight as familiar as if I'd just been here yesterday—right down to the dip in the ceiling where it met the upper cabinets. In spite of the popcorn texture applied in the years since, the waviness was still visible. Grampy assured me such sloping ceilings were typical of old houses, particularly after being fitted with new fixtures.

Memory welled as I gazed up...

I am terrified the ceiling will tumble down, but Grampy pulls me close, telling me not to worry. "Old houses were built by hand, my little Lizzie. By hand and by love. New ones are made with power tools."

He smiles, assuring me "the new ones might be straighter, but the love in this old house is too strong to let it fall."

I hadn't understood his words then, but I knew he meant I'd be safe. His love would always protect me. Here within these walls, I could still feel it.

Walking toward the window to distract myself from tears which threatened once again, my gaze was drawn across the driveway to the acres of corn beyond. Before I was born that field had belonged to my great-grandparents, but the land was sold off piece by piece over the years. Now, only the house and barn remained. I struggled to recall my family history, the year when the Platts had first come to Manchester, but I drew a blank. The facts lay buried somewhere in our family genealogy—now in the care of my much-more-orderly little sister. For the first time, though, I longed to know the whole story.

Climbing the switch-back stairs to the second floor, I made a quick tour. Flashes of memory encircled me as I stopped in front of the attic door. Watching Grampy ascend the stairs, Charlie and I listening hard in anticipation as he dragged something across the floor over our heads. Seeing him emerge moments later—to our delight— with a huge wooden doll house he'd made for us over the winter. Some of my favorite memories of the farm involve sweltering summer afternoons spent playing dolls with Charlie right here on the upstairs landing, an electric fan blowing hard in our faces.

Cracking the door was like opening an oven, and I closed it again as quickly as I could. If any of the furnishings I remembered were still here, the attic was where I'd find them. Curious as I was to uncover its treasures, though, the heat flooding down the stairs was overpowering. Any exploration up there would just have to wait for another—hopefully cooler—day.

The bedrooms looked as if not a day had passed—although in memory they were much bigger. The largest room boasted a queen-size bed and a view point past neighboring cornfields, far beyond transecting train tracks and all the way to the highway. A second window faced east, overlooking the large barn behind the house. In the smallest room, where Charlie and I had slept, I spied a bird's nest outside, its twig construction entwined in the ivy growing up the side of the house. I stood for a few moments watching through wavy glass as a mother bird hopped into the nest, carrying a cricket to her babies inside. The window itself must have been original to the house—single paned, wood-framed, the sill low to the floor—and I listened hard, thinking I might just hear the chirrups of baby birds through the pane.

Laughing at my imaginings, I realized I still had groceries in the car, and I was ravenous. Trekking outside to fetch them in, then depositing the bags on the counter, I was thrilled to discover the refrigerator was in sparkling condition. From what I could see, the rest of the appliances seemed functional as well.

Brand-new sheets and towels lay folded on the bed upstairs. Cookware, flatware, and dishes in the cupboards—and hallelujah, even a dishwasher. If the water heater worked, I'd be one happy camper.

I made a mental note to send the property manager flowers in the morning.

***

Early the next morning, a steaming coffee mug in hand, I opened the back door and stepped outside. The day awakened fresh and clear, a tiny breeze whispering through the fields even as it ruffled my hair. Tucking curls behind my ears to keep them out of my eyes, I couldn't help but admire the shimmering leaves in the surrounding stand of oaks. Watching as they seemed to shiver in the draft, I wondered how long they'd stood here.

Had it been these same trees which welcomed my Zizzie when she first came to the farm? A British war bride, she followed Grampy home to Iowa, six months pregnant when she arrived to meet her in-laws for the first time. On the mantle of my Seattle home, I have a black and white photo of her—young and smiling—sitting with Grampy under a tree. The sleeping baby who grew up to become my father lay swaddled in her arms. Three blissful faces dappled in sunlight.

Zizzie was the strongest woman I'd ever known. Facing life with a perpetual twinkle in spite of life's hardships—leaving her home and family on the other side of the ocean, losing her husband far too soon—she moved in to help my father care for my siblings and me when our mother died shortly before my twelfth birthday. Zizzie—like the trees facing wind, storms, and even the annual loss of their life-sustaining leaves—stood strong year after year.

I always wanted to be just like her...

Tugging myself back from the knife-edge of memory, I rounded a corner toward the back of the house. There I found the old water pump, its red paint worn and rusty. With my hand resting on the lever, I could imagine it was just yesterday...

Two little girls, barely more than a year apart—the younger one, blonde; the older, all brunette curls—arguing over who would get to ride the tractor when Daddy and Uncle Dean returned from the feed store.

"It's my turn! You gotta ride yesterday." Charlie glowers at me, arms held tight across her chest. "You always getta ride. It's not fair..."

"Lizzie! Charlie! Can you come here, please? I need your help. It's very important." Zizzie's voice grazes through the middle of our argument, just as I am about to deny Charlie's claim.

"Coming, Zizzie!"

We hurry back toward the house, and I lean over and hiss in Charlie's ear, her wheat-colored hair tickling my nose. "It is too, fair. No one got a ride yesterday—and it's my turn!"

As Charlie begins to wail, Zizzie intervenes, handing us a bucket, and assuring us "those poor thirsty cows by the barn have been waiting all day for a drink."

Though we immediately run for the pump, Charlie and I are still squabbling over who will work the handle and who will hold the bucket.

Our mother watches from the doorway, sheltering her eyes from the bright afternoon sun. Her body is already offering silent clues to the cancer that will steal her away from us before too many more years pass—but I know none of that in this moment. Calling out as we make our way toward the barn, she laughs as she cautions us.

"Be careful, girls! If you don't slow down, you're going to spill it all before you get there."

I can still see her smiling as we begin to measure our way ever so carefully over the gravel path and out to the barn.

With the sloshing bucket gripped tightly between us, we are quickly enfolded in black and white. Holsteins crowd the trough as we heft the bucket to pour in the water. I giggle with Charlie as we gingerly touch wet noses, wrinkling our own over the cows' "earthy" smell.

"Pee-yew! You stink," Charlie shrieks, all the while patting the nearest calf firmly on the head...

My heart squeezed a bit in reminiscence, realizing Zizzie merely invented a chore to pacify two bickering little girls. The house had long had running water and I was pretty sure even then there was a spigot down by the barn. We hadn't needed work so hard to bring water to the cattle—the few buckets we hauled couldn't have made much difference anyway—but it gave us something to do, making us feel a valued part of life on the farm. It was such fun to work the pump and watch the cows drink that we spent nearly every afternoon hauling buckets of water down the same path. At the end of our visit, when we were piling into the car to begin the long drive back home, Charlie sat crying in the backseat, wondering who would take care of the "poor thirsty cows" when we were gone.

I continued my exploration, but there were no longer any cows in the barnyard. Most likely, there hadn't been any since my uncle died. Heaving open the big sliding door, I saw a few hay bales piled deep inside. Stacks of lumber rested on the wall near the back, as if someone paused mid-project, meaning to return to it later. Leaning against the door frame, I closed my eyes and breathed in the smells of the barn—stale air, hot wood, and the honeyed tang of hay.

The familiar trace of ...*home.*

My memories of the farm were few, yet something about being back here brought the past very close. My father and uncle grew up here—my grandfather, too, if I remembered right. Grampy, Zizzie and their sons lived here among "the cows and the corn" on my great-grandparent's farm until a job at the Collins Radio Company called Grampy and his family away to Cedar Rapids in 1960. Three years later, Boeing brought them to Seattle. This final move made possible the auspicious—for my siblings and me, anyway—meeting between my mother and father at the University of Washington in 1967, and my own birth at Swedish Hospital just over two years later.

But there was more history for me here than my father's childhood and the early years of my grandparents' marriage, more even than the few visits I'd made as a child. A larger discourse dwelled within the walls of this house. My great-grandparents—people I barely remembered—lived here, raising their family, their crops, and their cattle. I wanted to know more about them, about this house. Had they, or their parents—or *their* parents, perhaps—been among Iowa's early pioneers, maybe building a sod house on this land before constructing the one where I now stood?

I wished one of them was here with me now—my father, or my grandfather—with ready answers to the questions about what life was like in Iowa a century or more ago. I wondered if there was anything left by one of my ancestors, something that could tell me what I longed to know. There was no longer anyone living who held the answers.

***

Pocketing a hastily-scribbled shopping list, I snatched up car keys and headed out the door. I needed to pick up a few things before I could feel settled in, and now was as good a time as any to go shopping. Yesterday, on my way here from the property manager's office, I passed a coffee shop on Franklin Street. In hopes of finding beans as well as a good cup of coffee, I decided to make *The Coffee Den* my first stop of the day.

As a historical novelist, there is little I like more than spending time sorting through boxes of old letters, diaries, maps, trinkets, and baubles.

~ Sara Sheridan

Chapter Four

~∞~

June 24th - There is something so intriguing about an attic—full of treasures undiscovered. Objects that sit today in the palm of our hands, but link us ever so closely to the past...

With a soy latte in one hand and a bag of whole-wheat bagels in the other, I was headed back to my car when I spotted a furniture store about half a block down on the other side of the street. Within an hour, I'd bought a cushy overstuffed couch and matching chair, and a set of coffee and end tables. I snatched up several lamps, as well, a small kitchen set with a couple of chairs, and even a day bed where Charlie could sleep when she came to visit. I also picked up a few rugs to make the place cozier. I told myself I'd sell the stuff with the house, so I might have bought more than I needed—but I wanted to be comfortable while I was there.

After the salesman assured me the furniture would be delivered by the end of the week, I headed off to find the rest of the items on my list.

By one o'clock, I was back home at the farm.

Thankful it was a bit cooler today, I grabbed a flashlight from the laundry room shelf and headed upstairs to change into the grubbiest clothes I'd brought with me. I could hardly wait to begin my quest. More than any place else on the farm, the attic called to me. If any of the things I remembered had been left behind after Uncle Dean's death, that was where I was going to find them.

With my hand resting on the doorknob, I hesitated—just for a moment. Was it my imagination or did the air seem charged with anticipation, as if someone had been waiting for me to finally open the door? Chuckling at such a ridiculous notion, I shook my head as if it was an etch-a-sketch erasing an image. The only impatient person here was me.

At the top of the steps was a large dimly lit space full of crates and boxes, and a few sheet-covered objects.

Great-gramma's furniture, maybe?

I hoped so, but from this vantage point it appeared to be little more than a whole lot of clutter. My flashlight exposed a view of aging cobwebs spanning corners of the levelled ceiling, and a thick layer of dust covering everything in sight.

Clearly, no one had been up in the attic in a long time. There were no windows, and the air was stifling. One solitary bulb dangled overhead to light the space. A tiny thread of light rimmed what appeared to be a hatch of some kind, up where the ceiling flattened out—likely offering access to the widow's walk circling the roof. I wondered if the door would even open, but if it did I'd have some extra light and fresh air at the same time. I'd only just climbed the stairs, but sweat was already beading my forehead.

Reaching the center of the room, I pulled the string on the light fixture, washing a faint yellow glow across the room. I needed something to clear those cobwebs before I would touch the hatch, let alone spend the time searching out the treasures those boxes might contain. So I headed back down to the kitchen in search of cleaning supplies.

I grabbed the broom and dustpan, some rags and a box of trash bags. Stopping on the upstairs landing, I tied scarf over my head before continuing back up the attic stairs. The last thing I wanted was spiders in my hair.

I really hate spiders.

A short time later, most of the cobwebs dealt with, I was ready to tackle the roof hatch. Dragging over a large wooden crate, I scrabbled to the top, reaching for the handle now right above my head. After positioning the flashlight, I grabbed a rag and scrubbed at the deadbolt, gripped it tightly and pulled. At first it wouldn't budge, then I felt it start to give—just a little. I jimmied it back and forth for a few breathless moments, then felt it let go. I pushed against the door as best I could and after yet another moment of uncertainty, it flew open at last. Sunlight flooded the room and the attic heat rushed to escape its prison. Rising on tiptoe, I could see enough to know the view of the countryside must be amazing. I made a mental note to get the roof checked out—it might be a terrific spot for some nighttime star gazing. In the meantime, though, I had work to do.

Pulling my head—quite literally—back into the game, I clambered down from the crate and turned to the surrounding boxes. There were a few more wooden ones, but most were cardboard containing little more than old clothes and blankets. Others overflowed with children's toys. An old electric train and its track were piled up next to several small boxes of paper-wrapped mercury glass ornaments. Some of the boxes might have been left by tenants who either forgot to check the attic, or just didn't want to make a trip to the dump.

Examining the sight before me, I spotted—leaning against the wall opposite the stairs, tucked behind a few more boxes—an old iron bedstead I was pretty sure came from Uncle Dean's bedroom, a writing desk, and a few much worn, cane-seated chairs looking as if they might have been part of Great-gramma's dining room set. Just what I was hoping for.

Maybe her old mantle clock is up here, too.

After spending several hours burrowing through boxes and trying to create some sort of order out of all the chaos, I was hot, tired and filthy. I'd bagged up a lot of the trash, separated out most of the things worth keeping—or at least worth looking over one more time before making a final decision—shoved all the furniture together closer to the stairs, and swept the floor. The clock I hoped to find was unearthed from the depths of one of the crates and sat atop the writing desk awaiting its return to its former home on the mantle. As soon as I had a few extra hands to help move them I wanted to bring the bed and desk down, too.

There was still plenty left to do, but my body insisted it had done enough for one day. But just as I'd laid down the broom, snatched up the handle of one of the overflowing garbage bags and dragged it toward the stairs, I spied a shadowy object tucked far back into the darkest corner of the attic right behind the chimney at the verge of the roofline—as if it had been placed there on purpose, then purposely forgotten. Only the light reflecting off the now-cleared floor made it possible to see it at all.

How on earth had I missed that?

In spite of my exhaustion, something about this discovery drew me in. Draped with a sheet and covered in soot and dust, the object—whatever it was—looked substantial, standing about three feet high, at least four feet in length and another yard deep across the bottom. I wondered how long it had been hidden away back there, just waiting to be found.

By me?

Smiling a bit at my whimsy, I tested its weight, tugging on a heavy iron ring visible on one end. If I could just get it out into the middle of the room. The shadows back there made it impossible to get a good look. Heavy cobwebs overhead made me nervous, but the broom took care of them in short order. I took a few swipes at the floor around the back of the piece, too, hoping I wouldn't be surprised by a nest of mice entrenched in the corner behind it.

Shouldering it—with more than a few grunts and groans—into a puddle of light on the floor, I finally had it situated so I could look it over. Standing slowly, I brushed off my grimy hands on the seat of my equally grimy jeans, wiping beads of sweat from my forehead and arching my back and shoulders in an attempt to relieve my aching muscles. I couldn't help but chuckle at my earlier enthusiasm and wondered if I would ever remember I'm not twenty-five anymore.

Now that a more thorough investigation was possible, I tugged off the sheet to see what I'd found. It appeared to be a trunk of some sort, but like none I'd ever seen before. Though showing its age around the edges, its finely-grained wood shone with a golden glow. With dovetailed joints and cast iron hinges, it looked more like an enormous desk than a trunk—its hinged front panel resembled the writing shelf on a secretary desk—a bit too low to pull up a chair to, though. There were lightly carved letters on the front that looked as if they might have once been part of a name or address, now too worn to read. The top and front sections were worn along their shared edge as if gnawed by a small animal, the gap allowing a sliver of light through to the inside. Hoping whatever chewed on the wood had departed long ago, I peeked through the hole, hoping for a glimpse of possible treasures within. I could hardly wait to get it opened.

The trunk itself brought back a flood of memory, of youthful dreams of long-forgotten treasure when my fourteen-year-old self rescued Mom's old steamer trunk from a trip to the dump after finding it in Gramma and Grampa Oliver's garage. Although it had been empty rather than filled—as I'd hoped—with the artifacts of some other era, the trunk found a home in the corner of my bedroom, and for the rest of my teen years, held close the relics of my own life. Perhaps because my mother was already lost to me, the trunk's still fusty scent embodied her life—the trace of memories not my own, but which I ached to hold onto nonetheless.

Surely this trunk isn't empty, though. It's just too heavy.

I reached for the latch, surprised to find it unlocked. I worked at the rusty bolt, hearing it drop with a satisfying metallic "thunk," then pulled at the bulky lid with both hands. Rusty hinges seemed reluctant to let go for a breath or two, but cracked open at last releasing a musty tang reminiscent of both the trunk of my youth and the antique shops my mom loved so much. For a moment, tears threatened, but once my curiosity got the better of me I knelt down and peered inside.

Two drawers extended across the top. One opened easily, revealing a few small books, an embroidery hoop with linen stretched across it, and a still-threaded needle tucked into the weave—as if the seamstress laid it aside for just a moment, but never returned. The second drawer was jammed shut. I tugged at it for a moment, but it wouldn't budge. Anxious to search through the rest, I decided I'd attempt to open that drawer later.

Two open sections lay below the drawers. A patchwork quilt with a lattice pattern lay folded atop the right side, stacks of books and a mass of small objects wrapped in yellowing paper filled the other. I didn't know how long these things had been there, but the quilt was in surprisingly good shape—probably due to the multiple mothballs which fell to the floor as I pulled it from the trunk. Running my hand over the aged fabric, I marveled at the pattern and intricate workmanship put into what was likely just a good use for the remnants of someone's clothing. Gently refolding the coverlet before setting it aside, I continued to unearth the trunk's contents one item at a time. A couple of calico dresses, a flower-bedecked hat, and several tiny shirts, all painstakingly folded and tied together with a ribbon. My mind began to race. Who had these things belonged to? The trunk was too old to have belonged to Uncle Dean—and somehow these things didn't look like a man's belongings anyway. Could this trunk have belonged to my great-grandmother—or some other, more distant, relative? Was it possible these baby clothes had been worn by my grandfather?

More quickly now, I gathered everything I'd uncovered so far and set it atop the quilt. A few loose papers covered with spidery writing, a couple of account books filled with algebra problems, a pottery pitcher wrapped in yellowed tissue, several small figurines, photographs, books, and a small, round cut glass bud vase surfaced next—all were set aside. There were wooden tools resembling nothing more than oversized sewing needles; framed needlepoint pictures and bookmarks. Finally, I came to a large paperboard box knotted with twine.

Had I found my treasure at last?

Releasing its bonds with hesitant fingers, I lifted the lid. Inside lay a muddle of loose papers, envelopes bound with ribbon, and several timeworn volumes. Almost without thinking, I reached for one, removed it from its shelter, and pressed open its yellowed pages. Written in a distinctly feminine hand, it began with a date—March 29, 1858.

My heart began to pound.

Laying the first aside, I took up another of the books, then another. Dates begin to diverge: August, 1861. January, 1882. May, 1868. Despite the disparity in dates, the handwriting appeared the more or less the same.

1858... more than a century before I was born.

Regardless of its absurdity, a single thought crossed my mind—

You've been waiting ... all this time.

One by one, I organized the books by date. In various sizes, they covered about thirty years' time, and I was fairly certain they were all written by the same person.

I wanted to look the trunk and its contents over in better light, but it was too heavy to move from the attic without help. For now it would have to wait. I'd call Alex tonight to see if he and one or two of his sons might come over tomorrow to help me wrestle it down the stairs. In the meantime, I gathered up the quilt, the bundles of letters, and all the rest of the items, placing them back into the trunk. Then, gently collecting what I'd decided must be the volumes of a diary, I carried them downstairs.

An hour later, well-fed and freshly showered—my grimy clothes churning in the antiquated washing machine—I flung my exhausted self down on the overstuffed couch, flipping on the lamp so I could examine my treasures. Ten bound volumes lay on the coffee table before me, just waiting for me to open them and begin my investigation. A sense of expectancy tingled through me as I ran my fingers over the books, marveling they had been hidden away up there for so long, but even more amazed I had found them. Having discovered the diary here in this house, the writer must surely be a relative—right?

Already stacked in chronological order, I snatched the first of the series right off the top of the pile. I gingerly cracked the cover and breathed in the musty trace of ancient books, evoking the library in my grandparents' house—books which had been stored in boxes in their basement until they had gained a room of their own when Uncle Dean returned to the Iowa farm right around the time I was born. I grew to love that fusty scent, defining those things I loved best. There was something so settled and comfortable, yet anticipatory about the fragrance of old books—like the promise of discovery in worlds yet unseen. My heart began to beat a swift staccato as I turned to the first page and read:

Diary—which may compose the reminiscences of the life, from day to day, of

Miss Emmie E. Hawley

A.D. 1858

Medina, Lenawee County, Michigan

Monday, 29 March - Today I commence to keep a diary...

Following that somewhat pretentious opening banner, Emmie recorded her days in the usual diarist's vein, listing events ("went to Uncle Benjamin Osborns, make a head dress for Aunt Mary...") and noting the weather ("pleasant only the wind blows, & is cold"). However, nearly three weeks later--she relates an episode that seems entirely different:

20 April, 1858 - Last Christmas & New Years I attended Cotillion parties at Canandaigua with Sylvenus Hamlin. Libbie wants him pretty badly, she can have him if he will marry her. I do not want him for a companion, no! no! not but that I like him. I do very much as a friend...

I had to smile. For nine days Emmie said little outside a recounting of her daily activities and chores, then out of the blue she began to tell a story.

I was enchanted.

For the next few hours, I skimmed through the first volume of the diary, noting the things she thought worthy of discussion, but especially her continued references to Sylvenus and Libbie. Between the threads of that story, she included remarks about other men who either expressed an interest in her ("Horace Jones ask me to attend a party with him. I refuse him again—tis at least the 20th time."), or declared their wish to marry her ("why is it? I ask myself that every young man one meets with must begin to talk of love & marriage first thing"). There were so many. I couldn't help but wonder, what was it about this woman which made her so attractive?

Emmie, just twenty years old, was one busy woman! She made (*and apparently, remade*) clothing for herself and her family, acting as seamstress for the entire neighborhood, as well. She "put up" strawberries, crocheted lace collars for her dresses, crafted hairflowers (*whatever those are*)—and taught school. All this was in addition to her chores around the house, things like baking cakes and pies several times a week and helping her mother in the garden. Emmie wrote poetry, read novels, and elected "Editress" of the local literary society. She complained more than once about the difficulties of poverty, but declared herself unwilling to be a servant to anyone.

A rhythmic thumping from an out-of-balance washer dragged my attention away from the seed of story entrenching deep within me, and returned my thoughts to the present. I set down the diary and walked into the kitchen to adjust the load in the washer. Through the window, I could see the last golden rays of the sun beckoning to me from behind the barn, enticing me to join them. Since my first morning in Iowa, watching the sun set had become the perfect end to the day—something I rarely took time for at home.

Miles of corn in the surrounding fields shushed and whispered in the breeze, rippling beneath illumined clouds—gilt-edged and splashed with fuchsia—reflecting the last light of the day. The barn nearly glowed as dancing trees cast rhythmic shadows across its side. Mostly hidden from sight, birds chirped from within those trees as if singing lullabies to their young, and a few stragglers flopped around the driveway taking dirt baths like drowsy youngsters at the end of the day, bathing under parents' watchful eyes before being bundled off to bed.

I've always loved this hour when it seemed like every creature of the day prepares for sleep just as those of the nocturne awake to perform. Bats would soon begin their summersaulting search for supper, and fireflies to flitter like Woodstock dizzily circling Snoopy's doghouse. Roving gangs of mosquitoes began their nighttime barrage, buzzing past my ears like fighter pilots. Twilight always seemed like a changing of the guard—the sun replaced by the moon and stars. One set of creatures for another. And although one watch stopped, another always began—to reconcile the hours.

If I was patient, I'd see it.

Watching the colors fade into dusk, I considered a change might be beginning for me, too. Jack had always been my sun. Our life together was the only story I knew—at least the only one left to me after so many others ended. Yet without my happily ever after, I had no idea how to write anymore—or even how to live. But that didn't mean there were no more tales to tell.

He promised my story was waiting.

Then... I will wait, too.

After all, although the sun sets, the moon always rises—in its own time.

Writers do not find subjects; subjects find them.
~ Elizabeth Bowen

Chapter Five

~∞~

June 25th- *If life is like a game of hide and seek, I think I was just tagged "it"...*

I awoke energized and eager to get back to exploring the diary—at least until I tried to get out of bed. Every muscle ached, and I had nearly decided I'd stay put for a few more hours when I noticed the time and remembered Alex would be over soon to help me haul the trunk down from the attic.

So much for sleeping in...

I—quite literally—rolled off the bed, groaning as my feet hit the floor. Righting myself and grabbing a robe, I shuffled my way into the kitchen to make coffee. Those yoga classes I'd taken with Alice a few years ago came to mind as I stretched for the mugs in the cupboard. Maybe I should consider taking it up again? Meanwhile, a hot shower would go a long way toward loosening up my stiff muscles.

An hour later, nursing both a second cup of coffee and still-achy shoulder muscles, I headed to the door to answer the bell. Alex and a freckled young man stood on the front porch—right on time, just as he promised.

"Mornin' ma'am! What's this about you findin' a treasure chest in the attic?" Alex chuckled at his own joke, before adding, "I brought these pirates here to help us with it. If it's as heavy as you say, we'll need them."

"Alex, thank you so much! I did manage to shove it over a couple of feet, but I knew I'd never be able to get it down the stairs alone. And please, call me Liz."

"Well Liz, I'd like to introduce you to my boys here." Turning to the young man standing next to him, he said, "This is Matt, my oldest grandson." As a third man—resembling nothing more than an older version of Matt, minus the freckles—walked up to the porch, Alex gestured in his direction and introduced him with, "And this is his daddy. Liz, this is Dan, my oldest boy."

As Dan stepped forward, I held out my hand to greet him, taken aback by his pleasantly weathered face and the brightest blue eyes I had ever seen—and I must admit was knocked a bit breathless. Pulling myself together and hoping I wasn't blushing, I shook hands all around and offered coffee. Alex and Dan were all business at this point, though. "Let's get that trunk moved and then we'll see about the coffee."

Thanking them again for their willingness to help, I led the way as we all trooped up the stairs. At the landing, I pointed to the attic door—although Alex seemed to know already.

With memory shining in his eyes, Alex told me the attic had been among his favorite places as a child.

"I haven't been up here for years. My brother and me...we used to play up here sometimes—mostly on rainy days—with your dad and his brother. We'd bring over our collection of toy soldiers and set up camps all over the attic. Bobby—your dad—and Dean were a few years younger than we were, but we all had fun. This attic was a terrific place to play." He chuckled to himself, remembering. "Your gramma was a real good sport about all the noise we made, too. All that stomping around up there... my momma wouldn't have put up with it"

Intrigued at finding someone who might know something about my family history, I wondered where to start with all my questions. But before I could set them in order, the first burst from my mouth.

"I found an old diary last night. In the trunk. But I have no idea who it might belong to. I don't remember any Hawleys in my family, do you?"

"A diary, huh? Might be interesting to see..."

Alex thought a minute, looked at Dan as if he might have an answer, and then slowly shook his head. "Hawley? Noooo....doesn't sound familiar. Let me think on it a while."

By then, we'd all marched up the attic steps and halted in front of the trunk.

"Wow...I've never seen one like this before. It is big." Dan scanned the trunk then turned back toward the stairs. I could see him mentally measuring the space. Was it even going to fit through the opening?

Alex had also assessed the situation and assured me they'd be able to get it down the stairs intact. "It might take some finagling, but we'll manage. After all, someone got it up here."

I offered to empty it, but after testing the weight between the three of them they insisted it wasn't too heavy, and Alex assured me the contents would be just fine. I climbed back down the stairs, clearing a path so they could set it into place without tripping over anything.

A considerable amount of grunting was heard over the next twenty minutes or so, and more than a few heads were banged against the sloped ceiling. There were also one or two flashes of panic on my part that the trunk would plummet and splinter into bits as they guided it down the tightly turned staircase to the main floor. But the three of them moved carefully, and in the end the trunk rested in the corner of the living room, right next to the window. Watching them set it into place, I was glad the room had already been painted—I certainly didn't want to have to move it again anytime soon. A few touch ups where the trunk had scraped the walls of the stairwell and everything would be good as new.

After setting four tall glasses of ice water on the table, I suggested coffee once more as we stood admiring the trunk—and this time they took me up on the offer. While I gathered mugs, cream and sugar, and arranged the last of the cookies I'd bought in Kalona on a large hand-painted tray I'd found in the attic yesterday, they trooped back up the stairs for the writing desk and chairs. By the time I carried in the loaded coffee tray, they were back in the dining room, mopping sweaty foreheads and gulping glasses of ice water.

Alex, clearly not one for small talk, got right to the point. "So, tell me about this diary you found."

"I was so surprised!" I said. "It was in a box at the bottom of the trunk. Ten volumes, covering about thirty years. But I'm not sure who the writer is...I don't recognize her name."

He thought for a moment. "What was it again?"

"She gives her name on the opening page as Emmie E. Hawley—from Michigan. In the first volume she is almost twenty, and obviously single. I skimmed through it, though, and found later places where she mentions her children so she must have married at some point."

Listening intently, Dan asked, "Did she talk about coming to Manchester, or mention a husband's name?"

Alex looked puzzled, like he was trying to remember a detail he used to know, but which was refusing to be found. "... And there are no Hawleys in your family?"

"No... at least not that I remember." I paused a minute, then asked, "Do you have any idea how long my family has lived here?"

He thought a moment. "I don't. My parents likely would have, but it's too late now to ask them. But don't worry, Liz. It shouldn't be too hard to figure her out. They have all kinds of ways now to help find out about people. Was there a date on the diary?"

I assured him I did, noting the entries seemed to run from 1858-1888. "If I can find a married name," I said, "that might be all I need to figure out whether she has any connection to my family—or even to this house. I paused for a second, thinking. "I suppose the trunk could have belonged to a tenant..."

Dan said he doubted a tenant would have moved such a heavy piece into the attic. "Too much work to haul it up there if it's not your house."

But about my mysterious diarist, he added, "I bet you'll figure her out in the diary itself, or with some help from the folks down at the County Courthouse."

Alex agreed. "If she ever lived here in Delaware County, they can help you find her."

I had to admit they were likely to be right. Once the diary had given me a more definitive name, county records would be a good place to begin my search.

***

The three men left with my promise to share anything I learned about the diarist's identity—vowing they would ask around and do the same—and I set about getting the house ready for tomorrow's furniture delivery. The sheets and towels I'd bought yesterday still needed to be washed before I could put them to use, and I wanted to get the curtains hung in the upstairs bedroom as well. Once all that was accomplished, I planned to sit down with the diary while I waited for the cable guy coming to link me up with the outside world. If I was going to start doing research on the Amish, looking for a possible book subject, it was essential I had an internet connection.

With the rental furniture moved out of the way, and laundry tumbling in the dryer, I sat on the couch to wait. The diary volumes were still stacked in front of me. I planned to skim through them one at a time to find the writer's connection to either Iowa or this house, and possibly a married name I might use to find her in the record books. I had enough research experience to know a woman was rarely discovered in historical records without the name of either a husband or father to identify her—particularly before the twentieth century. So, for the moment, all I was looking for was a name. Anything else could wait.

But what happened was entirely different.

Once I'd opened the first book and begun to read, Emmie's story sucked me right in. I can't say I was carried away by remarkable writing. Much of her prose was commonplace at best. Yet, her voice was so strong it was hard to resist. Her writing presented an image of

48

a romantic and idealistic young girl determined to make something of herself. Her greatest desire was to be a writer and she'd seeded her diary with poems and stories she'd written, as well as ink sketches and even building plans she'd drafted in the margins. She talked about books she read, naming several novels—although I'd heard of none of them. At one point, she even mentioned an opportunity offered her by a merchant in town: a chance to move to New York City and train as an artist with his sponsorship. Her mother nixed the idea immediately, leading Emmie to note with apparent resignation,

"I will stay at home a while yet, though I am sure I will regret it."

She spoke of young men (older ones, too!) who—on nearly every page—professed their undying affection and desire to marry her. Yet she seemed unmoved by it all, declaring time and again she would marry only for love. More than once I laughed out loud, muttering to myself that she must have read just a few too many of those novels. She just had to be making some of this stuff up.

No one is that irresistible.

Yet, at the same time I felt sorry for her. She was confined within a society which demanded things from her she had no desire for and kept her from doing what she wanted. I certainly didn't envy her lack of choice.

The next day, after finishing the first volume, I picked up the second, dated June 1860. I quickly discovered Emmie was still unmarried, but also still talking about various men who begged for her hand. She noted one in particular—in an entry dated June 3rd—who she clearly liked, calling him "a kind, intelligent and virtuous young man," yet she also claimed he possessed a trait she saw as his fatal flaw: "he likes and drinks intoxicating drink." She had written several times in the previous volume about her belief in the Temperance movement, and a man who drank was beyond consideration as potential husband material. She went on to note:

"I have vowed never to marry the best man that lives if he is addicted to strong drink, & with the help of God may I keep that promise."

Emmie was 22 years old in 1860, and from what I knew of the traditions of her day, her "advancing" age would have put her in danger of being considered a spinster if she didn't marry before too much more time passed. However, it was obvious she wasn't willing to settle for just any marriage partner. As long as the choice was hers, she knew what she wanted—and she wanted to marry for love. Emmie wrote about pressures from her family, though—from her mother's comments about her unmarried state, to an uncle who asked her to come and work for his family in November 1860, who "said so much, I cried." Yet just six months later, on June 26, 1861 she wrote she was "at home perhaps for the last time for I am (if no preventing providence) going to start for Iowa...My folks feel bad to have me go."

Now I knew she left Michigan in 1861. So...was this her Uncle's house? Had she married once she'd come out here? Feeling I was at last on the road to finding what I was looking for, I skipped to the end of the volume in my hand and started to work my way backward through it.

I didn't have to read far before I found, in July 1862, a reference to a man named James, along with a veiled hint she would have a new life and a new home as of October 1st. Scrambling for the next volume, I opened it to the date and discovered Emily was married by then, and on that very date she was moving with her new husband, James Gillespie, to her in-laws' home.

Gillespie.

Armed with his name, I—at last—had a way to find her.

A few hours later, laundry folded, cable and internet connected, and dinner in the oven, I opened my laptop and began a search for Emily.

Not knowing where else to start, I thought I'd just google her name and see if anything turned up. But aside from a half dozen

Emily Gillespies I'd found living in Florida or on Facebook, there was nothing of value—until I scrolled to the bottom of the page. There, on a website for Iowa cemeteries, I found a link, leading to an Emily Gillespie in a list of people buried in the Oakland Cemetery in Manchester, all with names beginning with "G."

My heart began to race as I clicked on the link and scrolled down the list: Gale...Garlick...Gibbons...Gifford... until I found Gillespies about halfway down the page. There were six listed—one of whom was Emily E., recognized as "wife of James." Her birth was logged as 1838—the same year as the Emily of the diary—and the date of her death as March 24, 1888. Picking up the final volume of the diary to corroborate whether I'd found the "right" Emily Gillespie, I opened to the last pages, and discovered an entry written in what appeared to be a shaky hand.

11 March, 1888- ...It seems sometimes unbearable to endure such pain, that my work is nearly done, yet there is a presentiment to stay yet longer.

Beneath this entry was another—clearly transcribed by someone else—in a younger, stronger hand noting the date of Emily's death as March 24, 1888. Along with the notation, I found what seemed to be a hand-written will, going on for several pages. This document specified which of her possessions should go to her son Henry and which to her daughter Sarah, before it became a narrative telling a tale of her husband James' deteriorating mental state over the course of their marriage. Beginning with a recitation regarding a bout with the "blues" James suffered less than two weeks after their wedding—one of his "spells," as she called them—it laid out a story of increasing marital strife over the years, and a growing litany of verbal and mental abuses for herself and her children, worsening until James was threatening suicide, terrifying Emily, and trying to kill his own son.

I sat back in my chair, overwhelmed with sadness this woman who died in such intense physical and emotional pain was the same one who just thirty years earlier longed for a loving marriage, happy home, and a life of personal fulfillment. Her idealistic outlook, so evident in the early pages of her diary had somehow been exchanged for a situation which must have been seemed unendurable.

I wanted to cry.

While she poured out her heart over the sorrows which defined her last days of life, recorded right there within the final act of her own life story, I began to get an idea. Rather than spending my summer scouring the internet, or talking with local historians, hoping to stumble across a story about some plucky Amish woman, why couldn't I just work with the woman whose life story unexpectedly fell into my lap? Surely, within this diary encompassing thirty years of a life, there would be more than enough material for my new project. Maybe she'd never been a Tudor queen or done anything most people would consider heroic, but didn't every life hold a story? If I set about a systematic study of Emily's own narrative, written by her own hand, I was sure to find her story within. And even if it wasn't a big enough story for a book, it would be such good practice for me. Besides, I'd written novels like this before—with much less to work with. This would be a great project to help me find my way back into the world I left behind when Jack died.

Jack.

He told me my story lay down the road, waiting for me. I only needed to be patient and it would appear.

I think maybe it just did.

We're all made of stories. When they finally put us underground, the stories are what will go on. Not forever, perhaps, but for a time. It's a kind of immortality, I suppose, bounded by limits, it's true, but then so's everything.

~ Charles de Lint

Chapter Six

~∞~

June 27th - *If I am a fish, and the diary bait, then I am well and truly hooked.*

The property manager stopped by as the furniture delivery truck was pulling out of my driveway. I shared with her my discovery of the trunk in the attic and asked if she thought it might have been left behind by a former tenant. After considering my find, now polished and gleaming in the corner of the living room, she agreed with Alex and Dan.

"They're absolutely right," she said. "It's just too big. Anyone who wasn't planning to stay here long term wouldn't bother to carry it up those stairs. Whoever left it up there was planning to be here a long time."

As she headed back to her car, I told her I'd let her know my decision as soon as I made up my mind.

***

Foremost on my mind was a desire to discover more about Emily's connection to the farm. Alex, stopping by the next day ("just to check up on you"), recognized the name Gillespie. When he was a boy, he said, he recalled a local man—"a pretty eccentric old guy"—named Henry Gillespie. Alex thought Henry grew up on a nearby farm, and was pretty sure he lived with his sister, "a schoolteacher, if I remember right." But reminding me that was a long time ago, he suggested I check out the name in county records if I wanted to discover whether either of them had any association with my farm.

Standing out by Alex's truck as he was getting ready to leave, I pushed my sunglasses up into my hair like a headband, and swiped at the perspiration puddling on my cheeks. Remembering my earlier discovery, I said, "I searched for Emily Gillespie's name on the internet the other day—and found her. She's buried right here in Manchester. In the Oakland Cemetery." Squinting up at him, I asked, "Do you know it?"

"Oakland? I sure do. My folks are buried there." He paused for a moment, jingling the keys in his pocket. "Hey, have you got a few minutes? I could take you out there. I know the guy who works in the office. I'll bet he could help us find the gravesite."

"Now?"

I'd been planning to head down to the county courthouse, but how could I pass up the chance to find Emily?

"Give me a minute to grab my purse and my notebook, and I'll be ready."

Already headed back to the house, I turned and smiled. "Thanks Alex. I appreciate all your help."

Not five minutes later, we were in his truck, headed toward town.

Alex assured me we'd be there in less than ten minutes, and he'd even drive me by the courthouse on Main Street on our way.

"It's just a few blocks off Franklin on our way to the cemetery. Practically on the way."

As we drove through town, I was struck again by the vision of small town Americana gleaming from Manchester's every window. The Delaware County Courthouse, its stone and brick edifice and steeple-like clock tower, was surrounded by huge purple-leafed shade trees—Norway 'Crimson King' maples, according to Alex—looking more like a Victorian hotel than a government building. Situated in a park-like setting on the edge of the mostly Italianate architecture of the downtown area, the whole area gave off more of a "theme park attraction" vibe than it did that of a real live town. The feeling continued along the wide tree-lined streets and sidewalks rolling through the residential areas and presenting a welcoming atmosphere that made me wish I could stay here forever.

I could almost hear Jack laugh, asking if we'd landed on the set of a Hallmark movie.

My reveries ended as we pulled up in front of the cemetery office. Checking my notebook to be sure I had Emily's death date, I stepped out of the almost-glacial confines of Alex's truck into the sweltering parking lot and followed him quickly through the office door, before I could start to melt.

A blast of cold air from an air conditioner hit me square in the face, an icy gust strong enough to blow my hair straight back from my forehead, but the minute I moved out of its path, the temperature shot up about 10 degrees. Clamminess seemed to crowd the rest of the room, so I decided it was better to brave the gale.

The office was small and stark—a desk, two folding chairs placed around a table in the middle of the room, dingy white walls, and blinds at the only window. It reminded me more of an automotive garage than what I envisioned the main office of a cemetery would look like. After a moment, the manager—Steven, according to a badge pinned to his shirt—came out of a back room, smiling and greeting Alex with a handshake. After Alex introduced me and I explained our purpose, Steven returned to the back room, reappearing several minutes later with two large volumes.

"What's the name again?" he asked as he flipped open the first of the books.

"Gillespie. Emily Gillespie.

He flipped open the book with Alex peering over his shoulder. He explained names of the deceased were listed alphabetically, so Emily should be easy to find. While Steven combed through the names, I wandered toward what looked to be a site plan of the cemetery, with names written in small boxes, like states on a map. But after several minutes of searching I hadn't found any Gillespies—and apparently neither had Steven.

"Nope, nothing here," he said. "What year did you say she died?"

I checked my notebook. "1888. March 24th."

"Hmm... I'll bet she's in the older section. Let me grab the other book." Retreating to the back room once again, Steven returned with a slightly tattered volume, larger and older than the other two. "This one should tell us what we want to know."

He leafed through this second book, looking for the name and date I'd supplied, finally turning to a page listing several Gillespies— "Hiram, Adaline, Lafayette, Lorindia, Clarra, Henry, Sarah, James...and Emily." Looking up, he said, "This must be it. 1888, right?" When I nodded, he said, "Yep. That's her then."

Flipping open another book, he searched out the location ("Must be the whole family there."), before turning to the map on the wall. Ruffling through the pages, he stopped at the third one. Running his fingers back and forth across it and muttering "Gillespie" repeatedly under his breath, he stopped at least and pointed out a line of plots—directly behind the mausoleum. "They're about two rows back. Should be easy enough to spot. Your Emily is near the end of the line."

Bracing myself for the furnace waiting outside the door, I once again shared a clammy handshake with Steven, thanking him for his help. Alex had waved his goodbye and was already headed toward the truck.

"Too hot to walk," he said. "Hop in. I can park right by the graves."

He didn't have to say it twice.

Parking beside the Greek-inspired mausoleum, we climbed out of the truck and began our search. The older sections of the cemetery weren't exactly laid out on a grid, but it didn't take too long to find the Gillespies. This part of the cemetery was full of white oak trees, their silver-backed leaves shading the ground all around and thankfully lowering the temperature a few degrees, yet still revealing a hint of dappling sunlight. Heavy air, searing and damp, enveloped me like a blanket, its musty scent filling my nostrils as I searched for the Gillespies that Steven assured us were here.

Laid out in uneven rows, the headstones ran in a jagged line ending with a single stone engraved with Platt. Although the first names on the stone weren't at all familiar to me, my heart skipped a beat nonetheless. Could this be a member of my family? The marker—right here in front of me—seemed like just one more link between Emily and me.

Pushing back the familiar sadness curling around the edges of my consciousness, reflecting all the cemetery visits I'd made over the years with my ever-shrinking family, I tried to force my attention back to the headstones in front of me. Finding Emily among this sea of those who passed on before.

Then abruptly, there she was—Emily Hawley Gillespie—just where Steven said she would be. A large granite stone, bearing the names of Emily and her husband James, stood at the end of the line of Gillespies, all with death dates between 1854 and 1955. With the exception of James, Henry and Sarah, all the rest died in the 19th century. Sarah, with the most recent date, must have arranged for all the markers since they all bore the same simple design—name, birth and death dates, with a cross and crown motif.

Looking up and down the nearby rows, I wondered what happened to Sarah's husband. Her name was recorded as Sarah Gillespie Huftalen, so she obviously married at some point, but there were no Huftalens nearby as far as I could see. A mystery for another day, perhaps?

I walked slowly down the line, reading each of the gravestones, wondering about their relation to Emily. In-laws? Cousins? Alex stayed with me until we found Emily, but then left me alone with my thoughts, telling me he was going to pay his respects to his parents.

Patches of sunlight splashed the grass around my feet, filtering through branches canopied overhead. The air, hot and damp, enveloped me like a blanket, its musty scent filling my nostrils just as memories of another cemetery filled my mind...

The late-January morning is shrouded in an icy fog, heavy and impenetrable. It hangs like a curtain so thick I can barely see the stand of trees less than thirty feet away. Quiet as death itself... the air still, as if the world has ceased even to breathe. Surrounded by dozens of people, I wonder...do I even know any of them?

My family and friends, Jacks' colleagues—all of them huddling together for warmth—are here offering their presence as comfort. They have come, I know, to honor Jack, to support me and the girls, to wrap us in their love in the face of his choking absence. Yet I sense none of this. All I feel is trapped. Caught like a fly in a web of confusion, yet compressed to a crystalline clarity—this isolated moment burns in my memory like ice. The pastor speaks of eternity while I wonder—absently—which direction Jack's headstone will face. Will the trees offer morning or afternoon shade?

"If you need anything, call us." Eager supplications echo in my ears as each one retreats from the graveside. Hugging me. Pleading with me. "Anything we can do. Any time. Just ask"

I have never felt so entirely alone...

Pulling my thoughts back to the present, I sensed I was somehow no longer alone. Emily was here. Not physically, of course, but I could feel her presence, nonetheless. Leading me, even here—just as she'd led me to the trunk. I couldn't begin to explain it, but I knew without a doubt it was true.

Stooping down, I picked up a sprig of silvered oak leaves from the ground at my feet and clutched it like a talisman. I gazed at the Gillespie headstones and marveled at the change begun in these last days. Emily was a stranger to me, yet since I found her diary she had become a significant presence in my life. For days I pored over her private thoughts, viewing the image she left behind. I still didn't know who she was or whether she had any connection with my family, but somehow I felt, in some small way at least, that I knew her—or at least, I was getting to know her. I had barely dented her writings but

I'd certainly seen some of the stresses she'd faced—the pressure to marry before she grew "too old." The burden of poverty and hard work. I'd seen the idealistic young woman she'd been at twenty juxtaposed against the miserable and pain-ridden woman she'd become by the time of her death. Standing there before her grave, I knew more than anything I wanted to discover who she'd been, what she wanted out of her life—and what kept her from getting it. She had a story to tell and she told it to the best of her ability for thirty years.

Right there in front of her grave, I made her a promise.

"I'll do my best Emily. Just tell me what you want me to say...show me how you want to be remembered."

Laying the branch at the base of her tombstone, I whispered, "I won't let you down. I promise." Then I turned away and walked back toward the truck.

My thoughts entangled in the commitment I'd made to a dead woman, I startled at the crunch of footsteps moving in my direction down the gravel path and looked up to see Alex walking toward me.

"Did you find what you were looking for?" he asked.

Did I? Well, I found a story so compelling I promised a stranger who's been dead for over 125 years I'd tell it. Did that count?

With a wry smile, I said, "I believe I did—and so much more."

I paused for a moment, not used to sharing my private thoughts with people I barely knew—at least not outside the printed page.

"I can't explain why I needed to find her. I'm not sure I understand it myself," I said. "But as soon as I found that diary, I knew my future was bound up with it somehow. Since I can't meet its author face-to-face, coming here seemed to be the next best thing."

I didn't know how, but I felt Alex understood I was working through something as I spoke. He listened intently, encouraging me to keep talking without saying a word. Jack would have done that, too— if only he'd been there.

I looked up from where I'd been scuffing at the gravel with my toe, meeting Alex' eyes again before I spoke.

"My husband died two and a half years ago, and ever since... I can't write anymore."

His faded blue eyes seemed to brim with understanding, but he still didn't speak.

"Have you ever lost anyone?" I whispered.

Somehow, as soon as the words left my lips, I knew the answer. Not only were his parents buried here, I was sure there was someone else. Someone he loved.

"My wife left when our sons were in high school, so I know what it's like to wake up one morning and find yourself alone," he said. "But that's a different kind of pain."

He paused, as if gathering his courage to continue. "Five years ago Dan lost his wife to cancer. It was a long, slow death—the end of a life not nearly long enough. Lindy was the love of his life, the sweetest woman who ever lived—and he and his boys were devastated by their loss. Me, too...I couldn't have loved her more if she'd been my own daughter." He fell silent, as if anguish snatched away the words.

I understood. That fathomless ache had swallowed my words, too, and had yet to return them.

"I'm so sorry, Alex. How awful it must have been for you all."

For all my experience with personal agony, I was at a loss for how to offer him comfort. To say I understood seemed so trite. Grief is definitely not 'one-size-fits-all.' Every loss is unique. For over two years I had mourned not only the loss of my husband, but the forfeit of those final precious moments of a shared life. When Jack died, he was alone, more than a thousand miles from home—and he was gone forever before I could say goodbye. Dan's wife had lingered, fading from life slowly and probably painfully. Likely, he had the chance to say the goodbyes I longed for, but in the end death stole his love away just as it had mine. Was his pain any less for having spoken the words?

Somehow, I doubted it.

But words were my stock-in-trade and for me they held such importance. Was the fact I'd never been able to share them in those final moments with Jack behind my writer's block? I had no idea. All I knew was the words were gone and I didn't know how to get them back.

We drove the few minutes back to the farm in silence. As he turned the truck down my driveway, Alex spoke at last.

"You should talk to Dan. It's been a rough road for him, but he's pulled through it. If anyone can understand what you're going through...well, he will."

I thanked him for his concern, and for taking me out to the cemetery to see Emily's grave. "It's given me a lot to think about," I said. "Her story is important to me. I don't know why—or how—but I know I need to find it.

Reading is the sole means by which we slip, involuntarily,
often helplessly, into another's skin, another's voice,
another's soul.
~Joyce Carol Oates

Chapter Seven

~∞~

June 30th - *I couldn't help but feel transported—as if I had traversed time and come face to face with the past. Not just history, but a living breathing woman...*

I returned to the diary again—starting again from the beginning. Although I'd skimmed bits of it already, uncovering a few facts—when Emily moved to Iowa, her husband's name, and several other details—I had now become more interested in the content. What sorts of things did she write about? What were her opinions on the world she lived in? What made her tick?

As I read, I made notes on events and people Emily talked about, creating a cast of characters for what I now hoped would become my next book. My own writing became a way to reflect on her thoughts about the events of her daily life, as well as the larger events of the world which she occasionally mentioned, asking the questions her diary brought to mind. These notes would eventually form the focus of my research, but they also helped me begin to get to know Emily.

After about three days of intensive reading, I began an exercise I'd never considered before. I began to contemplate my own reactions to Emily's words. How would I respond if I was in her place? If I lived in her world, spoke directly to her—what would I say? I wrote these questions into conversations, noting first her words, and then my responses to them. Since the tale of Libbie, and Sylvenus, the "man of her dreams," jumped at me from my first reading, I decided to return to it. I followed the threads, and made note of my own reactions. If I was going to act as Emily's audience, I needed to pay attention.

From my initial introduction to the diary, this first story she told intrigued me. I reread her first mention of Sylvenus, her discussion of the dances they attended at Christmas and New Year's, noting especially her vehement pronouncement that "Libbie wants him pretty badly, she can have him if he will marry her. I do not want him for a companion, no! no!"

Following her entry, I wrote:

Oh my gosh, so dramatic! Reading Emily's diary entry here just makes me laugh. Although her language is more formal and antiquated than mine ever was, this reads like it came straight from my own teenage diary—or one of many nineteenth century novels Emily must have read. I can almost see her now, her hand flung across her brow, swooning across the bed, crying out "No, no! I can not marry him. You can not force me, Father!" The whole scene unfurls through my brain, and I have the feeling as she wrote, Emily could see it, too!

Emmie returned several times to the theme of Sylvenus' (who she thankfully began to call Venus after a while) unrequited love for her, and her wish he would instead pursue her infatuated friend, Libbie. I couldn't help but wonder if she truly thought seeing her friend married off to someone who seemed fixated on her was a good idea—but if I took her at her word, it certainly seemed she did.

Meanwhile, I couldn't wait to see where the story took her. I didn't have to read more than a few pages more before I found another entry on the same topic.

Wednesday, 12 May - ...I am writing & meditating. I do hope Sylvenus will marry his cousin Libbie and not ask me for any company any more because I do not want to trifle with him; he is too dear a friend & I can not marry him. I do not love him as a wife should love a companion. tis pleasant to be home alone.

Again, I could picture the drama playing out in her mind as she wrote, and I continued with my own:

While I can understand your frustration over someone's continued interest in you when you've made it clear you are not interested, I'm not sure why you think their marriage to your friend is the answer to your problem. Wouldn't you be wishing on your friend a fate you do not want for yourself—a marriage where one is not in love with the other?

I sat back in my chair, a bit startled by my own words now scribbled on the page in front of me. Although I'd been responding to Emily's diary for several days now, this was entry was somehow different. I had written directly to her—not *about* her. Something had changed in the way I was viewing her story, something unforeseen. Without any awareness of the shift, I began to address Emily herself.

Hmmm...talking to someone who's not actually here? Gee, that's never happened to me before.

Grinning a little at my own eccentricity, my mind wandered back to a conversation I had with Alice a few days before. She texted while I was heating leftovers for dinner, wanting to catch me up on her first few days in Canberra:

Morning, Mom!

> Morning? I'm cooking
> dinner here!

Oh yeah--16 hour time difference! It's already
tomorrow here ;) Having breakfast soon
with some friends from school.

> Fun! Where are you going?

Local diner, nothing fancy .
Then library--for a group project.
How's the weather?

> It's hot here--and humid.

Weird it's summer there.
Only 50 today--
but sunny!

> Funny.
> What is the campus like?

SO modern! Not like New York at all.

Sending pics

Can't wait.
How are classes?

Good!! SO much fun.

Have you seen
much of the city yet?

Some. Beautiful!
Going to the outback next weekend
--maybe. How's the farm?

Good! I'll send pictures.
SO gorgeous here!

We texted back and forth for several minutes, sharing a few photographs and stories about our days— the same thing we did several times a week when she'd been at school in New York. Yet, we both kept returning to the strangeness of the idea that while we were chatting it was Wednesday for her, but only Tuesday for me.

Later, as I scrolled back through the text of our conversation, it struck me I had been speaking with someone living a day I had not yet lived—Alice's today was my tomorrow. It reminded me of those time travel novels I devoured as a kid, thinking about how incredible it would to actually speak to someone from the past—or even the future—someone whose daily reality was different than mine. Which got me thinking...

Could I do this with Emily's story—and how would a narrative involving someone long dead actually work? I'd have to play with the notion a while, to see how such a story could be constructed, but the idea was intriguing, nonetheless.

I should probably start with a traditional story, though. It had been a long time since I had written much of anything. Anxiety over the peculiarity of what I planned simmered around the edges of my consciousness, but the excitement which always accompanied a new project seemed to be overcoming it at the moment.

I decided to start with something simple. I'd create a short story based on threads taken straight from Emily's diary, but in the first person—just as she wrote it. I typically took the perspective of an "omniscient narrator," allowing me to stand beside my characters and offer an outsider's viewpoint of their lives. Yet somehow Emily's story felt it could only be told from her viewpoint—as if she herself were doing the writing.

But where would I start? I hadn't read too far into the diary, yet most of what I found spoke of sewing projects, family commentary, and discussions about men who wanted to marry her—ordinary words about ordinary days. In dozens of pages—out of the thousands she'd written—I uncovered just one story so far. Surely there were more? No one could write for thirty years without laying out a series of recurring themes. Her friend Libbie married a man who loved someone else, and to my way of thinking this was unlikely to end happily for either of them. Had Emily returned to their story in the months or years I hadn't yet read?

***

The next morning, I awoke with a sense of resolve. It was time to discover Emily's connection to the farm—and my family. Armed with her last name, the address of the farm, and the years of her family's deaths gleaned from their tombstones, I headed downtown to the courthouse to see what I could find. Although the landscape fairly sparkled with the remnants of last night's rain, it barely registered as I drove into town. My mind was spinning with curiosity as to what I might find in the county records.

I arrived a few minutes before eight, just before the doors opened for the day, and parked behind the building in a lot surrounded by those huge purple-leafed maples. The air was cooler than it had been the last few days, and wispy clouds streaked the sky. Overwhelmed with expectancy—I hoped I'd have my answers today—I couldn't help but wonder why I cared so much about Emily's identity.

There has to be a connection between us bigger than just her diary's presence in my house.

After heading up to the second floor and filling out several forms necessary to gain access to records not yet been digitized, I was

66

handed two large volumes and a box of files, then waved across the room to a large wooden table where I could go through them. The tap of my heels on the tile floors echoed through the space, ending with a loud thump as I dropped the books on the table top. The clerk thoughtfully suggested places to start my search in an effort to save me some time and hopefully make my quest more successful—information for which I was extremely grateful. Nonetheless, this was going to take a while.

In the end, after spending the better part of the day poring over census data, tax records, and property maps, I gleaned a bit of information, although not as much as I'd hoped. My great-grandparents bought the farm right after the First World War—but now I knew they purchased it from Emily's daughter, Sarah. Just as my grandfather said, he was born right there on the farm, a little over five years later.

Had my great-grandparents been arbitrary strangers, or was there some family connection? Nothing I found in the records offered an answer. I didn't remember any Hawleys in my family tree, but were there Gillespies? Maybe the connection was not by birth, but by marriage.

Surely the Platt headstone next to Emily's wasn't a coincidence.

Although I had solved the riddle about Emily's connection to the house, but why the trunk had been secreted into a corner of the attic was still a mystery. I knew now the house belonged to the Gillespies, having been built by James in in the early 1870s. The 1885 census listed Emily, James and their two children as living there, with James' occupation listed as farmer, while the sum total of Emily's life was concentrated in "keeping house."

Had the trunk been forgotten when the house was sold? Or had it been left with a relative for safekeeping? Honestly, unless the answer was contained within the diary itself, I was unlikely to ever know the truth.

Let's agree right here at the outset that memory is made up
of one part perception, one part intuition, and
one part pure invention.

~Liz Rosenberg

Chapter Eight
~∞~

July 2nd - *I remember my earliest beginnings as a child writer,*
thinking out loud through the scenes I imagined, speaking to my
characters and imagining they spoke back...

For several days my life consisted of little more than endless
rounds of reading and taking notes—plus copious amounts of coffee.
As time went on, though, I found myself moving from simply writing
in response to Emily's words, to beginning to talk with her as if she
was sitting right there in the room with me. It may have been a strange
way to work, but since there was no one else around to note my
eccentricities, I wasn't worried.

But in spite of my conviction that writing Emily's story was
something akin to destiny, I still struggled with how best to tell it.
Should I write it as non-fiction, beginning with my own story about
finding the diary and telling it from my point of view? I could also put
myself in Emily's shoes and write the story from her viewpoint. Or
should I stick just with Emily's tale, recreating her life story like a
biographer would do? Writing non-fiction wasn't my strong suit; my
imagination always wanted to take over. Besides, non-fiction would
no doubt end up being more about my life than Emily's.

So, fiction then. But, how to tell the story?

Maybe I should fashion a frame of sorts within which Emily's
tale could unfold, allowing me the freedom to reach her story's heart
without being wedded to its facts.

That's it!

Framing now decided, I turned to determining how Emily's diary could be discovered. Should it be found in an attic as I'd found it, tying it to a specific place—or maybe on a shelf in an antique store? I liked that idea. I needn't fashion Emily's now-fictionalized diary into multiple volumes like the real one—a single book would do—but I would definitely use Emily's name. Sure, I was redrafting her life—or bits of it, anyway—using her real name only seemed right.

It was her story I wanted to tell, after all.

Next, I considered how to begin. Not the first line of the book, it was much too soon for that—but an opening scene. Do I use first person—or third? Definitely not second; I had always found that point of view so confrontational.

Too many choices...

I decided on third, just to set it apart from the rest. I'd set Emily up as the chronicler of her own life, but when introducing the diary's discoverer—its reader—I'd act as narrator. Creating an audience outside of myself simply by offering Emily's story through the eyes of another would be a good way for us to collaborate, and I was excited by the idea of telling her story with two voices.

It was time to let her speak.

I closed my eyes, and let the scene fill my mind, willing the character I'd imagined to appear.

Ah, there she is now...

***

Wandering the aisles, the shopper almost passes it by as she peruses row upon row of objects lining the shelves. Spotting a pile of books lying on a tabletop, a pair of lacy gloves draped across the top, she almost skips across the floor in her eagerness to see. To explore.

Fingertips dancing along spines, she studies titles. Probing for hints of what might lay within. But one is somehow different from the rest, and she stays her search when she reaches it.

She is spellbound. Overcome with the need to hold it in her hands. The unassuming, slightly shabby cover certainly offers her no recommendation, but beyond reason she pulls it from the stack. Is it just in recollection her fingers seemed to tingle as she did?

Running her hand over its bindings, reveling in the soft, worn leather, she opens the book at last and breathes in the musty tang of its pages. Skipping past the flyleaf, she reads:

Diary—which may compose the reminiscences of the life,

from day to day,

of

Miss Emmie E. Hawley

A.D. 1858

Medina, Lenawee County, Michigan

"Oooh ...it's a diary!"

Realizing she has spoken the words out loud, she takes a quick peek around her chuckling to herself at her enthusiastic reaction. But she has to admit, she is intrigued. Fingers kissing pages, she skims a few entries then flicks ahead to read a few more. Captivated by her find, she clasps the volume tight to her chest and rushes the counter in her excitement. Ignoring the shopkeeper's attempts at conversation, she sidesteps her usual practice of bargaining for a better price and willingly pays the sticker-price for her prize. Stuffing the now paper-bound volume into her purse, she gathers the rest of her packages, and exits the door, opening her umbrella and running for her car through the rain.

Not thirty minutes later, hair toweled dry and swathed in her favorite sweats, she pulls the diary from its brown paper bindings. A steaming cup of tea by her side, she settles into her favorite chair, pulls a blanket across her lap and once more carefully cracks the cover of the book. Poring over the words on the page, she gradually becomes alert to a voice within her head, growing ever louder, as if the diarist herself is speaking aloud. Disconcerted, yet oh-so-curious, her mind's eye crowds with vivid images. Antiquated prose rises, dancing the distance of space and time, until at last the continuous present of a diarist's world is all she can see or hear...

***

I can see it all. Every word sprung to life.

By now the reader has—hopefully—been pulled into the world of story. Intrigued and curious, she is ready to listen. But where to begin?

Which story would Emily want to tell first?

I imagined I could hear her—clearing her throat, preparing to speak. Her voice confident and strong.

"I'm ready," she says. Are you?"

I wait, her voice filling my thoughts. Picking up my pen, her words seems to pour from my fingers.

> *We write to taste life twice, in the moment and in*
> *retrospection.*
> ~Anais Nin

Chapter Nine

~∞~

Emily

11 October, 1858- I promise to go, although I would not if I had not told Sylvenus I would attend his wedding the last time I went with him. Yes, Old Journal, I promised that if I could not marry him that I would not refuse to see him married to my dear friend Libbie...

It is well past sunset. The colors which earlier splashed the sky have faded to a glittering black as the wind draws gauzy clouds across the sky. A glow of moonlight, nearly bright enough to read by, pours through my window, washing the page as I sit, pen in hand, preparing to record the events of yet another day. This volume in my lap has been a constant friend, "my only confident" at times, and today—the day before Libbie's wedding—it feels especially so. Reluctant to commit my recalcitrant thoughts to its pages, I leaf through them instead, recalling the chronicle of moments which preceded this one. My twentieth birthday. Parties and Church meetings. Weddings, births, deaths—and the early-September announcement of the engagement of my dearest Libbie and her beloved Venus. In this moment, 'tis this event which captures my thoughts. Pursuing an October wedding before an anticipated move west, their preparation time seemed far too brief. Yet, in spite of the brevity of time, both seemed so happy on that day.

But then I began to sense a shift. Not simply in the circuit of the year—crisping leaves and mellowing sunlight—but, I saw a change begin in Libbie, too. The wedding fast approaching, she put on a blissful smile whenever our friends offered their good wishes or asked about plans for their move. She smiled and chattered as if she hadn't a care in the world. Yet behind her eyes, I saw a rising panic, like a church bell growing ever louder, as the wedding day loomed nearer.

Overcome by welling memories, I set aside my diary and rise from the chair. Drifting to the window, I stand silent sentry over the moon-soaked landscape, watching silhouettes of wind-tossed trees pirouette along the side of the barn, listening to the groanings of barn walls and the cattle inside, and shivering in the chill of the night. In spite of the lateness of the hour, my brother mends a harness by swaying lantern light in the barn's open doorway—doubtless assisted by the brilliant moon suspended overhead. My eyes turn farther afield, drifting slowly over sacks of newly-threshed grain piled high on a wagon, and wandering out to the fields along the horizon—toward Libbie's father's farm.

I return to the chair, pick up my diary, and prepare yet again to write of my day. But I can not do it. Not yet. Instead I ruffle through the pages and read, remembering...

20 April - Last Christmas and New Year's I attended Cotillion parties with Venus Hamlin. Libbie wants him pretty badly, she can have him if he will marry her. I do not want him for a companion, no! no! not but that I like him. I do very much as a friend...

A small smile twists my lips when I recall my imaginings as I penned those words, clearly fancying myself the overwrought heroine of one of my favorite books, as I begged to be released from a hateful proposal. Yet there was no one forcing me to marry. I said no to his proposal with no regrets or repercussion—although I never did speak of it to Mother. She would not have approved my resolve.

Venus and I had been childhood playmates, and fast friends since. It seemed hard to believe it was only eight months ago, after midnight at the New Year's Cotillion, when he proclaimed to me his undying affection. Although I loved him dearly as my friend, I simply did not love Venus as a wife should love a companion—and I knew neither of us should be forced to settle for that.

Outside, an unforgiving murmur rises from the trees which seem to shake their fists toward my window—and I shudder. I can almost hear within their lurid whisperings my mother's words telling me I am too choosy, that I will "sometime take a broken stick" of a man, just to avoid the humiliation of becoming a spinster. But I will not—I know I will not. And yet...

25 July - Libbie & I had been there only a short time when Venus came & visited with us. Ah me, I verily know we can never forget the past. I almost dread to be near him; he seems to be lured away into thought...

In spite of our long friendship, I did all I could to avoid Venus in the months which followed the Cotillion. I eluded his attentions in town, at church socials and neighbor's picnics, careful to escape being discovered alone in any place he might approach to discuss his eternal devotion. Even the blazing July afternoon Libbie and I fled the stifling heat of the church Quarterly meeting—in hopes of spending a few peaceful hours reading and gossiping in the cool green shade of the Medina cemetery—became a snare when Venus found us there.

"Emmie... and Libbie," a voice called out. "How fortunate to find you both out here! Was the meeting not to your taste?"

Libbie's voice faltered in her reading, and looking up from the book in her hands, we both turned to see Venus approaching across the churchyard. Groaning inwardly, I pasted a smile on my face, but noted the softening in Libbie's eyes as she looked at him. Wearing a lovesick gaze, her attention was fully turned on him as she nearly dropped the book to the ground and fumbled for something to say. Noting her response, my smile became genuine. Maybe there was a way to make us all happy in this. I remembered her family's clear regard for Venus, and obvious desire that not only would Libbie wed soon, but choose a husband from amongst her kin. Marrying a cousin, particularly such a distant one as Venus, would be a solid choice in her family's eyes. Clearly, Libbie was already smitten. It was merely a matter of turning Venus in her direction. Surely, it would not be difficult.

But the afternoon did not progress as I hoped. Venus paid little attention to anything Libbie said, focusing instead on my every word or movement. Even my attempts to point out to him Libbie's many talents ("You should see the hat Libbie is making—it is the prettiest I've ever seen. And her cakes? Light as a feather. Whoever makes her his wife will be the luckiest man in the world") fell flat, making Libbie alternately blush and blanch as Venus responded with only the slightest hint of interest. My continued rebuffs of his attempts to turn the topic to our past friendship eventually led him to lapse into silence, whirling a fallen leaf between his fingers, and in spite of my apparent failure to turn his regard toward Libbie, I was relieved—it was the only peace I'd felt since he first appeared.

Like the heat, his continued devotion was suffocating.

Over the weeks which followed, there at last appeared to come a quiet change—Venus seemed struck by Libbie's obvious devotion. Budding in the few, small attentions he paid her in the Medina cemetery, her earlier interest began to flower, finally opening fully before me in an ardent declaration of her love for him. Denying a desire for anything more from life but the prospect of living it as Venus' wife, Libbie claimed only such a marriage would satisfy her. I wanted to see her happy, and if becoming his wife would make her so...well, 'twas my wish, too. She must marry someone—and soon—to please her parents. I truly believed his notice would become her happiness. All would, at last, be well; I was sure of it.

Provoked once more from my reveries by the unforgiving wind whipping across freshly-harvested fields, I turn toward the window. Hours have passed. The moonlight has shifted across the floor while clouds scuttle across the sky, alternately revealing and obscuring the room. My oil lamp sputters, and recognizing the night's chill, I reach for the comforter on my bed, pulling it around my shoulders and snuggling deep in a quest for warmth. But a chill remains, for its source is not wholly the night air. I continue to read and think of Libbie...

15 August - Libbie & I rose at six, breakfast at seven. ...Libbie & I lie on the bed and read a story, "The Doomed Sisters"...

Closing the book with a satisfied sigh, I rolled over from my position sprawled sideways across the bed, and squinted at up at Libbie. She was seated on its edge in a wash of afternoon sunlight, seemingly lost in her thoughts.

"I do love that book, I said." It is so very dramatic! Yet no matter how many times we read it, I am always saddened in the end. It seems so unfair, the way the bad sister is treated by her family and friends—and for such a paltry thing as refusing to marry the man of her father's choice. How sad it would be to grow old all alone without love."

As I spoke, her face seem to stiffen and shutter—as if all previous sentiment was being pulled inside her and locked tightly away. Was this fear?

"How good to know we will never suffer this fate," I said quickly in an effort to deter what seemed to be a pooling of tears in her eyes. "Venus truly seems as fond of you as you are of him—and your parents are so happy at a possible match. You will marry well, Libbie, and live long and happy. Myself? Well, that remains to be seen, but..."

In spite of my words meant to offer comfort, the tears filling her eyes spilled at last.

"Oh Emmie...I don't know what to do. Father is so determined I will marry soon, and Mother reminds me almost daily it is well past time..." She stops, drawing a few quavering breaths, gathering herself and her thoughts lest the tears continue to roll down her cheeks. "I do love Venus so, but I am not sure... what should I do? How can I marry anyone simply because it is expected of me?"

What could I do or say to make it better? I knew as well as she that marriage was what was expected of us.

Her mother's voice at the door interrupted our conversation, telling us Venus had arrived for tea. Dabbing at tears, and pasting on a smile, she leapt at her mother's call, straightened her skirts and went out to greet him—with me trailing along behind her.

Once in his presence, Libbie's mood turned slowly to misgiving. All is not well, I see in a moment. In spite of the smile fixed on her face, I can see she is worried by her choice—or its lack. In spite of his recent attentions to her, his affections still seem fixed on me—and his behavior does nothing to assuage her doubts. Every time he so much as spoke a word to me or glanced in my direction, her demeanor nearly glowed with distress.

Libbie's fears threatened her happiness, and I did not know how to dispel them...

***

In the heavy silence of the house I note the rhythmic ticking of the clock on the bureau, and I am shaken by the realization it is already...tomorrow.

This is the day my dearest friends will be wed. And I...?

There is nothing I can do that might help. The dread which holds me captive now confines the words I would commit to the page. How can I admit—even to myself—the mistake in judgment I have made.

But what can I do? I am not the one compelling her here—it is custom that forces her choice. An unmarried girl is simply a drain on her family's resources; it is her responsibility to her family to marry. If she finds love, so much the better for her, but marriage is her responsibility, nonetheless. I know this to be true...hasn't my own family made it clear?

Somehow these reflections do not comfort me. I had encouraged Libbie in her quest for Venus' affections, assured her of his regard, and helped her plan her wedding. I was so sure that once he found someone else—someone who actually loved him—his infatuation with me would fade away. I was sure this marriage would be the perfect solution for them both—resolving the pressure to wed from Libbie's parents, gaining her a loving husband and Venus a wife who would truly love him.

I am not so certain anymore.

In my wish for my dear friends' happiness, I had never considered the possibility that, in spite of all their smiles and plans, nothing had actually changed.

I close my diary and close my eyes. I must believe all will be well.

* * *

After a restless night, dawn arrives at last—the air quiet and clear. Yet, as the day progresses, the wind begins to rise once more and clouds blow in to half-conceal the sky, like mounds of uncombed cotton bolls scattered across the blue. Mother worries against a likely rain, yet I scarcely notice the darkening skies. My time is spent in battling my growing dread—and baking a cake. Libbie's brother Royal arrives at two, as we had arranged, for a supper of Mother's baked chicken. At five we leave for the wedding in his brand-new covered carriage. Yet I am heedless of all save the renewing wind and the fading light of day.

All too soon, I find myself standing—cake in hand—outside Libbie's front door. Festooned with flowers, the house is already filled with the genial voices of family and guests. The rich aroma of foodstuffs brought by neighbors drifts on the air as they arrive from farms all around the county to become part of the celebration of a neighbor's marriage.

12 October - Mr. Pack was there & all the guests had assembled. I went to Libbie's room...

Setting the cake on the already heavily laden sideboard, Libbie's mother leads me away down the hall, babbling on about the beauty of the bride and the quality and stability of the groom, reminding me once more of Libbie's eagerness to see me as soon as I arrive.

Knocking on the door, her mother calls out, "Libbie, dear. Emily is here."

Fingers now resting on the doorknob, my heart pounds wildly in my chest and I can feel my stomach churn with an icy dread at the moments to come. Inside, my dearest friend is preparing to marry the man she loves, and I am here to wish her well. To share in her joy—all the while knowing his heart still yearns for me. Inside, she dons her happiness, unwittingly tangled in the unseen and unraveling threads of her life. I hesitate another moment, gathering my thoughts with a final deep breath.

Squaring my shoulders, I steel myself with a smile and push open the door. Standing in front of a mirror, she catches my eye in the glass before she turns to face me.

"Emmie! You're here. What took you so long?" Voice quavering through a veil of anxiety, she flutters toward me, her hands draped with flowers.

"Help me? I can't get it to stay on."

Tamping down my earlier trepidation, I chuckle and grasp the offering in her hand. 'Tis only bridal nerves. With a wry sort of smile, I stroll once more the familiar playful paths of our friendship.

"You have always been a bit helpless. How do you ever manage a day without me?"

Setting the wreath on her head and frowning in concentration I silently work hairpins through the profusion of fragrant blooms and glossy black curls until all are secure in their place. Taking her by the shoulders, I spin her back toward the mirror, taking a step back to admire the effect. Beaming at her, I force a brightness I do not feel.

"There, you are perfect. See?"

Watching intently, eyes wide and dark, she regards her reflected image. She wears a bewildered expression, as if she is searching for a response within her mirrored gaze.

The quiet thickens like a fog, until I can hear nothing but the sound of my own jagged breath. Restless at her lack of reply, I pat her hair, smooth the fabric of her dress across her shoulders, and try one more time to quell my increasing unease.

"Do you remember when we were little? The day we..."

Yet before I can finish my thought, Libbie bursts into tears. Reeling back from the mirror, she flings herself at me and buries her face in my shoulder.

"Oh Emmie!" In her despair, she can find no other words. Tears trace her cheeks, searching in vain for some small corner of reassurance.

Shushing her softly, I enfold her in my arms, gently rubbing her back and murmuring soft, nonsensical words about this day being the happiest of her life, reminding her of the wonderful future that lay ahead with the man she loves, and whispering that she shouldn't cry.

But there is no answer to her quandary. Hoping for love, she is instead succumbing to the same business arrangement every woman must make in the end—she accepts a love-sworn proposal of marriage, but receives instead an arrangement meant to secure her future. She is freed from society's censure of spinsterhood, but consigned instead to a life of hardship and drudgery, moving from sweetheart to chattel. And without love, how unbearable a fate that will be.

I can not ask her why she cries.

A brisk tap on the door reminds us both of the world waiting outside. Gently freeing myself from her embrace, I kiss Libbie's damp cheek, straighten her dress, and secure a smile to wish her well once more before opening the door to her mother. Crossing the threshold into the hall, I hear a quiet "Thank you, Emmie," then move to join those gathering for the ceremony.

Moments later, a white-faced groom leads his tremulous bride to the altar.

Libbie's tears do not reappear. She wears in their place an air of acquiescence which surrounds her like a smothering vapor, choking the life from her face. Standing up with Venus, she looks more the condemned prisoner than a blushing bride taking the final steps delivering her from single life to wedded bliss. I wonder if anyone else sees her distress.

Like marble figures before their families and friends, the two are flawless in their loveliness, yet stiff and icy-cold. The time-honored rite goes on as custom requires—shared vows and a golden band, weeping from a mother and admonitions from the Good Book—until Brother Pack at last declares them man and wife. Slipping on a stilted smile at the cue, she waits for her new husband's kiss—yet it never comes. In the muddle of merriment which follows, perhaps no one else notes its absence, save Libbie—and me.

At the preacher's pronouncement, as is custom, all present spring forward to kiss the pair and wish them happy. I have been to enough weddings to know what follows. Libbie's mother surely dabs away a few lingering tears, and wrings her hands in joy at seeing a daughter married at last. Her younger sisters certainly skip 'round the couple, laughing and declaring their delight in the beauty of the ceremony, unquestionably looking ahead to the day when they, too, will become brides. Her father undoubtedly offers a hearty handshake, and a booming "Welcome to the family" to the groom. But in this moment, I am aware of none of it. Standing on the fringes of the fete, I can see only one thing.

Seemingly spellbound in the midst of the celebration, he stands at her side—looking only at me. In this moment, as Venus abandons his bride—my dearest friend—I find myself mired in disbelief at his actions

He approaches, reaching for my hand.

This can not be happening.

Raising it to his lips, he gazes into my eyes and gives his first wedded kiss not to his bride, but to me. In my desire to avoid both my family obligation and a husband I do not love, I wished on my friend a husband who did not love her.

Tearing my eyes away, I pull my hand from his, but not so violently I gain the attention of the well-wishers gathered nearby; I would not have Libbie see this for the world. Hurrying like a ghost from the room, I am soon standing alone on the porch taking deep gulps of air, fanning my heated face and trying to sort my jumbled thoughts.

Surely, it will all be right. Certainly, he will grow to love her and forget this silly infatuation with me. Undoubtedly—in time—all will be well.

12 October – I respect them both and sympathize with his past devotion—may all end well...

Hesitant once again, I note the tempest outside my window, and face at last the truth of my thoughts:

I can not believe that it will.

***

At the chime of her grandmother's clock in the hall, the reader is pulled back to the present. Alien images recede as quickly as they came, leaving her with the text on the page and her own jumbled thoughts. Still settled in her favorite chair, her tea—untouched—has gone cold. Has she somehow left this place, she wonders—or has her imagination merely run away with her? Feeling the warmth of the chair beneath her, she recognizes that whatever happened, it was all inside her head. She smiles at her whimsy and rises from the chair with a stretch. Glancing toward the window, she realizes the rain has stopped, and patches of blue peer out from between the grey.

Here's what I think: it's one thing to know that rejection is coming, and it's an entirely different thing when it arrives.

~ Autumn Doughton

Chapter Ten

~∞~

July 9th- *Whatever this turns out to be, writing Emily's life in this way is a chance to get her story out into the world—and it gets me writing again. Both good things...*

I pushed away from the desk and laid down my pen. Stretching my arms wide and reveling in the feeling of accomplishment, I knew something good had happened here. Somehow, we did it—together. I still wasn't sure whether I could actually turn these scribbles into a novel, but hoped I could at least cobble together a series of short stories. Maybe I could title them something like "Diary of an Iowa Farm Wife."

Seriously? Is that the best you can do?

Still, the writing had felt like a collaboration as I read and reread portions of the diary and let Emily's words funnel through me, allowing my imagination and her memories free reign as I worked.

I couldn't wait to call Amy and let her know I was working again.

***

The next morning arrived cloudy and hot, the air filled with a fevered sense of foreboding. The previous night's enthusiasm over the story I'd written gave way to a haze of anxiety, a sick feeling that no matter how much I might believe in this project, Amy was likely to hate it simply because it wasn't what Avalon was known for. I kept reminding myself my last few books were pretty successful. That I could make this work. Yet, no matter what I longed to believe, I wasn't buying it.

This conversation isn't going to go well, I just know it.

It had only been about a month since we spoke, so I could put the call to Amy off a bit longer if I wanted to. But my more realistic side realized I was avoiding the issue. I needed to convince her so she could convince them—and the sooner the better.

Since Charlie wasn't here to do it for me, some positive self-talk was in order. Reminding myself I'd done it before. I'd taken the sparsely-told stories of some pretty obscure women and made them sing, so I assured myself I was sure I could do it with Emily's diary, too. The story I'd written was good, and once I had a chance to work on revisions—tightening the prose, fluffing the descriptions—it would be even better.

I'm not sure I was convinced.

Maybe the best thing to do at this point was to type it up, and send the story off to Amy—along with an explanation of my plan for the larger work—giving her a chance to read it through before we actually talked about it. I'd spend the afternoon writing up a synopsis, attach the story to an email...and wait to hear from her.

Unfortunately, I didn't have to wait long. I sent the story and synopsis off to Amy that same evening, and within two days I received a reply:

Liz,

So glad all is well there on your Iowa farm, and I'm especially pleased to hear you're writing again. Once you get your feet under you, I know it will all pick up steam and you'll be churning out another winner in short order. Go girl!

As far as the work you sent, I know it's preliminary, but I just don't see Avalon wanting this one. It's a sweet little story, but who was this woman? What did she do? I don't believe your readers will care much about someone who lived and died on a farm in Iowa 150 years ago. Where's the romance in a story like that?

But don't be discouraged. I know you have another book in you. I just don't think it's this one!

We'll talk again soon. When you come up with another idea, I absolutely want to hear about it!

Take care,

Amy

Sitting there at my desk, those carefully cheerful words mocking me from the screen, I heaved a huge sigh. Although her reaction wasn't entirely unexpected, it still stung a bit.

Ok, more than a bit!

Amy was trying hard to be supportive, I knew, but as far as I was concerned her answer boiled down to, "Really? Is this all you've got?"

I've lost it. I'll never write another book...

But—a "sweet little story"? My reaction careened like a ping pong ball, bouncing from self-doubt to irritation.

I wasn't some first time wanna-be writer with an enthusiastic query letter and an overwrought manuscript. I was a published author with several best-selling books to my credit. Publishers came to me offering contracts.

Don't be discouraged?

Just who does Amy think she is to offer me this verbal pat on the head?

I must admit I wallowed a little—allowing irritation to build for a while. Whether I'd anticipated it or not, the rejection of my idea hurt. In spite of the fact Amy tried to sound encouraging, her email was nothing less than a full-scale dismissal.

Maybe I should give the Amish story idea another thought.

Yet... I truly believed I was meant to write this story. Emily left an important tale contained in the daily writings of a woman considered insignificant by the world, but no more so than the rest of us. I believed her story was worth telling.

But if no one is willing to listen?

As I always did when I hit some sort of roadblock, I picked up the phone and called my sister.

Charlie and I had always been close, but the loss of our mother so early in our lives drew us even closer, and we remained so, in spite of living on opposite coasts. Charlie rushed to my side when Jack died, and several years before, I dropped everything to be her support when she left her husband after discovering his infidelities. There was nothing we wouldn't do for each other.

When I told her about my discovery of Emily's diary, she was nearly as excited as I was, wanting to know everything I'd learned about her through my reading. I called her again after finding Emily's grave in the cemetery, promising to let her know once I'd scoured the county records, hopefully discovering her connection to the farm and our family. What I hadn't mentioned was the story I was writing based on the diary—or the fact I'd sent an early draft off to my agent. I didn't want to tell anyone until I'd gotten some sort of feedback on the work.

Well, now I had—and I was devastated. Where else would I turn but to Charlie? Pressing the numbers and waiting for an answer, I launched into my sorry tale as soon as I heard her voice.

"Oh Lizzie, I'm so sorry. I can't believe she said that, but... she's just wrong." I could hear the frustration in Charlie's voice. She was clearly incensed Amy couldn't see in this diary what I saw.

"Well, in her defense... I haven't written anything in over two years. Maybe it's not the subject matter. Maybe the writing was just... awful!" At the height of the pity party I was throwing for myself, I could feel the tears welling in my eyes, but I was determined not to cry. If I broke down over this, Charlie was likely to hop on the first plane for Iowa. I wanted to see her, but having her run to my rescue wasn't exactly what I had in mind.

"No way, Liz. You are a phenomenal writer. Amy just can't see past the demands of what passes for popular fiction these days. If there's no bodice-ripping sex or sappy love story, she's not interested. She wouldn't know a good story idea if it walked up and bit her."

I could tell Charlie was getting wound up over Amy's rejection. But much as I appreciated her defense of my writing skills, I wasn't sure she was right about it this time.

"I don't know, Charlie. It is kind of a strange concept. Would anyone want to read about a woman who was a... a nobody? Amy was right. Emily lived on a farm 150 years ago—in Iowa, of all places.

She wasn't famous. She didn't do anything worth writing about. She didn't even marry anyone that *anybody* had ever hear of...how interesting can she be?"

Pausing a moment, I asked, "Honestly? If I wasn't your sister, would this be a book you'd want to read?"

I could almost feel her bristle on the other end of the line, as if I challenged her character with my question. "I haven't read your Emily's diary, but I know you can take her life—whatever it was like—and make it sing on the page. If Amy can't see that...well, she's an idiot."

Not quite convinced by her words, but feeling immense gratification at Charlie's outrage over my "honor" as a writer, I told her I wasn't ready to give up just yet. "I don't know if it will ever turn into anything, but I'm going to keep writing. It's hard to explain, but I feel like I need to do this. That *I* have to be the one to take Emily's story to the world."

At this pronouncement, Charlie laughed. "Lizzie, are you going all metafictional on me now?"

Joining the joke, I told her I just might.

*It may be that the strongest instinct of the human race,
stronger even than sex or hunger, is curiosity:
the absolute need to know.*
~ Jack Finney

Chapter Eleven

~∞~

July 12th - *When I was a little girl, I used to wonder about the people who lived in my house before me. Had another little girl slept in my room? Looked out my window? Sat under my favorite tree?*

There was something compelling about the idea that other people, before I was even born, lived their lives in the spaces of my own. With Emily's connection to the farm now established, what I most wanted to know was how she lived her life in this house which now belonged to me.

Having finally discovered how my family came to live here on the farm, I had not yet found any familial link between Emily and me. I could take some time to try to track down a connection through one of those internet genealogy sites—or I could just ask Charlie. She was the one with Zizzie's copy of the family genealogy. If there were either Hawley or Gillespie branches on our family tree, she could find them. I may have been the one who loved to go trolling through the past, but my sister was the organized one, the family record-keeper.

It was obviously time for another call to Charlie.

"Lizzie!" Charlie was practically squealing when she picked up the phone. "Your ears must have been burning all afternoon. I was talking to Maggie, telling her about your book idea for the diary. She was absolutely fascinated by the whole thing. She wants to know more—anytime you want to talk about it."

She'd been talking to her boss about my idea? I appreciated her support and eagerness to help, but my story had already been rejected once. It wasn't ready to face another editor so soon. Especially not when it wasn't really written yet.

Nope, not happening. Not yet.

I must have been silent too long. Charlie spoke again to fill the gap.

"Don't worry, she knows you have a book contract with Avalon. But if they don't want it, maybe someone else will."

Charlie can get pretty excited about things and has been known to exaggerate from time to time, so I always take her enthusiasm with a grain of salt. But Maggie was the executive editor for fiction. If she liked my idea, maybe it was still a viable project. Could I step past Avalon, though—assuming Charlie's boss was even interested? Maggie hadn't actually seen a proposal yet—or even a chapter—so how could she know whether or not it was a good concept? Heck, no one had seen it since it didn't actually exist, except for a short story in a word doc, a few pages of scribbles in a notebook, and the skeletal structure erected inside my own head.

Changing the subject in an effort to avoid any more discussion of my not-quite-existent book, I asked Charlie about the Platt family tree. "Is it handy? Could you check something out for me?"

"I think it's in a box in the hall closet. Why? Did you need it for something?"

I filled Charlie in on the information about Emily and the farm I'd gained through county records: Our great-grandparents bought the Gillespie farm back in the early 1920s, but if there was a family connection between them and Emily, I hadn't found it at the courthouse.

"And then there's that Platt headstone at the end of the row of Gillespies...."

I stopped for a moment, thinking about the odd feeling that left me with. "It can't be a coincidence. I was hoping Zizzie's family tree might help me figure it out."

"Well, I'll fish around for it, and let you know what I find. I can bring it with me when I come down the end of next week, if you like."

"Charlie! You finally made reservations? I'm so excited. Wait until you see this place. It's so amazing..."

"I know, I know. You've been telling me about it for weeks. I don't remember the farm the way you do, but I am anxious to see it anyway. I have to admit, though, it's the diary I can't wait to get my hands on. But I haven't made flight reservations quite yet, I wanted to talk to you about airports first."

I suggested Charlie fly into Cedar Rapids since it was much closer to Manchester, but she wanted me to meet her in Chicago. I wasn't sure I wanted to do a nearly eight hour round trip just to pick her up at the airport, but before I could suggest she take the train from Chicago if she didn't want to fly into Cedar Rapids, she started trying to bribe me with a night "on the town" in Chicago.

"C'mon Lizzie. A night out in the big city could be fun," she said. "We could go out to a club, or at least have a fabulous dinner somewhere. Maggie told me about this restaurant... And when was the last time you went out for the evening, anyway?"

"If you include the high school production of "Guys and Dolls" or parent-teacher conferences, then maybe a couple of months ago. If you mean something like a date, well..." Although Charlie couldn't see me, I winced, knowing what was coming.

"That's exactly what I mean, and you know it." She was getting irritated with me now. "If not a date, then a night out with friends or coworkers. Please tell me you're at least doing that."

I could tell she was concerned about me, but I didn't have the heart to admit I had basically withdrawn from all my friends. Between some pretty extensive wallowing, getting used to being single, and going back to work, I pretty much cut everything—and everyone—else out of my life. It wasn't healthy and I knew it, but what could I say? I had said no so often people just stopped asking. It was easier to stay home, grade papers and read.

"You're not, are you? Ok, little Miss Recluse, that's it! I'm flying into Chicago and we're going out on the town for the night before we head back to the farm. As soon as I've booked my flight, I'll start looking for a hotel. All you have to do is meet me there. If I can book an early enough flight, maybe we can even work in a spa day and some shopping." Like every other little sister on the planet, Charlie was determined to get her way.

I guess I'm going to Chicago.

***

Two hours later, the phone rang—Charlie had found what I was looking for.

"Hey Liz, I've got it. Did you know we had a great-great-great grandmother named Harriet Hawley? I don't remember Zizzie ever mentioning the name. But when you get back that far, I don't recognize many of the names on the family tree, anyway. But does Harriet sound familiar to you? She married a John McGee, and had ...well, a whole bunch of kids. Long story short, their granddaughter Lillian was our Great-grandma Platt."

I was so excited I almost fell off my feet.

Sinking into the nearest chair, I asked, "Harriet? Charlie, are you sure? Harriet was the name of Emily's youngest sister! That's just too much of a coincidence not to be a connection."

Although, I did consider for a minute the myriad repetitions of Emily, Sarah, Henry and James among Emily's neighbors in the diary (*seriously, did no one in the 19th century have any imagination when it came to naming their children?*), I finally asked the question that would clinch it.

"Does it say where and when she was born?"

I knew Emily was born in Medina, Michigan in 1838 and her sister Harriet was about seven years younger. If the place and time were right, Harriet had to be my missing link.

"I can't read Zizzie's writing very well, but I'm pretty sure it says Michigan," Charlie said. "Michigan, 1845, I think... yeah, it's 1845. Does that match with Emily's sister?"

Emily, bless her heart, left a family genealogy right here in her diary, recording the birth dates of her entire family. Her youngest sister Harriet was born in 1845. This had to be the same Harriet. That would make Emily my—our—Great-great-great aunt!

I could hardly see straight. Now more than ever, I was determined to discover all I could of her story. I knew what brought Emily here to Manchester, and I assumed her sister—my direct ancestor—came to Iowa for very similar reasons. Now that I understood her connection with this house, I realized Emily's story was, at least in part, my own. After all, Emily and Harriet were sisters—just like Charlie and me.

My great-grandmother must have been charged with keeping the family history when she and her new husband bought the Gillespie farm—hence the trunk in the attic. Someday I'd search out the story of my Great-great-great grandmother Harriet, but for now this connection was enough. Emily had grown larger than life in my eyes, and hers was now the only story I could see.

***

A week ahead of Charlie's scheduled visit, I started drafting another short story inspired by Emily's diary, based on a series of entries she'd made over three or four days as she left Michigan and headed west to Iowa.

She talked about leaving her father's home to travel with her uncle to take on a job which sounded distinctly like that of a housekeeper, as well as becoming a caregiver for her motherless cousin, Susan. Considering her earlier reluctance to take on a position that in any way resembled a servant's, I was a bit surprised she agreed to go. Clearly family pressures on an unmarried young woman played some role in Emily's decision, as well a piece of unsavory gossip about her circulating her neighborhood. Although she never spelled out what it was, she was quick to assure her diary none of it was true, noting her "character is unblemished." Nearly a year had passed since it was first heard, but the story was apparently still making the rounds.

She may have been looking for a way out of town—or maybe she was just looking for a bit of adventure.

Whatever it was which drove her, in late June 1861 Emily boarded a train in Morenci, Michigan—heading for a new life in Manchester. Now twenty three, her romantic notions were still largely intact, and she spoke several times about a man she met on the train. Someone whose intelligence and character appealed to her, enforcing her belief there might be a man she could come to love and marry one day. And for someone who spent nearly three years insisting she'd never yet met anyone worth considering as a potential mate, that alone made her words about this man exceptional.

Emily's idealistic nature, and my own life-long desire to take a cross-country train trip made this story a natural to write, so I went at it with enthusiasm. With the diary open before me, I had the facts down, but let my imagination run a little farther afield as I wrote, living vicariously through Emily's experience. Traveling on a train from Morenci to Dubuque, Emily got her first, and probably only, glimpse of a big city. Chicago. It was also the early days of the Civil War, and I couldn't imagine such a major event as a war wouldn't be a constant topic of conversation among those traveling the country by rail. It seemed a natural thing to include.

Just as I had before, I picked up my pen and began the tale as if Emily was recording her days in her diary...

All we are, all we can be, are the stories we tell," he says....
Long after we are gone, our words will be all that is left,
and who is to say what really happened or even what
reality is? Our stories, our fiction, our words will be as
close to truth as can be. And no one can
take that away from you.
~ Nora Raleigh Baskin

Chapter Twelve

~∞~

Emily

I can feel the rumble beneath me as the train hurtles down the tracks, propelling me ever farther from my childhood home. Outside my window, the daylight is beginning to fade over vast prairies dotted with the riotous colors of wildflowers like I had never before seen, and along the horizon I can just make out the hazy outline of the largest hills I ever saw. We spent last night at a hotel in Chicago, but tonight we are on the cars all night, hurrying toward the boat which will deliver us across the Mississippi River to Dubuque in the morning. With the rhythmic shudder of the tracks beneath me, I am sure I will be rocked swiftly to sleep.

Yet before I can close my eyes for the day, my diary beckons. Much has happened that I wish never to forget. I crack open its well-worn pages, remembering these last few days...

***

27 June, 1861 - This morning Edna and Henry take me to Morenci. I leave home half past six...Alas tis hard to leave home and friends, but the words "we cannot always live at home" are too true...

Kissing my mother and little sister Harriet good bye, I turned toward the wagon ready to carry me the first leg of my journey to Uncle Henry's home in Iowa, to help him run his inn and care for my motherless cousin. Excitement mingled with a nameless unease as I took one last look at the home I'd known all my life. Childhood memories rushed at me from all sides and threatened to undo me as my brother Henry reached out his hand to help me into the wagon already holding Uncle Henry and Cousin Susan. Kissing me on the forehead, Pa—with a wry smile—offered one last word of warning:

"Take care to not get your cape caught in a buggy wheel, Emily."

Touched by the concern hidden within his practical words, I was also somewhat confused at the meaning behind Uncle's sudden snort of laughter. Still, I gathered my skirts and promised I'd be careful.

Somehow I felt, even then, he was speaking of more than just the wagon ride ahead of me.

Driving through my hometown of Medina and on to the train depot at Morenci several miles away, I thought of all I was leaving behind. My sister Edna chattered of her beaus, and the parties I would miss, wondering in my ear whether our cousin Susan would—once home—act the saucy girl she had always been, in spite of her good behavior on her visit, and musing over the sights I would see on the trip. I wondered how I would like living in Iowa, and how my life might change there. Surely, Uncle would not treat me as a simply a servant, come only to cook, clean and serve at his whim. I did not think I could abide such a life; even being relieved of the pressure from my parents to marry was not worth that.

Arriving at the station, Edna's mood shifted, and she threw herself into my arms, weeping as though her heart was breaking.

"Emmy, I will miss you so... when will we ever see you again?"

I had considered this move for months, yet in that moment it felt so jarringly sudden. In spite of the desire to escape my untenable situation—unfounded rumors which although proved untrue, had damaged my own sense of a good character, and pressure from Ma and Pa to marry—the anticipation of great adventure had carried me through the preparation, so even bidding farewell to acquaintances and friends had not made it quite real.

"Edna, hush," I said. "Of course you will see me again. Iowa is not so very far, is it?"

In my heart I wondered at the truth of my own words. Most who move so far west never return, and the cost of a journey by train is very dear. This might well be our last conversation short of heaven. But I said none of this, instead speaking of the things we might do if ever Edna came to visit.

With a swirling column of smoke hovering over the crowd on the platform, I considered their faces. All were strange to me. What would it be like to go through each day without seeing familiar neighbors on the road or in town? How long would it take to view these strange new faces as acquaintances—or friends? I thought of the likeness I had taken for Edna, and hers now resting in the locket hung 'round my neck—a parting gift from Ma, meant to remember them by. Fingering its chain, I considered the strangeness of my future—a future hidden from my view, but commencing along the railroad tracks stretching out before me.

That evening as I wrote in my diary, I considered my fate...

far away from home in a land among strangers, I will have to form new acquaintances & associates, yes we may find as true friends among strangers those we have never seen, as we have at home...

I smiled to myself as I remembered a particular stranger standing on the station platform as we awaited the next Chicago Central train that would carry us on our way west to Iowa. How handsome he was.

Edna spied him first, standing near to us, lean and tall, with dark wavy hair. He gazed down tracks just beginning to hum from the approaching train. His bearing put me in mind of a preacher or professor—he wore a fine gray coat and vest, a bowler hat, and an air of sophistication—yet in seemed an agreeable gentleman, as well. As we stared in his direction, our curiosity cloaked in the guise of watching for the train, he turned and stepped toward us, approaching our brother Henry to politely ask the direction of train and inquire our course in turn.

Trading introductions amongst our group, he presented himself as Mr. Hathaway, late of New York City, and begged our pardon for interrupting our conversation. Querying my long-anticipated trip, he asked if this trip on the train was my first.

"Oh, yes," I said, noting for the first time his clear blue eyes. "And I am so delighted for it, although I am sorry to be leaving my family behind. It is always sad to say goodbye. Yet imagine, we will be traveling such a long way in so short a time...and sleeping on the train in one of the new Pullman cars. I am so looking forward to that. How modern and progressive we've become. Someday we might hope to travel the whole world this way."

He laughed, showing beautiful even teeth and deep dimples.

"Clearly, Miss Emmie, you are destined to see much of the world! I remember my first trip across the prairies not so long ago...the sights were remarkable, but the comfort was not. However, the railroads cars are much more comfortable now. You will surely enjoy your rest on the train."

In an instant, I was smitten—and so, it seemed, was Edna. She smiled and coyly asked of his travels, but his attentions were fixed on me.

"But, surely you aren't traveling alone?" He smiled at me, with something unreadable in his eyes. Admiration? No, it seemed more like confusion.

"Oh no, I am with my Uncle and cousin—see, here they are now."

Uncle Henry and Susan approached at that moment with our tickets, and introductions were again made all around. Uncle peppered Mr. Hathaway with questions about his business and travels, and we discovered our new friend was indeed well-traveled—having once been as far from home as Paris, France. Susan begged him to repeat a few lines in the language, and as we said our final goodbyes to Henry and Edna, and boarded the train, he delighted us all with a brief poem recited in French.

I was beside myself with admiration for him in that moment, convinced I had at last met the kind of man I had dreamed someday to marry—the kind of man I had given up hope of ever meeting.

Uncle and Mr. Hathaway spent the long hours of our first day on the trip west, talking and sharing tales, while Susan and I considered the passing scenery, walked the aisles, read, or drank in their conversations with rapt attention. The two men hit it off so well that next I knew arrangements had been made for us all to meet for supper during our stop for the night in Chicago. Mr. H— recommended a good restaurant near the Hotel, and volunteered to make a reservation for eight o'clock.

On our arrival at the station in Chicago—and what a beautiful building it was—we and our luggage were loaded into a carriage for the short drive to the Hotel, and once there, we settled in quickly. Not wanting to waste a moment of our time in town, Uncle, Susan and I went out walking after tea. We climbed to the observatory of the Court House— about eighty feet high—where we could see all over the City of Chicago, even so far as the ships sailing on the deep blue waters of Lake Michigan. Never had I seen so much water—so vast it may as well be the sea. It was a beautiful sight indeed. After spending a lovely few hours exploring the city, we turned back toward the Hotel, and dressed for our supper with Mr. Hathaway.

How pleasant 'tis to listen to the conversation of one that is well educated and can talk on any subject...

And well educated he was. Over supper, Mr. H— told us tales from his years at university, spoke of the cotton business of his merchant family, his travels abroad and learning French phrases in Paris cafés, and—over our meal in the hotel dining room in Chicago—he recommended to us some of the sights of New York City.

"When you someday travel to New York, Miss Emmie—and surely you will, such an adventurous girl you are—you must go to the Metropolitan Opera. The most heavenly music! There is assuredly none its equal anywhere in the world, not even in the opera houses of Paris."

Susan hung on his every word—and I? I yearned to absorb and remember it all—the wondrous smells wafting from the restaurant kitchen, the heavy velvet draperies at the windows, the gleaming silver and crystal, and elaborately folded napkins. This was a world I had never known before, and one I feared I might never see again.

Over our meal, I spoke of my desire to become a writer, and the essays I had written and delivered at lyceum. I revealed a long-past prospect of travel to New York to study painting, and nearly cried when I recounted Mother's many words against it. He commiserated with my regret over the missed opportunity to gain not only an education in the art I loved, but the chance to discover a larger world than I had previously known.

"I had such a desire, too," I said as we walked back to the Hotel after dinner, "to someday learn another language, and visit museums and libraries. I want so much to go to college, and maybe become a teacher one day."

Mr. H— pulled my arm through his, and patted my hand in a friendly manner, before leaning in close to whisper in my ear the promise to one day teach me French— "you can teach it to your little cousin, if you like." I smiled at his gesture and the tickle of his warm breath on my ear, but also noted Uncle's unexpected scowl in our direction. Remembering Mother's lectures on proper decorum, I pulled away slightly, yet left my hand resting on his sleeve. As we continued back toward the Hotel, Mr. Hathaway seemed to walk more slowly, stopping periodically to point out some landmark or other, until for a moment it seemed we were entirely alone—with no sign of Uncle or Susan.

Stopped before an elegant storefront, Mr. H— turned toward me, and drawing his arm from mine, reached out to grasp my elbows before he spoke in a hurried hush.

"Miss Emmie...I have not often met so lovely and intelligent a girl as you. I know the hour grows late and we will soon be back at the Hotel, but may I ask you to meet with me later—for just a few brief moments after your cousin has gone to sleep. I have something I must ask you, and have no wish to speak of it in company. Would you consent to meet me on the Hotel stairs at midnight?"

Drawing a sharp breath of surprise, I opened my mouth to speak, but as swiftly as they had disappeared, Uncle and Susan reappeared just ahead—and I could feel Uncle's glare in my direction. Calling to me to hurry, declaring it was growing late and we had an early train, his previous friendly manner toward Mr. H— changed abruptly. We continued the walk in silence, and on reaching the hotel, Uncle snapped a brisk "good night, sir," and marched Susan and me swiftly toward the stairs. I turned, smiling, to offer a "good night," but remembering his interrupted request, I instead nodded my assent and whispered "midnight."

After what seemed like endless hours, when Uncle had finally ceased his lectures to Susan and me on the impropriety of young ladies allowing close conversations with virtual strangers, and the inherent dangers in foreign travel, he announced his intentions to go to bed. Susan, I feared, might never stop talking and go to sleep, as I watched the time slip swiftly across the clock face. Although I could hear my mother's admonitions on the value of maintaining a respectable reputation ringing in my ear, I knew I must speak with Mr. H— before I slept.

At last Susan's declared delights in the day ceased and her breath grew soft and slow. I tip-toed toward the door, eased it open as silently as possible, and hurried down the hall toward the stairs, praying I would not be discovered.

Flushed with the intrigue of meeting a man alone at midnight, I quietly descended the last flight before the lobby until I saw him at last, standing on the bottom stair and checking the time on his pocket watch. Smiling at the sight of his dark head bent over the glimmering time piece, I quickened my last few steps, anxious to be in his presence at last.

"I'm here!" I wanted to call out. Yet in the interest of discretion, I waited until he at last heard my approach and looked up.

"Good evening, sir..."

"Miss Emmie, here you are at last. I had nearly decided you weren't... Oh, never mind, I am so pleased you've come. I have something important I must speak with you about." He shuffled his feet, betraying the apprehension of his thoughts

"Mr. Hathaway, of course I have come. I said that I would." Pausing as if to slow my racing heart, I took a deep breath before asking him to please tell me what was on his mind.

Reaching for my hand, he clasped it tight, and began to pour out what seemed a well-rehearsed speech.

"Miss Emmie, did I tell you where I was headed to on this trip? Unbeknownst to my family and friends, I am taking the train south to New Orleans, to join the southern Cause. I know it must seem strange to you, but many among my New York acquaintance are Southern sympathizers, and would join the fight if they could. I know that, for a Northern girl like yourself, this may be unwelcomed news and possibly carry a treasonous intent, yet I truly believe in State's Rights." His demeanor became hard with his words, and he began to raise his voice from its whisper as he said, "The Confederacy is in the right in this fight, I am convinced of it."

Taking a deep breath, he considered me intently and began again. "But my purpose in meeting with you was not to tell you solely of my political inclination, but of a much more personal one instead. I believe that I have come to love you, and would wish for you to wait for me, in the hopes that we might one day—after this war is over—marry. As much as I might like to ask you to come with me tomorrow, I know it would not be fair to you, and it would certainly not be safe.

Yet, I would hope you might wait for me. I would very much like to see the world with you."

Smiling at last, he asked, "Do my words shock you?"

Shock did not begin to describe my feelings. Overwhelmed with the significance of both his Southern sympathies and sudden declaration of love for me, I was—quite literally—dumbstruck. I am by no means an Abolitionist. I had despised John Brown's histrionics, but still did truly believe the Northern cause to maintain the Union was just and true. How could I love someone who would go to war against it?

Seeming to sense my distress, he continued his speech in a cooler voice. "Please forgive my haste in declaring myself? Were we not parting so soon, I would bide my time and court you properly. Yet, here we are... In less than two days' time, you will cross the Mississippi toward your Uncle's home in Iowa, and I will board another train heading for Missouri and then south. If I do not declare my intentions now, I do not know when I might have the opportunity again. We might never see each other again—and that I simply could not bear." He paused for a moment, as if gathering his courage. "Can you possibly forgive my politics, and wait for me?"

Too stunned at his words to think clearly, I mumbled I would give him an answer in the morning, and turned toward the stairs. Yet, he did not easily let go of my hand, and I wondered at his actions. There was such a desperate sadness in his eyes, I forgot myself for a moment, and leaning toward him, I pressed my lips to his cheek. He dropped my hand and threw his arms around my waist, drawing me close. His lips found mine, and in spite of my surprise, I returned his fervent kiss. Thus we stood for several glorious moments, until I—at last—reluctantly pulled away.

With a tremulous smile, I promised we would speak in the morning, and wishing him goodnight, hurried back to my room.

***

In spite of the softness of the feather bed, I slept little. Tossing through my mind were thoughts of the ever-encompassing War creeping ever closer—so many had died already, just last week a boy I had known since childhood—and a strong desire to stay as far from it all as possible. I remembered talk I heard yesterday among the men on the train, about a bloody battle at a place called Manassas, with thousands dead and wounded. The thought of this awful war made me ill. Yet mingled with all this was an intense admiration for the man who just hours ago declared his esteem for me.

What did I care for politics? How could I not forgive when he was all I longed for? Hearing Mother's admonition—delivered mere days before I finally agreed to travel to Iowa with Uncle—ringing in my ears, I fixated again on the biting words she spoke. Declaring to me, "if you do not marry soon, you will likely spend the rest of your life as a most pitiable figure—the spinster sister that your brother will be forced to support," she summed up my current situation to a tee. I know she was desperately hoping I would find someone among the Iowa farmers who would not mind that I was well-past twenty, while I lived in dread she might be right. Knowing all this, how could I say no to any man who would take me, let alone one whose person was all I had nearly given up hope I would ever find?

In spite of my sleepless night and the turmoil in my heart, the day dawned bright and clear. As the first rays of the morning sun began to flicker through the breeze-ruffled curtains, Susan awakened, squinting and stretching, as I sat with my diary in my lap, contemplating dark thoughts.

28 July - This morning arose at five o'clock. Wrote a letter home before breakfast. Uncle, Susan and I went walking, we saw a great many splendid buildings...

My gloom began to lift as we headed out the door to explore the city on a glorious summer's morning. Although the summer air would soon grow stiflingly hot, the early morning sky was a cool and brilliant blue, and the wonders outdoors beckoned. Before we hurried to the station to board the train at nine, we strolled through a park near the hotel and across a swing bridge drawing its circuit as we watched, allowing a steam boat to pass by. Yet our enjoyment of the city sights was of necessity short-lived—before it seemed an hour had passed, it was time to board the train to Dubuque.

After finding our seats in what seemed a very crowded car, Uncle launched into a succession of orations on decorous behavior for young ladies which echoed the lectures both Mother and Father subjected me to after I declared my intention to go to Iowa. I squirmed and endeavored to look contrite, yet in the end my eyes drifted toward the window, observing the billowing black smoke rising from the engine, then scattering to the wind.

Once he felt he had made his point, we settled into a much less interesting journey than that of the previous day. In spite of the same colorful prairies and the expansive blue skies strewn with swiftly-passing clouds which had entranced us the day before, there has been a pall cast over my enjoyment of the day. Susan and I continued to read aloud to each other, yet our book was much less compelling, the colors did not seem so bright, and my mood grew ever duller as my contemplations once more turned to Mr. Hathaway's proposal—and his noticeable absence from our company.

For he was nowhere to be seen—at least until shortly before we reached our final stop. In the hubbub of brakes and baggage filling the air as the train prepared to stop in Dubuque, he was at my elbow, tugging me aside for a word. Removing his hat with a small bow in my direction, he began to speak in a formal, detached tone.

(We were, after all, surrounded by a great press of people.)

"Miss Emmie, I do apologize for my absence today. Although I had hoped to converse with you—and your relations, of course—further today, I am afraid a need to complete some business correspondence has kept me from you until it is nearly too late. I have so enjoyed your company, and would wish it might continue. One always prefers the company of those whose thoughts and principles are like his own, and I feel I have found that in you."

Furtively glancing around, and not finding my Uncle nearby, he moved a little closer and began to whisper fervently in my ear. "I must ask—quickly before any can hear—have you considered my request? When I return—if I return—will you allow me to call? Will you consider becoming my wife?"

Pausing briefly, he seemed to study my expression, looking deep into my eyes as if to gauge my reaction before continuing.

"Were it not so dangerous, I would ask you to accompany me now, but I know you are promised to help your Uncle with the care of your young cousin, and I would not, for the world, ask you to break your word to enter such dangerous circumstances with me. May I please call on you to restate my intentions, on my return?"

I hardly had the chance to even open my mouth, to say "Yes, of course you may!" when Uncle was grumbling in my direction. "We are pulling into the station just now. Take hold of your things; we must go quickly."

We disembarked the train in a rush, hurrying to collect our luggage from the porter, while Uncle reminded Susan and me we must make haste to catch the boat which will ferry us across the Mississippi River. Mr. H— climbed down with us, helping to collect our bags, and even contacting a driver to convey us to the dock. Although Uncle seemed to snub him as much as possible—shy of outright rudeness—I was so desperately sorry to see him go. His presence not only made the journey much more enjoyable, but offered me a glimpse of a world I would likely never know. Even more, with his declaration from last night still ring in my ears, I know that, whether he returns or not, my life will never be the same. Before I met Mr. Hathaway on the train platform in Morenci—not three days ago—I thought I might never find someone I could love or respect enough to marry, someone whose mind challenged my own, and who cared for more than just crops and chores, yet there before me stood such a one.

Lifting the last of our luggage into the buggy, Mr. H— turned toward me, and quickly captured my hand. Bowing his head over it, he pressed a fervent kiss to my gloved fingers and whispered "I promise I will come back, Emmie...for you," before tipping his hat to Uncle and smiling at Susan. Offering a final "Adieu," he climbed back into the carriage to return to the station, holding tightly my gaze as he drove away. In that moment, I feared that in spite of his declaration of affection and determination to make me his wife on his return, it was doubtful I would ever see him again. Too many who march off to war would never come home. Yet I knew, no matter how long I might live, I would never forget him.

I believed then—and still do—that I was irrevocably in love.

The last thing I heard, as the carriage turned the corner out of sight, was Uncle muttering something sounding distinctly like Pa's final warning to me.

"... warned you about those buggy wheels."

It was much too late for that.

***

Settling into my new life, I thought about Mr. Hathaway every day. As I washed dishes or baked pies, I hoped I might hear from him someday soon. Washing Uncle and Susan's clothes, I prayed he would stay safe in spite of the war. Dusting and sweeping, I longed for a day that might bring him to my door to keep his promise to return and make me his wife. Surely this war could not last much longer.

Not a week after my arrival, Mr. Parker—a regular guest at Uncle's inn—shared over dinner the news of a railroad disaster he read of in the local newspaper, just yesterday. It had occurred on the St. Joseph road as it traveled across a bridge over the Platte River in Missouri, mere days after my arrival in Coffins Grove. As he described the crash, my heart stopped as I counted the days back from the accident to my arrival here.

"For a time it was feared nearly all on board were killed; there was such chaos. Yet, in the end it seemed there were fewer than twenty deaths—yet over one hundred badly injured."

My disquieted thoughts reeled, searching for answers. Surely this could not have been the same train Mr. Hathaway was traveling on—could it? How many days did it take to travel to New Orleans? Would his train have travelled in that direction? Surely he could not be among the… dead.

The disorder of my own mind was echoed in the outcries of dismay from all at the table. It seemed everyone was talking at once, wondering aloud whether it was connected to the war ("Was it an attack by southern sympathizers, do you suppose?") or whether any they knew any aboard ("Mrs. Nelson's grandson was on a train headed to Memphis, was he not? Could this have been his train?").

Uncle's voice finally boomed above all the others, inquiring whether the cause of the crash was known, before Mr. Parker finally answered him. "It appears the bridge may have been tampered with in some way, causing the fires. There are still examining it."

As soon as I could, I excused myself and returned to the kitchen to be alone with my thoughts. The weight of Mr. Parker's news pressed in on me like a stone on my chest until I was breathless with panic. Bile rose in my throat, and my hands would not cease shaking. How could this be true? If Mr. Hathaway had indeed been killed on the train, how would I ever know it for certain?

I had no name or address to contact for news, yet surely there was a list of the dead in a newspaper somewhere. Where would I find it? Could I ask without looking suspicious? I had no proper connection to Mr. H— outside a few days spent travelling on the same train.

He had declared himself to me, and asked me to consider one day becoming his wife. Yet no one else knew—nor likely ever would.

As my tears began to flow, I hurried up the stairs to my room. Cleaning the dishes would have to wait until I regained control of myself. I simply could not have anyone asking me why I wept.

Writers are liars, my dear, surely you know that by now?
And yet, things need not have happened to be true. Tales
and dreams are the shadow-truths that will endure when
mere facts are dust and ashes, and forgot.
~ Neil Gaiman

Chapter Thirteen
~∞~

July 18th - *Dreams are funny things. Sometimes they become the star*
we set our life-course by, and other times they stop us dead in our
tracks. They force us to consider ourselves...

"Just what do you think you are doing? This is my life you are toying with."

Startled by an unexpected voice, I glance up to see a woman seated across from me angrily waving a sheaf of paper—the same pages I had just been writing. She is dressed peculiarly, as if from another century, yet in spite of her clothing she still seems oddly familiar. Looking around me, I see I am no longer at my writing desk, but seated instead at a large oak table, surrounded by empty chairs. Everything about the room is somehow wrong—yet I still know it is mine. It is evening; I am sure of it. I've been writing all day, but the windows stream with a white light so bright the room is practically glowing with it.

What is happening here?

Turning back toward the woman, I ask, "Who are you? What are you doing here?" It is a ridiculous thing to say, I know, but in my confusion it is the best I can do.

"What am I doing? That is what I am asking you." She rises from the table, knocking her chair off its feet and worrying the pages in her hand as she stomps around the room. Face flushed and etched with irritation, she raises her voice. "I am not a character in one of your novels to be moved around whichever way you will." Almost skidding in her tracks, she whirls around to face me. "This is my house, and my life you are muddying. What gives you the right to construct such lies about me?"

Continuing once more her heated circuit of the room, she flings my carefully written pages into the air, muttering under her breath all the while, "She has no right."

As the sheets of paper flutter to the floor, their edges flicker in the light, looking for all the world like the fireflies which should be flitting over the fields outside. All at once I realize why she looks so familiar. She is the woman in the photograph I'd found bundled with letters in the trunk—Emily Gillespie! Right here, in my bedroom, in my house.

Her house.

Wait...this just isn't possible.

Yet, here she is... Emily.

"But you're dead," I say, weakly. "What are you doing here?"

It is such a stupid thing to say, but what do you say to someone—a really infuriated someone standing solidly in front of you—who can't possibly be there?

Glaring at me, she says, "My presence among the living is not the subject at hand. Answer my question. What gives you the right to playact with my life? To rewrite my story?"

She pauses a moment, brows knit tight and eyes filled with frustration, before she speaks again—more softly this time, as if she is holding back tears. "It was my story, to tell as I saw fit."

Your story?

Stronger now, her voice pulls me back from my internal question.

"I will admit I thought Mr. Hathaway a charming and intelligent man when we met on the train, and yes, I thought of him as someone I could possibly grow to love one day—but I would never have considered such a precipitous proposal... and none was ever made!"

In a heartbeat her anger flares again. "I am a virtuous and godly woman—and you are making me sound like a...a..." Her sentence sputters to a halt, as if there are no words to convey the depths of the wrong I have done to her.

She continues in a whisper. "You have no right!"

The room grows silent. My own breath the only sound.

She raises her voice, accusing me once more. "And just how did you know about Mr. Parker and the train disaster? I never wrote of it in my diary. I would remember if I had."

Feeling chastened after her tirade, I answer meekly. "I found a letter to your father in the trunk. When I saw what you said about the abolitionists, I thought..."

"You read my private letters? How could you dare?"

She is practically spitting fire.

What can I say to her?

Her voice grows plaintive as she speaks again. "Why can you not listen to me before you decide how to tell my story? Why can you not hear *my* voice?"

She stands quiet before me, her face shuttering, her earlier anger shifting to a sort of sadness. My failure to see her as she wanted to be seen has clearly upset her.

But while thinking about how best to answer, I grow aware of music—a faraway, yet oh-so-familiar tune. As I listen, it seems to grow louder, pulling me away from Emily's presence, until my eyes fly open and I find myself head down on my desk in a room flooded with early morning light, my phone singing in my ear.

Night had given way to morning—I had fallen asleep over my writing.

Blinking in the morning light, I sat—a bit confused at first— trying to figure out what was happening to me. Had it been just a dream, or had Emily actually been here in this room? Her presence seemed so real—I could still feel her anger practically pulsing around me. I wasn't sure what to make of it all, but I knew she wasn't happy about the direction her story had taken.

My phone—its alarm inexplicably set for six am—was still humming, but I was less concerned with my reason for waking than with what just happened. Emily's reaction to the turn of the story was what concerned me now—even if it had only been my own subconscious telling me I'd gone too far. I stayed up too late, and I've always tended toward melodrama when I am overtired. Clearly, I let my romantic imagination run away with my writing.

What was the harm, though? It made for a much better story in my opinion.

But the whole train crash thing…where had that come from? Maybe the thought of Emily possibly finding and then losing the love of her life on a train simply hit too close to home for me, since a train was where I'd lost Jack. Had I used the story of Emily's "cross-country romance" and her letter about the train accident to play out my own pain over Jack's death??

Adding her fear and uncertainty over Mr. Hathaway's death certainly delivered an emotional punch which the tale—as she told it in her diary—lacked. As a writer, I knew that was important, especially in envisioning a far different audience for my story than the one Emily must have had in mind.

That presents the question, though…just who had Emily been writing for?

If Emily's diaries were meant to be as private as I considered mine during my teenage years—locked and buried in the back of a drawer, hidden away from Charlie's prying eyes—then the only possible audience would have been Emily herself. There were times when the diary read like that, too, a simple chronicle of the day's events, things she wished to record and remember. In other places, though, her entries read like scenes straight from a novel. As if she'd been imagining her life through the eyes of a character from one of her favorite books—trying on a persona different than her own.

Was she writing to someone other than herself? It sometimes seemed that way. There were times I could sense a shift in her imagined audience through the words she chose to commit to the page.

Since the day I'd discovered it, buried and forgotten in the trunk on the attic, I spent a lot of time with Emily's diary, reading into the wee hours most nights. I reflected on her words, her actions, her choices—not simply through what she chose to write, but in the life she was obliged to because of the times in which she lived. Sometimes I admired her choices and sometimes I was critical. However, once I decided to take her tale as my own, I had begun to think about little more than what would make it a good story, what a contemporary reader might like to read. I gave little thought to the truth behind it—not the facts, but Emily's truth. By allowing my imagination to run free, and adding or subtracting those things I thought summed up her life in a way more appealing to a twenty-first century audience, I was revising her history to suit my needs. Telling the story I thought was important.

Was I wrong?

Yet wouldn't her story simply die if I didn't tell it? Hidden away for over a century, it slumbered in the bottom of a trunk until the day I excavated it from its hiding place. If my mother was right and all the little moments of our lives lead us toward our destiny, then I was meant to find and read Emily's diary. To return her words to the world where she once lived. And as the reader of those words, didn't I have a right to interpret them through my own point of view? Through my own experiences?

In my efforts to make Emily's story "accessible" to a contemporary audience, was I actually trying to tell my own story— just jazzing it up a bit to make it more attractive to contemporary readers?

But a book's readers do it, too—working out their own feelings through the words on a page. That's why we can recommend our favorite book to someone, begging them to love it as we do—but so often they don't. They just can't see it through our eyes.

If I was going to tell Emily's story, I wanted to stay true to her life—and her times. She was not a twenty-first century girl and it would be unfair to portray her as if she was. I may not be able to view her through any eyes but my own, but I needed to be certain I was making an effort to see her—and not myself! Maybe it was time for me to just listen.

What is a diary as a rule? A document useful to the person who keeps it. Dull to the contemporary who reads it and invaluable to the student, centuries afterwards, who treasures it.
~ Sir Walter Scott

Chapter Fourteen

~∞~

July 22nd - *Reading Emily's diary, I can't help but think about those I kept when I was younger—I wonder what someone who might find them in 100 years would think of my life?*

I had spent long stretches every day—and often well into the evenings—reading Emily's diary and making note of what was happening with her year by year. There were so many pages to cover, I was doing little more than skimming most of it, lighting now and then on sections which seemed to especially pull me in. Like any diary, not every day was what could be called fascinating, but there was a regularity to most of it which made some of the events she recorded jump out at me. For the moment, though, I was determined to see her life as she saw it—giving weight to those things she saw as important.

Emily's diary contained all the fine points of her life, those things she deemed worth remembering. If I was going to write her story, the diary was obviously where I'd find it. So, grabbing a roll of left-over shelf paper, I tacked it up on the kitchen wall, picked up a marker, and sketched out a timeline of the major events of her life.

Emily started keeping her diary just a few weeks before her 20th birthday. She left Michigan for Iowa at 23, married James at 24, and a year later, she gave birth to son Henry. It was another two years before their daughter Sarah was born—tiny, but healthy—while her twin brother died before taking his first breath. Emily had only wanted two children, but she mourned her baby son's death nonetheless. After that, there were no more children born to Emily and James—an unusual thing in a time when so many of the women around her were giving birth every year or so until they died.

She and James worked hard, first on a rented farm on his parents homestead, then on acreage of their own. Their children grew, and Emily began to raise turkeys to help with the family's expenses—and to have a little money of her own. Emily wrote frequently about women's suffrage, as well as the temperance movement. In her era, women had almost no rights to property—or even their own lives—and one of the things that she saw as the source of difficulties for many of the women around her was the consumption of alcohol, particularly on the part of husbands who drank away the family income then proceeded to take out their frustrations over their financial condition on their wives and children. She spoke of the subject so often it clearly must have touched people she knew and loved. She wrote essays about both suffrage and temperance, sometimes sending them off to local newspapers or presenting them at the local Lyceum—a local, sometimes traveling, organization sponsoring public programs and entertainments. She handed out literature for both causes to neighbors who seemed interested and attended more than a few lectures on the topics. She even noted several arguments with her uncle on women's rights, and was unafraid to share her opinions.

About ten years into her marriage, a deep recession devastated many of their neighbors, including some of their own family members. Emily and James somehow escaped the worst of it, most likely because of Emily's frugal ways and good business sense. During the worst of it, James had "gifted" Emily with the deed to their farm, although she was wary of the gift. It was also a source of contention which drove a deep wedge between the two of them in the long run.

As her children grew older, Emily returned to the writing and painting she loved in her youth, submitting poems and essays to newspaper writing contests, and entering paintings for awards at the fair. But her children were the true center of her life—everything she did seemed to ultimately come back to securing their future and happiness. Her relationship with James had definitely fallen to, at best, second place.

Emily wrote at length about the importance of education and she wanted her children to have the best, working hard to pay their tuition at a private school in town—much to James' chagrin. He felt she was putting on airs, and thinking she was too good for anyone else. According to some of the things she wrote, it was would seem he must have included himself in that assessment.

I was often dismayed by the image she painted of her husband. He was clearly a hard-working man—no one could farm successfully and not work hard—but she so often wrote of him as if he was not good enough. Once, after buying new furniture and rugs for the parlor, Emily declared it all "too fine" for him, wishing he would never have a reason to be in the room.

Emily's depiction of her children—Henry and Sarah—on the other hand, was simply too perfect to be believed. Time and again, she remarked they were named by their teachers as "splendid readers" and "far advanced in their studies," and Emily herself declared them "most worthy noble Children." She prayed for their health and safety, more specifically pleading with Providence to foil James' efforts to force them to quit school and work with him doing farm chores. More than once she declared she would do all in her power to help them get to college, in spite of the fact James saw no value in it.

Emily also wrote about larger events of the world she lived in: the Civil War, America's Centennial, a World's Fair, the deaths of two Presidents, and even astronomical events—including the appearance of two different comets which terrified many of her neighbors who feared they marked the end of the world.

All these things comprised the written details of her life, but not the story she was trying to tell.

I just needed to figure out what it was.

The world isn't just the way it is. It is how we understand it, no? And in understanding something, we bring something to it, no? Doesn't that make life a story?

~ Yann Martel

Chapter Fifteen

~∞~

July 27th - *There's just something about a brand-new journal…*

Time passed quickly. I'd be headed to Chicago to meet Charlie in less than three weeks, but due to my growing obsession with Emily's diary, I had let much of the housework fall by the wayside. Oh, I'd kept up with laundry and dishes *(I might be a bit disorganized, but I'm not a complete slob)*, however, things like dusting and vacuuming—and keeping track of all the scraps of paper on which I'd been scribbling notes—had been completely overlooked since the day the furniture was delivered. If I wasn't going to have my neat-freak little sister coming unglued over the mess, I needed to set the diary aside for a while and get a few things done.

I need a list.

My incessant need for lists is probably why the paper in my life has a tendency to reach sometimes awe-inspiring heights. But I couldn't help it. I was a list maker from the time I was first old enough to write one. I loved my lists so much if I ever did anything not on my list, I would add it, just so I could have the pleasure of crossing it off to show I'd actually accomplished something. Clearly, I needed to make a list before I could begin to actually clean my house.

I'd like to say I wrote up a quick one and was vacuuming within five minutes, but that didn't happen. I did start a list of chores, then moved to writing a grocery list *(also a useful thing)*, but before long it regressed to scribbling notes on the diary, asking myself the questions I wished I could ask Emily, and doodling in the margins while I considered how she might answer. It wasn't until the doorbell rang I remembered what I was supposed to be doing.

Opening the door, I found the mail man standing on the porch with a package.

"Mornin' Mrs. Benton. Here you go" he said, handing over a large padded envelope, too big to fit through the slot in the mailbox down by the road. "And here's the rest of your mail."

He bundled a rubber-banded stack of catalogs and advertisements into my waiting hands, and scurried back down the steps to his waiting vehicle.

Waving as he backed up the gravel drive, his van skidded out down the road and sped off toward town. "Must be late for lunch," I muttered to myself, waving back at him before turning to look at the package. The return address told me it was from my baby brother.

Smiling because I knew what it was likely to be, I did my best to open the envelope carefully. But in the end, an overabundance of sticky packing tape got the better of me and I ended up practically shredding the envelope in my impatience to uncover its contents. As I'd guessed, it was a book of some sort, wrapped in tissue and tied with a string.

Will...such a thoughtful brother, and one who loved books as much as I did. He was always on the lookout for something he thought I might like, and his owning a used bookstore didn't hurt either. Over the years, I'd gotten my entire Vonnegut collection from him, an exquisite leather-bound version of the 1908 edition of Sir Thomas Malory's *Le Morte D'Arthur*, and for my birthday last year, a signed copy of *The Thirteenth Tale*, a British novel about a reclusive author and the woman she hires to write her biography. This past Christmas he sent me a first edition of Hawthorne's *Mosses of an Old Manse* he'd unearthed at an estate sale. Will always seemed to have a nose for finding the most remarkable books.

How come that sort of thing never happens to me?
Oh, wait...it just did!

Peeling back the wrappings, I could see the book in my hand was different. Bound in exquisite hand-tooled leather, its gold-embossed cover begged for my attention, practically pleading with me to open it. Cracking the cover and breathing in the heady scent of brand-new leather, I found inside it nothing but blank pages waiting to be filled and Will's familiar handwriting on the flyleaf:

The pages are still blank, but there is a miraculous feeling of the words being there, written in invisible ink and clamoring to become visible.

~ Vladimir Nabakov

Work your magic, Lizzie J—make them visible!

I couldn't help but smile at the quote he included. Sometimes writing did feel like that—filling blank pages with words that were somehow already there. And how like Will to offer such a beautiful object of support for my plan. I had to admit, there was something about this lovely book which made me want to just sit down and start writing in earnest.

***

Emily settled into her new life—away from her family for the first time in her life—filled with new places, new people, and a lot of hard work. Her diary chronicles her second day in Coffins Grove as filled with visiting with neighbors, baking, washing windows, and the "rest of the work"—a schedule that repeats itself in one form or another nearly every day for the rest of her life.

In finding a way to share Emily's account of her life, I decided another tale worth exploring was her courtship and marriage to James. Emily met and married James Gillespie about 15 months after arriving to live with her Uncle and cousin in Coffins Grove, a few miles from the farm where James lived with his parents and younger brother on the outskirts of Manchester. Their first meeting must have made little impression on Emily. He isn't even mentioned until the day her uncle tells her quite off-handedly he'd dropped by to see her the day before.

119

After this brief announcement of his existence, James isn't spoken of again for over two months.

It was with James' introduction I would begin.

Whether my earlier experience had been "just a dream" or not, I believed Emily wasn't happy with the way I had taken and embellished the tale of her journey to Iowa on the train. I felt as if the dream had been her way of telling me to sit back and simply listen to her story as *she* told it, rather than trying so hard to tell it my own way.

Settling myself into the overstuffed chair in the living room, a tall glass of iced Earl Grey at my side as the ceiling fan whirled overhead, I tucked my hair behind my ears, opened the diary to October of 1861 and eavesdropped as Emily began another story.

Emily

13 October, 1861 - Uncle said James Gillespie was here this afternoon. Milton here a short time, after evening meeting, pleasant. 'Tis ten o'clock. I'm writing. Wonder where I may be one year from now. Ah, I know not, no...

I had been at Uncle's inn in Coffins Grove for about four months, my life settled into a predictable routine: cleaning, cooking, and baking—as well as serving tea or meals to our many guests and visitors. Caring for Susan was not challenging work, but she was often disagreeable and uncooperative, making it difficult at times to get my kitchen work done. There were times I despaired of ever again having a moment to myself. Neighbors came and went, visiting for the evening, or stopping by for tea and gossip in the middle of the day. Although I enjoyed the visits, the hurried pace of my life was exhausting. Peddlers and other travelers came by frequently, always ready with news from other places both near and far. It was not a lonely life by any means, but I was homesick nonetheless. Mother, always reminding me of my family responsibility to marry, would have been pleased to know several local young men clamored for my attention—one among them was Milton Nelson, the younger son of Uncle's nearest neighbor. Milton often worked for Uncle during the day and escorted me to parties or dances in the evenings.

However, Milton would be headed off to war in just two days.

He stopped by this evening to tell me he had enlisted and would be leaving day after tomorrow, so I thought I should like to make a kind of farewell party for him. His sister Emily and her mother were sorrowful indeed over his departure and I hoped having all the neighbors in to bid him good bye might make them both feel better as he says his farewells.

In the morning I sent Ted, our hired boy, out with invitations to all our neighbors and friends, telling of the party to be held in Milton's honor that evening. With nearly the whole neighborhood coming out, it was a merry group at first. Yet by the end of the evening, many were weeping—some for Milton, and others for those who had already gone off to war—sons, brothers, husbands. All gaiety was muted by the time everyone drove home at the end of the evening. Hanging back as his father handed his mother and sister into the buggy, Milton gave me his Daguerreotype and begged me to come to the train station in the morning to bid him adieu. I promised I would.

The mood at the train was somber. There were ninety-four soldiers starting out for Missouri, accompanied by the sounds of much weeping from family and friends who feared they might never return. Milton kissed my hand, looking deep into my eyes before turning away to embrace his mother and sister, and shake his father's hand. He then climbed the steps into the train car and waved his hat to us as the train pulled out of the station. Mrs. Nelson began to weep as the train pulled away, and cried all the way back home. She was terrified Milton would die. Considering how many had already died, many before they saw even a single skirmish, I understood her fears.

After they dropped me at the inn, I entered the house through the kitchen thinking back over the last few days. A deep melancholy settled over me. What would the next year bring? Would more of my neighbors be called to fight this dreadful war? I wondered if I would ever see Milton again when so many men had left, never to return. Moments later as I heard Uncle come in through the front door, I remembered his announcement yesterday that James Gillespie had been here to see me. I was barely acquainted with the man—what could he possibly want to speak with me about.

26 December - James Gillespie came in, commenced talking, so we sat and talked till nearly eight (may we never forget the conversation that passed between us, how much I would give to know if he really means all he said) then I went into the kitchen to get breakfast...

It had been two and a half months since James' first visit to Uncle's inn to see me, although we have actually been keeping company for only a matter of days. Smiling at the thought, I considered how much had changed in such a brief time.

Milton had come home to visit the first week of November, striding through the crisping leaves on the lawn to put a ring on my finger, declaring his love and offering his wish that I would wear it until he returned. Although not certain of my feelings for him, I agreed to keep the ring, vowing to consider his question until he returned from war. We exchanged a few letters over the next weeks, and his sister Emily always shared with me those he sent to his family. As time went on, however, I realized that although I valued his friendship, I did not love him as I had always hoped to love a companion. I never spoke of this in my letters, though. I couldn't bear the thought he might feel abandoned so near the time he might go into battle.

Thinking of those days brings back Mother's words that I would "someday take a broken stick of a man" to avoid being alone. I am determined that will never be true, yet I am also aware time is marching on, leaving me—still unwed—alone in its wake.

It was at the Christmas Day dance for the Soldiers Relief Society, held in the ballroom of the Inn, that James and I truly became acquainted. Constant at my side, he brought me cups of punch between dances and helped me keep the dessert platters filled. After the party had broken up—about five in the morning—I went into the parlor to lay down and rest a while, when who should come in to sit beside me but James. We talked for hours and he declared great affection for me, claiming he'd had his eye on me ever since I had first come to live at Uncle's inn. He said so many sweet things, hinting at a future with me at his side, that I was promptly smitten. He spoke of my beauty and virtue, intimating I would one day make someone a wonderful wife. Speaking of the farm he would own one day soon and the family he hoped to have, he was so convincing in sharing his dreams that I almost began to believe they might include me.

3 January, 1862- I went with James to the dance. We came back around 11 o'clock. When we came in all was still. We sat down by the fire and enjoyed ourselves in conversation that we may never forget, no. Never...

I could hardly believe it had only been a week since James and I sat in the parlor as he shared the longings of his heart with me. I thought my own heart would burst when after the New Year's dance, we sat by the fire and James declared himself to me.

"I love you so, Emmie. Could it be possible that you might one day love me, too?"

I was so overwhelmed by emotion, I feared I might not be able to speak. Yet as tears threatened to spill from my eyes, I nodded happily. "Yes. O, yes, James. I believe I might."

We sat before the dining room fire, reveling in the quiet for hours, murmuring words of love and making plans for a future together someday. James did not actually speak the words asking me to become his wife, yet we still vowed to each other the day would come when we would one day exchange hearts and hands in marriage. The short time of our courtship has passed so quickly; can it really be only since Christmas that we have spent time together? Yet, it seems that promises have been made between us. I pray that if we do not change our minds, it may soon be God's will that we be joined as husband and wife.

James came to visit as often as he could, sometimes coming just for dinner before returning home to his father's farm, and other times staying all night at the inn. When he would stay over, we would sit up half the night, talking and making plans. Although he was an ardent lover, I held him at bay, not quite trusting in his affection for me as yet. I couldn't quite label it, but there was something about him that disturbed me. Mother would say I was borrowing trouble, but my uneasiness wouldn't be denied.

On one particularly long and tiring day, I had laid down on the sofa in the parlor to rest a moment before finishing up the dinner dishes and readying things for the next morning's breakfast. Uncle and Susan had been out to the Lyceum, earlier in the evening, and I had just finished mopping the barroom and kitchen. The few guests we had were still out for the evening, but Susan was already asleep upstairs. The house was so quiet, I fell asleep almost immediately. Yet, what seemed only seconds later, I was awakened by a whisper in my ear and a gentle kiss on my cheek.

"Emmie. Wake up, my dear! I have brought you a surprise."

Rousing from a deep sleep, I yawned and rubbed my eyes. "James? What are you doing here? It's so late."

"Oh Em, it is not so late. It's barely eight o'clock. Wake up, I am here to take you on a sleigh ride. The moon is full and it is so bright outside with all the snow."

I had sat up by this time, and although I would have much preferred my bed, I could see the excitement on his face at presenting his surprise.

"Alright James. Give me a moment to get my things. Is the sleigh already waiting?"

Smiling broadly, he assured me it was. I went to the closet to fetch my hat and coat—and the new woolen mittens Mother had sent me for Christmas—bundling up quickly before meeting James at the door.

Snatching up my hand, he tugged me—laughing at his enthusiasm—toward the door. "Hurry Em," he said. "You must come see how beautiful the snow is in the moonlight."

Long before I wrote stories, I listened for stories. Listening for them is something more acute than listening to them. I suppose it's an early form of participation in what goes on. Listening children know stories are there. When their elders sit and begin, children are just waiting and hoping for one to come out, like a mouse from its hole.

~ Eudora Welty

Chapter Sixteen

~∞~

August 1st - *Memories are so subjective. How can someone else's feel so real to me?*

Closing Emily's diary, I pulled my thoughts away from the scene Emily painted with her words. I could see it all so clearly, as if I had been a fly on the wall during her conversations with James. Opening the beautiful journal Will sent, I picked up my pen and began to write, speaking directly to Emily:

So here it is—James' first appearance in your diary. It seems like almost an afterthought to even mention his visit as you did. A virtual "oh, by the way..." for the man who would one day become your husband.

Of course, you didn't know that yet, did you?

Was your Uncle playing matchmaker, or was this something you remembered in retrospect and added to your diary later? Had you even met James before the day he turned up at the inn looking for you? Clearly you weren't lacking for company in Coffins Grove. In the picture you painted here in your diary, men seemed to flock around you continually—just as they had in Michigan.

Still, your James moved fast, didn't he? After you brief remark on his visit in October—where you never even saw him—you didn't mention him in your diary again until the day after Christmas when he comes to the party at the inn. Yet some spark was surely struck between you for you to sit up all night talking, sharing a secret conversation you wouldn't even commit to the pages of your diary.

But isn't that the way keeping a diary often works? People assume what finds its way onto its pages are the deepest secrets of a life. Things that—good or bad—you hold closest to your heart. Yet in my own experience, it seems those things are often least likely to be found within a diary. If the happenings are good, you're sure you'll never forget them. If they are not, you can scarcely bear to record them at all, lest they somehow gain strength through the writing.

However, I believe your conversations with James were the former, not the latter. I can imagine he shared the longings of his heart with you, and your only fear was that writing them down might make them disappear like stars in the full light of day.

Barely a week has passed since your first "date," and yet there he is, declaring his love for you. As someone whose wedding followed her first date by just over six months, I certainly understand that love sometimes moves quickly, but even for me it seems he moved a bit fast. Did you feel the same—and if so, did it worry you? It would seem that you did. Or were you so anxious to find a way out of your situation with your uncle that you were ready to be satisfied by any solution that came your way?

I can't imagine feeling so desperate. So anxious about your future you would take anyone that came along just to feel secure.

Or maybe I can...

A year ago, when my neighbor mentioned the local high school was in need of a long-term substitute for a literature teacher who was going on maternity leave, I jumped at it. Not because I wanted to teach, but because I was afraid of being alone with myself any longer.

With my literature degree, teaching experience, and several published novels under my belt, I was apparently the answer to their prayers. The hired me practically on the spot.

For myself, I figured that if I couldn't write, I could at least hang out with writers. So, for three periods a day, I introduced high school students with the glories of English literature. It was so much easier to surround myself with beautiful words written by others than to face the fear I'd never again produce any of my own

So, I led my students in discussing great books and graded their essays. For a while, it kept me busy, and it was enough.

But it isn't anymore. I know that now. And more than that, I don't think the life you chose was enough for you either.

Oh, I believe you did your best to convince yourself it was—just as I did. But I think even before your marriage, you knew—deep down—that marrying James would be nothing more than a way to feel secure in the moment. Not the way to a truly happy life.

Unfortunately, a moment is rarely enough...

I laid down my pen, and gazed out the window toward the neighboring cornfields. The afternoon was giving way to evening. I could see the neighbor's tractor turning onto the road, its driver likely headed home for dinner. Life on a farm seemed ordered by the sun, especially this time of year. The sun got a farmer out of bed to tend his stock or start his day in the fields. The sun provided the energy by which his crops grew, and the sinking sun directed him home at the end of the day to again feed livestock and spend a few precious hours with his family. It might be different in the winter when daylight was scarce and the sun often hid behind clouds, but when the summer sun danced the sky it seemed a constant reminder of the swift passage of time.

Had Emily seen the sun this way? As it rose and set every day, was she also conscious her life was passing? As I read her diary, listening as she spoke about James, I couldn't help but wonder why she turned to him so quickly when Milton had given her a ring and made his feelings for her so obvious. Was she hedging her bets? Trying to assure herself that no matter what happened she wouldn't end up unmarried? At nearly twenty-four, Emily's "shelf life" as a prospective bride was almost past, and all which lay beyond it was spinsterhood and a life of dependence on others. A spinster daughter or sister was seen a burden on fathers or brothers, as well as a source of unpaid labor, working to care for nieces and nephews and living as an unpaid domestic servant charged with making life easier for the lady of the house. If they had no home of their own, most were destined to care for the homes of others.

Was she just doing whatever was necessary to assure that the time in which a family of her own was possible wouldn't pass her by? Or had she just fallen so much in love with James she was willing to forget another man already made her a promise.

A bird in the hand, maybe?

Emily wanted only two things from her life—the ability to live it as she chose, and a loving home of her own. With James' obvious interest, I'm sure it began to appear she just might have found her last chance at the latter.

Whatever the reason, her interest in James seemed clear—at least to me.

Turning back to the diary, I pressed open the pages and once more began to read Emily's life.

We tell our stories, especially as young people, in part because we want them to be true. We want life to be full of adventure and creativity and daring that might, just might, be real.

~ Dana Frank

Chapter Seventeen

~∞~

Emily

19 February, 1862 - This evening we all went to Lyceum (snow some in evening). James came home with me. We sat & talked awhile after the rest had all retired, ah, those questions...

It had been quite a long evening. After cooking for eighteen people at dinner, James and I went to the Lyceum for the evening's presentations. I always enjoyed those events; they put me in mind of so many times back in Michigan I recited a poem or essay I had written. Several townsfolk, in addition to a few speakers from out of town, read works or gave talks on various topics. Sometimes there were even entertainments such as songs or plays. Tonight's event included a spirited debate on the abolition of slavery, and I listened with great interest to both sides of the issue.

It was snowing again as we exited the schoolhouse. James very solicitously tucked a blanket tightly around me as I sat next to him on the bench for the drive home while Uncle and Susan huddled in the back, also wrapped up in quilts. I tucked my hands into James coat pocket and we sat snuggly together in his carriage, enjoying the crisp air and laughing at the thick fog swirling with our every breath. Yet as we drew closer to the inn, his mood grew pensive.

Uncle took Susan straight upstairs after we arrived home, however James lingered for several hours. I tried to engage him in conversation, yet in spite of his reluctance to leave, he seemed to have nothing to say. In an effort to fill the silence and ease some of his apparent distress, I talked of home, telling him stories of my childhood, my school days, and my friends from home. He appeared to listen, yet with only half an ear. Finally, I asked if something was amiss. Had I offended him in some manner?

Looking quite serious, more so than I had seen him before, he seemed to unwilling to meet my eyes. Finally, he swallowed hard, and with a quavering voice, he spoke at last. "Emmie, do you love me?" Looking up, he took my hand and asked one more question. "Will you be my bride?"

Although we had spoken on this same subject more than once before that night, I was still surprised at his words. All the tension of these last hours was caused by those two simple questions? I smiled at his nerves before leaning in close and whispering in his ear, "Yes, James. I do love you. I will be your bride."

His relief was immediate. A huge smile spread across his face as he pulled me into his arms and let out a loud whoop. "You said yes? You really said yes?" Dancing me around the room, he kept repeating, "You said yes."

Once he left for home, I sat down with my diary, wanting to remember this night forever. I was filled with such happiness that I'd found a man I could love, that I would gain my own home at last. But I felt tempered by a certain sadness as well. It was so hard to be so far away from my parents and friends at such a moment, yet I prayed that all might be for the best—that James and I would ever prove to be all we now think each other to be.

In the morning I would write a letter to Mother, telling her of my news, but in that moment, I simply closed my diary and my eyes, trusting all would yet be well.

***

Two weeks later, after the next Lyceum, James and I once again sat up all night, speaking of our future. We decided we would marry in one year—on the first day of March 1863, hopeful he would have his own farm by then. His mother long ago promised him that on his marriage she would deed over one hundred acres of the farm that

131

she held title to, and he hoped she would keep her word so we might begin our married life in a home of our own.

We vowed to hold true to this date and to each other, and my prayer would continue to be that God's will would be done in our relationship. Although I would not wish him to know it, I am still somewhat anxious at the thought of forever leaving my father's home—even if I have not lived there for nearly a year, for tis a great thought to think of leaving childhood's home to take a companion, yes indeed.

14 March - To day heard the news of Milton's death. He died in the Hospital, at St. Louis with typhoid fever on the 18th of February. I composed some poetry on his death today...

In spite of my growing relationship with James, I faithfully corresponded with Milton all these past months, doing my best to keep his spirits up and informed of the news at home. Yet I felt such guilt that he passed still holding tightly to the hope I might one day agree to become his wife. I can only hope the thought brought him comfort in the end.

My own comfort, however, was not so easily assured. As the weeks went by, James seemed to be reconsidering our plans to marry in a year. One evening after dinner, he told me he thought we should not plan for a certain day, but leave it to providence to decide when would be the right time. His unwillingness to make plans caused me to wonder if he changed his mind about our marriage altogether. I considered returning home for a time, simply planning for a visit. But by the time of my twenty-fourth birthday in April, I told Henry Nelson and his father that I would be leaving in just five or six weeks. Aside from my homesickness, I couldn't bear the thought of staying in Coffins Grove and having James humiliate me by breaking off our still not-widely-known engagement.

"I think you will not go—and if you do you'll come back." Mr. Nelson looked at me smugly, as if the thought of my leaving was simply beyond my own choice. "James is sure to have something to say about it."

Mr. Nelson may not have known of it, but I had no intention of breaking the promise I made to James—yet, as Mother is fond of saying, "there is many a slip 'tween the cup and the lip. A thing is not done till 'tis done." For myself, I would put my faith in James' intention when I was certain he would keep his word.

12 April - O Dear, how can I stay here any longer; Susan is so saucy. But may she, as she grows older, learn to use more judgment...

The last few weeks have been such a trial. Susan's defiant behavior has been nearly unbearable at times and Uncle is no help at all. I am so tired of dealing with not only the difficult work of keeping house and cooking for guests who come and go at all hours, but with Susan's impertinence as well. At times I despair of whether she will ever learn better. It has been forty-one weeks since I arrived here in Uncle's home and, although I have James' declaration of love and marriage, I still feel as if I have nothing of my own. In spite of the personal affection he shows me, there are times when it seems he doesn't even remember what he offered. Is it any wonder I doubt his assurances?

I am uneasy, and I am often quite gloomy. My friends here are wonderful, supplying my every want in the way of company, yet still I have a longing desire I do not comprehend. Guilt also rakes my heart as I consider the past; may I not do again the evil deeds which I know to be wrong. Ah, may the will of God be done, not mine.

I pause at this thought. My heart is so heavy over my past transgressions, I can not shake them. I can not even bring myself to name them lest someone might someday read my words and think ill of me. If James knew, what would he say? Would he withdraw his words of love and his promise of marriage? Would my past cost me my future? I can not bear to even think of it.

In the midst of this upheaval, I miss my home and my family so much. I am once again considering a visit home in June. Just seeing Mother and Father, and being their child once more would mean so much to me.

27 April - Went to meeting but did not stay...James came to Uncles with me.

Sunday afternoons usually brought a visits with the neighbors after meeting time, but on this day I simply could not face it. I was so disheartened by James' apparent renunciation of the promises he made me that I told Uncle I would just walk home. The walk was not far, but I felt the time alone—something I so rarely had—would do me good. But I had not ventured out more than a few minutes when I heard a buggy come close behind me. Turning, I saw James in the seat, smiling and waving.

"Emmie! Where are you bound? I was hoping to speak with you today. Can I carry you wherever you are headed?"

His expression was so eager, so genuinely pleased to see me. I set aside my melancholy as best I could and accepted his offered hand to pull me up on the seat beside him. Thanking him for his care, I smiled as brightly as I could manage, and tucked my skirts away from the wheel. I attempted several topics of conversation, beginning with the subject of the sermon, until it became obvious he was not disposed to speak.

"You had something you wished to say to me?" I asked.

I hated that my speech was so formal toward someone I was pledged to marry, but our relationship seemed to teeter on such a precarious balance these last weeks—I had no certainty about his intentions any longer.

Without so much as a smile, he nodded. "I'll tell you once we've arrived."

Once we'd reached the inn, James handed off the horses to Ted and we went inside through the kitchen door. After helping me off with my coat, he took me by the hand and led me into the parlor. The room was dark and somewhat chill in spite of the sunshine outside, and along with his silence, gave me a sense of foreboding that whatever he had to say might be bad news. Leading me to the lounge, he seated me carefully and sat at my side. My stomach was chock-full of butterflies, and I hoped whatever it was, he would just get it over with. I was tired and discouraged, and simply hoped there would still be time for me to enjoy some quiet before everyone else came home later in the afternoon.

In spite of my qualms, I saw he looked pleased about something. He could hardly contain his excitement and I became curious as to what it might be. Finally, without saying a word he knelt before me, reached into his pocket and held up a golden ring. Looking up at me, a grin began to spread across his face, until it occupied even his eyes. Taking my hand in his, he slipped the ring onto my finger.

After weeks of hearing little more than silence on the topic—or excuses for why we couldn't set a definite date for our marriage—James decided to surprise me with a ring. This was surely a commitment, since all would see it and know of his intentions. I wanted more than anything to ask him when we might be wed, but I did not want to spoil this moment with my questions. I would try to be patient a little longer.

Throwing my arms around his neck, I knelt beside him on the floor, kissed his cheek and snuggled in close. "I love it, James. Thank you!"

"It was my grandmother's," he said, his fingers fiddling with the ring now on my finger. "She left it to me for my bride—and that, my dear Emmie, is you!"

For the next several hours, we sat in the darkness sharing kisses and caresses. And we made plans for the future—our future. Although we had spoken of it many times before, in this moment I was finally feeling secure in our promised future, and in his love. This time I believed I could finally begin to plan for our life together.

Every reader finds himself. The writer's work is merely a kind of optical instrument that makes it possible for the reader to discern what, without this book, he would perhaps never have seen in himself.

~ Marcel Proust

Chapter Eighteen

~∞~

August 9th - *Although I've known all along Emily eventually married James, I've been so drawn into her story, I can hardly bear to set her diary down. I feel driven to know exactly how it happened, to understand why she acted as she did...*

Finishing the last bite of my sandwich, I brushed the crumbs from my fingers and picked up my pen. It felt so natural speaking to Emily it was as if I was writing a letter. Although never quite as satisfying as speaking face-to-face, a letter did have its advantages. Writing offered time to think, to consider more carefully what to say and how to frame it.

Taking up my pen, I began...

Less than two months after your first date, James proposed and two months after that, his grandmother's ring rests on your finger. I can so easily imagine the way he worked up his courage to propose, his utter happiness at your answer—and yours as he finally offers a token that will make his commitment to marry you visible to the world. Your story reminded me of Jack's proposal—all nervous laughter and shallow breathing. I have to admit, it was kind of endearing. Although Jack and I dated quite a bit longer than you and James had been keeping company, my parents still managed to seem shocked that it happened so quickly.

But it didn't seem that fast to me.

Still…waiting a year to marry? Such a long time, yet if it brought you the home and family you craved, I supposed you thought it worth the wait. You always claimed you wouldn't marry without love— and that you wanted a home of your own. I can also imagine the thought of living with your in-laws would not be a pleasant one.

(It's ok, really. I wouldn't have wanted to live with mine, either!)

Intent on my writing, I stopped when I heard the rumble of the train which passed every night at this same hour, the blast of its horn reminding me of Emily's brief mention of Milton's death. She wrote of a poem she penned at the news, and I couldn't help but feel she somehow saw herself as a tragic heroine who lost a lover in the war. Musing over the idea, I turned back to my journal and again addressed Emily directly:

I almost forgot about Milton. And so—apparently—did you. How sad he died of sickness…and before he even reached the battleground, but that happened so often in those days. A quick Google search informs me more of the men who fought in the Civil War died from disease than from battle wounds—some two-thirds of the total deaths.

Did you feel guilty? Knowing Milton died hoping—maybe even believing—you and he might have a future together, did some sense of remorse drive you to stick with James even when it seemed like maybe planning a future with him might be a lost cause?

Did you ever wonder if things were moving too fast with James—or whether his indecisiveness meant he simply changed his mind about marriage?

I know I did…

I'm sure that it would have been a comfort for you to return home to visit your family at that point, even if it was just for a brief visit. Surely some time away from Manchester could have offered you some perspective on your life. But you made a promise to James, and for some reason you felt that alone should keep you from visiting home.

I can't help but wonder whether things would have been different for you if you had gone home…

Laying the pen down, I rose from my chair—stretching my aching neck and shoulders. I felt as if I'd been writing all night, and a glance at my great-grandmother's clock told me it was nearly true.

2:36 am.

Carrying my dishes back into the kitchen, I couldn't help but think there was something about Emily's relationship with Milton—short, and apparently one-sided as it was—that drove her relationship with James. Something made me wonder if her commitment, in spite of his indecisiveness, grew out of more than desperation to marry simply to avoid becoming a spinster. Was there—just maybe—some sense of guilt behind it?

Emily took Milton's offer for granted and he died--still hoping for a future with her. Regardless of whether she felt anything more than friendship for him, couldn't guilt over his unrequited feelings have made her cling all the more tightly to James? To his promises? If only so she didn't have to view herself as someone who couldn't keep a promise.

Maybe I'm reading more into her words than I should, but I know a thing or two about guilt...

***

I was eleven when my mother died. In one of our last conversations—probably the first time I truly understood she was dying—she asked me to help my dad, to look out for Charlie and Will. I cried and cried, begging her not to leave me, but vowing I would always watch over them.

"I'll take care of them Mom, I promise I will. I won't let anything happen to them—ever!"

Holding my hand tightly, she lifted her other hand to my head. Brushing her fingers gently over my hair before resting them on my cheek, she smiled—and in remembrance her words took on the weight of a sacrament, becoming more a charge than a commendation.

"You are my brave girl, Lizzie. I know you'll always do the right thing.

From that moment, I knew—whether it was what my mother meant or not—my brother and sister were my responsibility.

But it wasn't until a few years later I first understood the terrible weight of it...

Fourteen years old and annoyed I was stuck spending Saturday afternoon watching my little brother. Not exactly my dream day...

"Lizzie! Push me again."

Will's whining is starting to annoy me. He begged to come to the park, and in spite of wanting to go to the movies, or just curling up in my room and reading the afternoon away, I agreed to bring him down here to play.

But I've been pushing his swing for over half an hour now, and I've had enough.

"I just want to read for a few minutes. Can't you play on the monkey bars?"

I know he's only six and I'm trying not to let him see my irritation, but he's driving me nuts. "Come on, Will. I need a break. Play by yourself a few minutes, or we'll have to go home."

None too happy with me, he's pouting now. But he finally heads over to the bars and starts to climb. Maybe now I'll finally get to finish my chapter...

Turning the last page, I look up, expecting to see Will inching his way across the top or hanging upside down off the bars—but he's not there.

Didn't I just hear him talking about a cloud shaped like an ice cream cone?

"Will? Where are you?" I call. "Will!"

I am screaming now, but there is still no answer.

Nor is there any answer for the next five minutes.

No answer...

No Will.

I can hardly breathe. He is nowhere I can see, and my throat is raw from screaming his name. Tears streak my cheeks—the same cheek my mother caressed as she charged me with his care.

He is gone—and it's all my fault.

I hope she can't see me now. One simple thing she asked of me, and I couldn't do it.

This is all my fault.

I found Will a short time later sitting under a tree on the other side of the park, completely oblivious to the chaos he'd caused. Caught up with watching a squirrel stuffing pine nuts in his mouth, he claimed he hadn't heard me calling his name. I was so relieved—and so angry—but mostly overwhelmed by guilt. I'd let my own desires override my responsibility for my brother. I'd ignored his calls for my attention and nearly lost him forever.

I scolded him all the way home, reminding him that he was never to wander off without telling me, but I knew I was the one who failed. I'd broken my promise. I didn't deserve my mother's confidence in me.

I vowed to never let her down again.

The muses are ghosts, and sometimes they come uninvited.
~ Stephen King

Chapter Nineteen

~∞~

August 10th - *I've got to admit I expected more. This place looks so ordinary, I might have driven right past it without a guide...*

I woke late the next morning—the sun long since risen above the trees outside my window—not surprising since I stayed up late reading, finally falling into a fitful sleep sometime after 4 am.

Just as I drifted off, I decided it was time to search out the inn where Emily lived with her uncle and cousin when she first arrived here in Manchester. So, as the coffee brewed I opened my laptop and typed "Henry Baker Coffins Grove Iowa" into the search line.

Talk about easy! Before the coffee was ready, I had discovered the location of the inn and the cemetery where Emily's uncle was buried; a digitized copy of his will; information about his wife, daughter and grandchildren; plus drawings and both old and new photographs of the Inn itself.

The Coffins Grove Stagecoach Inn, now on the National Historic Registry, even had its own Facebook page—complete with street address and phone number.

The number was disconnected, but I decided I'd just take a drive over there to take a look around. Alex had warned me though, the GPS maps weren't quite "right" on this side of town, so—since I needed coffee anyway—I decided to stop by *The Coffee Den*, pick up some beans and, hopefully, a few basic directions. The baristas proved to be a fountain of information about Manchester so far. I was sure that if they didn't know how to find the old inn on Candle Road, no one would.

I was so right.

***

With a soy cappuccino steaming on the counter in front of me, I scribbled the directions to the inn on the back of a bag of coffee beans. The barista enthusiastically filled me in on what she knew of the inn's history, its proximity to the cemetery where Henry Baker was buried, and local gossip about restoration plans with a new owner. Now anxious to be on my way, I picked up my drink from the counter, dropped the bag of coffee in my purse, and began to back slowly toward the door as she chattered on and on. She was relaying tales about ghost-sightings near the cemetery when I heard someone call my name.

"Liz? Is that you?"

Whirling a bit too quickly at the sound of a familiar voice, I nearly knocked over a display rack of coffee bags when I saw who it was.

"Dan? What ..." Startled once again at the vivid blue of his eyes, my heartbeat frantic in my chest—but it wasn't just with embarrassment over my clumsiness. Scrambling to right the rack without spilling the coffee in my hand, I was at a complete loss for words.

Why can I never seem to a form a coherent sentence around this man?

Thankfully, he moved to fill the gap, offering his drink order to the barista as he helped me gather the bags which had fallen to the floor before turning back to speak.

"So, what are you up to? Other than rearranging the store, I mean." A twinkle in his eyes belied his serious tone as he dipped his voice, and in a stage whisper asked, "Have you found any deep dark secrets in the diary yet?"

Ok, this I can talk about!

Placing the last bag back on the rack, I took a deep breath and willed myself to relax. Summoning what I hoped was a serene smile, I found my voice at last. "Well, as a matter of fact, I did discover something interesting. I figured out the location of the inn where

Emily lived when she first came to Iowa—and I'm headed out there now to see it."

Taking his coffee from the barista, he turned back toward me and asked, "Is it nearby?"

As we walked toward the door, I told him what I'd discovered about its location. Waving a goodbye to the barista, he assured me he knew exactly where it was.

"It's not far. I could drive you out there—or you could just follow me..."

Less than ten minutes later, after a drive which led through town and past both of our farms, Dan's truck pulled up in front of a mildly impressive mid-nineteenth-century Greek Revival brick house set back in a wide sweep of lawn and surrounded by tall oaks. As I parked not far behind him, his door opened and his passenger—a golden retriever—bounded out of the cab and loped in my direction.

At the sound of a loud whistle, the dog wheeled around and sauntered back toward Dan who clicked a leash on his collar.

"I usually let him run," he said as he came up beside me, the dog now contentedly trotting by his heel, tongue lolling as he seemed to smile at me. "But Bill here gets pretty excited over meeting new people. I didn't want him rushing you, not knowing how you feel about dogs."

"Oh, he's fine," I said, leaning over to scratch his head. "He reminds me of a dog we had when my daughters were young. Goldens are wonderful with kids, but...Bill?"

He looked sheepish as he said, "My youngest boy named him Billy Bones. You know...Treasure Island? But it's a mouthful, so after a while he just became Bill. Still, named after a pirate or not, he's a great dog—even if he is a little excitable."

Squinting in the bright sunlight, I wished I hadn't left my sunglasses on the kitchen counter. But in spite of the glaring sunlight, my attention was drawn toward the house. A fly buzzed past my ear, a stiff breeze rustled through cornstalks on the neighboring farm, and on the road a black buggy passed—its driver waving from behind his horse as my focus slips to the past.

I can almost see a stagecoach, full of weary travelers, turning off the road and pulling up to the inn in a cloud of dust.

Is that Emily at the door, preparing to greet them?

Realizing Dan was speaking to me, I turned back to face him, a bit sheepish at being caught daydreaming. "I'm sorry, I spaced a bit there. What did you say?"

He grinned at my confusion. "I said, 'Is it what you expected?'"

Noting the incongruity of the setting—from the satellite dish perched precariously on the edge of the aging roof and the rusty milk box tucked into a corner on the porch, to the decaying foundations of what had probably been a barn and the ever-present cornfields surrounding the house—I asked myself, is it what I expected?

I couldn't help but laugh.

"Dan, from the moment I arrived in Iowa, nothing has been what I expected!" I paused a minute, shaking my head before continuing. "But I'll bet you meant the inn, didn't you?"

Turning back toward the house, I considered it carefully. "It's smaller than I thought it would be. I don't know why, but I expected it to be huge—not just a big house."

I paused again, looking up at the windows circling the façade, and tried to imagine what the place would have looked like when it was new.

"Emily wrote about peddlers who made the rounds of neighboring town, travelers who stayed here on their way from one place to another, large groups who came for dinner or dances."

Looking back in Dan's direction, I asked, "How could they possibly hold neighborhood dances in a place so small?"

"Small neighborhood?" he said, the twinkle in his eye belying his quizzical expression.

We both laughed at that. But Dan was right, considering the current size of the local population, how many people could possibly have lived here in Coffins Grove in the 1860s?

We continued toward the house, talking about the possibility of finding a buyer interested in restoring the place and the now-absent barn. He even told me tales he and his childhood friends used to tell of ghostly apparitions spotted through then-boarded-up windows.

"It's haunted?"

"Well, according to local folklore..." Dan cocked an eyebrow and chuckled as he continued. "Some people say Henry Baker and his family haunt the inn and the cemetery..." He turned and pointed off to our right, "just over there."

"Have you ever seen them?" I asked. With its aging headstones and monuments barely visible through a stand of oaks at the edge of the property, it looked like the kind of cemetery likely to have its own congregation of ghosts—or at least a collection of neighborhood legends.

"No, but some folks claimed to," Dan said. "When I was a kid, a lot of my friends used to camp outside in the summer, sometimes taking walks out this way in hopes of spotting a ghost or two. A few of them even insisted they'd seen old Henry Baker roaming the neighborhood looking for the hand he lost in a reaper accident."

"Really?" I couldn't help but chuckle at the thought of a ghost wandering the countryside looking for a lost hand.

"We were only ten, remember? A bunch of boys trying to one-up each other...exploring with flashlights in the dark, vying to see who could tell the scariest story."

"Like slumber parties," I said. "My girls used to do that, too. But it always backfired and someone would end up crying, wanting to call her parents to pick her up in the middle of the night—too freaked out to sleep in a strange place."

"Exactly," he said. "But there really are local stories about the place. In the early 90s there were even people who came here from who-knows-where to do some sort of 'ghost experiments' in the old inn. Everyone thought they were nuts, but those people were convinced the place was haunted."

Peering through windows, I could see that no one lived here now. The room to the left of the front door must have been the ballroom Emily wrote about—and in spite of my initial thoughts about the size of the house, it did look able to fit a fair-sized gathering. I could easily imagine couples spinning around the floor—as long as there weren't too many of them.

Across the floor was a doorway leading toward the back of the house and stairs climbing up from the entry, but I could see little else. However, at that moment Dan dropped a question which stopped my assessment in its tracks.

"So, are you here chasing ghosts, too?"

I laughed uncertainly, unsure why the question felt so probing. I glanced up at Dan's face and could see he hadn't meant anything by it. It was clearly meant as a joke, but it threw me nonetheless. I managed a quip about leaving the ghostbusting to the professionals and steered the conversation back toward the architecture. We discussed crooked lintels and the motif along the roof line for a few minutes until his phone rang and he announced he needed to head back to his farm. Shielding my eyes with one hand, I waved with the other as he and Bill-the-dog drove off, then returned to my still-churning thoughts.

Am I chasing ghosts?

What was I doing if not trying to find those things which had seemingly left me behind? Trying to pacify those ghosts which refused to give me peace. Haunting my waking... and now even my sleep.

That wasn't it, though. In spite of all those I lost in my life—my parents and grandparents, even Jack—they were not what haunted me. My ghosts were fears for the future, not traces of my past.

I suppose that was what drew me to the diary.

When Emily began to write, her whole life was ahead of her. But as time moved on, she grew more fearful of what lay ahead. Life changes—it always does—but she grew more aware of how little of her life was actually within her control. She was raised to marry, bear children, and work alongside her husband—in spite of her personal desires. Surely she began to realize, particularly after coming to Iowa, her future was dependent on someone wanting her. Offering her the life she was told she must live—whether it was what she wanted or not.

Did the specter of spinsterhood cause Emily to accept a life she wouldn't have otherwise chosen? Was she doing whatever was necessary to assure that the time in which a family of her own was possible wouldn't pass her by? Or had she simply fallen so much in love she was willing to forget another man had already made her some sort of promise. Did she promise to marry James—in spite of her concerns—out of fears for her future?

Whether she was running toward her future or away from her past, it was clear she was looking for something. In spite of her desire for a home and family of her own, she had come to this place to take on someone else's. Adamant she never wanted to be a farmer's wife, she became exactly that.

I turned back toward my car, ready to dive into the diary once more. Visiting this place hadn't exactly given me what I hoped to find, but then—as I told Dan—nothing about this trip was what I expected. But I had come to understand this inn—for local travelers and for Emily—as an in-between place. Marking time before they made their way to the places they belonged.

Just like me.

In spite of my curiosity about the reasons behind Emily's choices, a niggling little thought just wouldn't let me go...

Was I also running away? Were there ghosts—uncertainties about my future, guilt over my past—keeping me from living the life I wanted, too? Shaking my head as if to clear my thoughts, I pulled myself back to considering Emily's story of her life at the inn.

After all, I had a book to write—and Emily was waiting for me.

Every man has his secret sorrows which the world knows not; and often times we call a man cold when he is only sad.
~ Henry Wadsworth Longfellow

Chapter Twenty

~∞~

Emily

1 June, 1862 - James is sad today, he wept but told not why...

We still had not set a date for the wedding. James explained that until his mother deeded over to him the hundred acres of her farm as she promised, we could not do so. He was determined that, although it might be necessary to live with his parents for a time after our marriage, he would only do so to make possible building a house on our own farm.

His mother holding the deed to the farm was an unusual circumstance. James' father gave it to her long ago in an effort to save the farm from his creditors. Yet, even years later, it still remained in her possession. Rarely did women own property, even in the second half of the nineteenth century. Times may have been changing, but they were not changing so quickly as that. James' mother may have been the legal owner of the property, but as a married woman she still had no legal right to its control. It was James' father who must be convinced. I know this arrangement troubled him greatly for his father seemed unwilling to let any of the acreage go.

One day during James' evening visit, we sat under a large oak, silently watching the changing colors of the evening sky. Inexplicably, he began to weep. His mood had been dark all evening—for several days, if truth be told—but he never cried in my presence before. No matter how I tried, I could not coax a reason for his sorrow out of him. He merely held me tight and wept into my shoulder. James had been given to spells of unsociability from time to time, even occasionally suffering with "the blues," but I had never seen him so apparently troubled before—and I was clueless how to make things better.

"Hush, James." I soothed him as I would a small child, making shushing sounds in his ear and gently caressing his hair. "What is worrying you, my darling? Please tell me." We sat thus for what seemed a very long time, yet he said not a word. Eventually, however, his breathing began to quiet. The sun had set, dusk was spreading, and bright stars flickered one by one into view. Heaving a final sigh and squeezing me tightly, he kissed me deeply and then pushed me away as he stood.

"I am so sorry, Em. I am so sorry." He rubbed his face with one hand, and turned away toward the barn. "It is growing late. I must get home."

"James? Must you go?" I jumped to my feet and reached for his arm, but he shrugged me off, striding away toward the barn.

I followed after him, calling out for him to stop. "Something is wrong," I said. "Will you not tell me what it is...please?"

He muttered something I couldn't understand and the next I knew he was astride his horse, waving as he turned down the road.

I stood for a while watching the stars spark the sky, wondering what had happened—and whether it was likely to happen again. James was so thoughtful, and worried so. How could I help him through his troubles? I offered a prayer that God would lead me always and turned toward the house—and my diary. I was so thankful to have a place where I could lay down my fears.

15 June - I am pondering on the past, thinking what may be my future lot, & writing in my diary...found James here. We sat in the Parlor & talked & c. till near two, it will probably be the last time this summer as I intend to commence teaching school next Tuesday...

Days went by, and slowly James' mood returned to normal. I hoped there would be no return of his troubled tempers, and in spite of the fact our lives were still unsettled, he appeared much happier. Although we never discussed what happened that night, his melancholy did seem to be behind us, and for that I was glad.

We did discuss our plans for marriage though, deciding I would teach school in Masonville for the summer. It would earn me thirty dollars, and with our hope to marry within the year the money would be handy.

With twenty-six scholars looking to me for guidance, I stayed quite busy. I boarded with a different family each week (which was not an ideal arrangement, but necessary), and yearned for the weekend visits James promised to make. He came to visit the first week, and brought me home to Uncle's for a visit over the second weekend—the Fourth of July holiday. We attended an afternoon picnic in the Grove, then went into Manchester for an evening dance, finally arriving home just as the sun was coming up. It had been such a lovely day, but I had to return to Masonville on the morrow.

27 July - this afternoon James came to see me. It seems but tis as the words of God & may it be his will, the first of October if no preventing providence may perchance find me in another home, ah, my dream of last June...

Trudging back to Mr. Martin's farm, I reflected on the day. My students were uncooperative and sassy, and the heat in the schoolroom nearly unbearable. As I made my way home, an ill-tempered parent waylaid me with complaints about his child's lack of progress in reading. Nearly choking with the dust from the road, I was deeply exhausted and longed for nothing more than a few moments rest in a quiet room before I prepared tomorrow's lessons.

Yet, seated on Mr. Martin's front porch, an unexpected visitor awaited me, nearly invisible in the shadows. I was startled when a voice called out as I walked up to the house.

"Emmie!"

Looking up at the sound of my name, I could not have been more surprised. Walking toward me with a huge smile on his face was

150

James. Picking up my skirts, I began to run, nearly dropping my book bag and tripping up the stairs in my haste. "James! I can not believe you are really here."

Hurling myself into his arms, I was lifted off my feet as he swung me around, kissing me soundly as he did. He laughed heartily at my reaction, asking, "Did you miss me?"

"James! It's been three weeks. Of course I missed you."

Drawing me toward the settee on the porch, he asked how my teaching was proceeding, teasing me as to whether I would be willing to give it up at the end of the summer.

"Oh, James. It is just awful. Some of the students refuse to listen, and others do nothing but misbehave all day long—especially the larger ones." All my romantic ideas about educating bright and curious minds were being soundly trounced by my summer experience as a teacher.

He laughed again, and wondered aloud if they were just looking for extra attention from a pretty teacher. But I knew that was not the problem. Some felt they were too big for schooling and simply did not want to be there.

"I wonder to myself regularly, how many times does a teacher have to weep for the misconduct of some pupil?" I shook my head, and said determinedly, "No, I can not wait for this summer to end."

With a look which promised he was pleased by my answer, James proceeded to assure me I need never go back to teaching. "Em, would you be pleased to hear we might be married by the first of October?"

"Truly, James? No more hindrances?" I had walked this path before, so was hesitant to truly believe it. Yet, he seemed so certain, so joyful.

"Truly, Em. You would have to postpone your visit to Michigan, of course. Yet, if God wills it, we shall very soon be wed."

I wanted so much to be married and away from both my service at the inn and my trials as a teacher. I wanted a home of my own, a haven. I wanted a family.

So I chose, in that moment, to believe him.

6 August - O dear, 300,000 more men called for to be ready by the fifteenth of this month or they are going to draft. Ah, horrible indeed to think so many of our associates & friends must be slain on this dreaded battlefield...

With all that James and I contended with as we planned for our future, never did it cross my mind the War might threaten to intrude. Still teaching in Masonville, I occasionally worried about whether James might be forced to go off to fight, especially when so many young men around me seemed pulled to war every week. In his letters James assured me he would not go unless he was obliged to, yet still I feared he might change his mind. Men too often seemed to be drawn to what they saw as the heroic acts of war. My brother Henry had already joined the Army of the Potomac, and I was terrified I might never see him again. I couldn't bear the thought of James joining as well.

Invited to tea by the mother of one of my students, I looked forward to what I hoped would be an afternoon which did not include complaints about my teaching. Mrs. Rose and Mrs. Dutton were there as well and we had a lovely time talking of the neighbors' new carriage and Mrs. Rose's soon-expected baby, when the conversation turned to the lecture planned for that evening at the schoolhouse—an effort to gain volunteers for the war.

"Mr. Dutton tells me they need 300,000 volunteers by next week or they are going to begin to draft." Mrs. Dutton sat back, looking directly at me before continuing. "Will your James volunteer? Our country needs good strong men to fight for it."

My thoughts were in turmoil. 300,000? How could we be asked to spare so many? I saw a sea of faces before my mind's eye— Milton Nelson, Horace Jones from the farm next to Father's, and so many of our neighbors and friends who had already given their lives to this war. Men who would never again work their farms, kiss their wives, or raise their children—and what would become of those wives and children whose husbands and fathers were killed? They would have no way to support themselves; forever dependent on the charity of others. War was often as terrible for those left at home as those who went off to fight.

What would I do if James were to fight and die?

I was terrified at the thought of being alone—of losing him. The conversation carried on without me, all present debating whether there would be enough volunteers, and who might be drafted if there were not. They hardly seemed to notice that I had grown silent. Holding in my tears and worries as best I could, I excused myself on the pretext I had a lesson to prepare before the evening lecture, and walked the path back to Mr. Martin's farm.

I must admit I cried on my way home, but sat down immediately to write James a letter, begging him not to go to war. If a draft came about, there was nothing I could do—but he must not volunteer.

7 September - James was here all day, most & evening, too till eleven. Can it be that next week Emmie is to be a bride? Yes, yes, if James fulfills his promise—but may I trust that all will be well, that the will of God be done.

My summer teaching ended none too soon. School closed on September 5th with examinations, followed by a presentation where the scholars recited their pieces and sang their songs. James came to collect me the next morning and I left Masonville with hopes to never return--at least not to the schoolhouse.

The draft I feared never happened, and James did not volunteer to go off to war. I had the thirty dollars earned from teaching, and the future before me shone bright. James and I decided our marriage would take place in a week, but in the end nearly two more weeks passed before we wed. Uncle and James went to Dehli to get the license on the 17th, and on the 18th—to the surprise of all in attendance we stood in the Parlor of my uncles' inn, ready to make our vows to each other. Later that evening, I wrote in my diary for the first time as a married woman:

What a pleasant day to day has been, just sixty-four weeks ago today I started for Iowa with Uncle now there is to be on my mind new cares, yes, I am married now—and may it ever be my desire to make James a happy home...

On my wedding day, it was my dearest wish.

We must be willing to let go of the life we planned so as to have the life that is waiting for us.

~ Joseph Campbell

Chapter Twenty-One
~∞~

August 14th - *It's less than a week until I meet Charlie in Chicago, but I can't seem to think about anything but Emily's troubles...*

According to her diary, Emily was at least a bit concerned about James mental state, yet she made no move to escape the engagement. Was it because she was so in love she couldn't bear the thought of living without him—or simply because she felt marrying him was her only option? I wished I knew. I wanted nothing more than to sit down with her and ask, but the diary in my hand was all I had. I snatched up my pen and began once more to write:

Sitting here in my comfortable 21st century life, I can't help but wonder why you didn't just call the whole thing off. If James can't make up his mind to marry you, why don't you just move on? But then I remember you are not standing in my shoes. You don't have the choices that I did—that I do. An unmarried woman—through 19th century eyes—was considered at best a child in the eyes of the law. In some places she might be able to own property, but she could not manage it for herself. She cannot control her own money (assuming she has any), or vote, or—in most places—gain access to higher education.

You must have felt trapped.

Through reading her diary I came to believe Emily was just looking for the security of a home and someone to love her. I couldn't blame her—that's what we all want, isn't it? For all the grander goals and plans that wrestle for our attention, nothing is stronger than our desire for the sanctuary of home, for a place and people to belong to. She'd lost her place in her father's home, and deep down I believe she knew she could never get it back. Did she see James as her last hope to avoid a life composed of little more than servitude to other people's families? Other people's children?

The threat of war was possible roadblock to her plans. Fears of losing James to a hated war must have loomed large—and that was one fear I understood. How would I have felt if I had even an inkling Jack might die when he left for the conference on that January morning? That he was had headed out for a known danger, instead of being caught by something I never even considered?

Teetering on the brink of memory, I turned my thoughts back to what the encroachment of war must have felt like to Emily. If war intervened, she could have lost a husband before she ever had him. She'd seen other women lose husbands, fathers and sons—losing homes right along with the breadwinner. The wives (or more particularly, widows) left were left to fend for themselves, dependent on the charity of family or friends to survive. No wonder she was terrified by the thought of a draft.

Yet if Emily's greatest fear was spinsterhood, it appeared she avoided it. She was now a married woman, with hope for the happy future she wanted so much.

Unfortunately, things didn't quite work out as you hoped, did they?

I couldn't help but wonder, though, how her life might have turned out had she not married James. Her children—who became the center of her life—would not have existed, but neither would the emotional pain she lived with because of James' instability, and giving up on her dreams. Would she have ever been able to life the kind of life she desired? In her time, was such a thing even possible for a single woman—for any woman?

***

Out on the front porch watering the flower baskets I bought in town the previous week, I heard the crunch of tires on the gravel drive and glanced up to see Dan waving from the driver's window. Although we'd passed a few times on the road, I hadn't spoken to him since we visited the inn together. He asked me then if I'd ever figured out whether there was any connection between Emily and my family, but I hadn't found one yet.

Now I have.

As he walked up the path in my direction, I couldn't help but notice—once again—the brilliant blue of his eyes, their corners crinkling as he smiled. With the same nervous flutter as the last time I'd seen him, my breath seemed to catch in my throat.

Get a hold of yourself, Lizzie. You're being ridiculous.

"Hey, Liz. How's it going?"

Taking a deep breath, I quickly launched into a story about my upcoming trip to Chicago and how much I missed my sister. Anything to cover my jitters from his presence. But when he asked if I'd learned anything new from the diary, I relaxed a little and let my enthusiasm for the topic take over. Inviting him in for coffee, I promised to tell him the whole story.

As the coffee dripped into the carafe, I pulled a few mugs out of the cupboard and launched into my tale.

"I did find out something fascinating... Emily's my aunt!" I said. "Well, my great, great, great aunt, anyway."

Starting with what I'd learned at County Records, and moving on to Zizzie's family tree, I recounted the whole process of figuring out just who Emily was to me.

Dan, clearly amused by my enthusiasm, laughed and said, "I don't think I've ever seen anyone so excited over finding a dead relative."

"It sounds ridiculous, I know, but it's almost a relief. I think I would have been incredibly disappointed if I'd discovered the diary hadn't belonged to someone in the family."

Pausing for a moment, I looked Dan square in the eye and acknowledged something I hadn't even admitted to myself.

"On some level, I needed Emily's history to belong to me. My life has been one long succession of losing the people I love, and each loss took a piece of my history with it."

"Dad told me you lost your husband. I'm so sorry... How long has it been?"

Fearing his face wore the pity I'd grown used to from others who heard my story, I turned away for a moment. But when I looked back, it wasn't pity I saw there. Considering what Alex had shared about Dan's loss, I knew what I saw on his face was empathy. He'd been where I've been. His loss may have come in a slightly different form, but it was pain nonetheless.

"Jack was killed about two and a half years ago—a train accident in LA. I was home working on a book when it happened..."

For all the times I had told this story, it should be easier by now. The words shouldn't still stick in my throat.

"I never got to say good-bye." I paused a moment, struggling against the words. Steeling myself against them. "He called me just before he got on the train, but I didn't answer the phone because I was busy writing."

I couldn't believe those final words actually came from my mouth. I had never spoken them aloud before—not to anyone. Oh, I hadn't known when the phone rang that it was him, but I'd lost the chance for a final 'I love you' because I was too busy with my own concerns to pick up the phone. To pay attention.

Just like I'd done with Will...

But, unlike Will, Jack was now lost to me forever.

For a breath or two, the room was so silent I could hear a bee buzz past the open window.

Dan spoke at last, his words reaching deep into the guilt I had stockpiled, almost begging me to let it go.

"Don't be so hard on yourself, Liz. You didn't know he wouldn't call back in an hour. Life doesn't come with a schedule of events. Much as we might wish otherwise, there is no early warning system for tragedy."

Dan fell silent again, looking away as if deciding whether to carry on or not.

"You know, he didn't die because you let the call go to voice mail..."

How could he know...?

He looked at me closely, as if willing me to believe him. "Even if you had answered, you'd still feel cheated of your goodbyes."

He sat for a moment, staring down at the cup in his hand, then took a deep breath and continued.

"I was with Lindy at the end, but she didn't even know the boys and I were there." He pushed a hand through his hair. "We'd known the end was coming fast and were as prepared as you can be— but I still felt like her last moments were stolen from me."

His voice, quiet until now, grew stronger as he said, "Death doesn't play fair, Liz. It wasn't your fault."

The rational part of my brain realized he was right, but guilt still stirred my heart just as my finger swirled the rim of my now-empty cup. I couldn't meet his eyes, but asked the question I'd been turning over in my mind for weeks now.

"How did you... get past it?"

He was silent for a long moment. The sound of a tractor, probably coming from the farm across the road, drifted in and filled the room. The bee still buzzed at the window. I began to wonder if my question was out of line and opened my mouth to apologize when he began to speak.

"If you mean, 'how did I get over it?' I don't think I ever really will. But, past it?"

Once again, he grew quiet. I could almost hear his thoughts shuffling into place before he spoke again.

"I'd love to say I woke up one morning and the pain was gone. That I was happy again. But you wouldn't believe me if I did—and it's not true anyway."

Nodding toward the coffee pot, he asked for another cup. While I poured, he spoke again.

"The pain never fully goes away. You know that. But you learn to live with it—by living." He paused again, stirring sugar into

159

his coffee. "I knew what Lindy would say about the kind of life I was living. Breathing, yes. But brooding... She'd have been so mad at me. She was gone and nothing I could do would bring her back. But I had a choice to make. I could either dig my heels in, continuing to wallow in my misery—refusing to live without her—or I could set out to make a new life for myself. Even if it was without her."

His blue eyes searched mine, holding my gaze as if willing me to believe him.

"I knew what I had to do. I had to make the choice to move on with my life."

He was right and I knew it. I'd tangled with this same thought for months now—especially since coming to Manchester. It couldn't have been easy for him to say these things, but I appreciated his honesty. He understood in a way few did—but I still struggled with the question.

How do I just get past a gaping hole in my life?

As if sensing he'd said enough for now, Dan gently steered the conversation back toward Emily's diary, asking if I'd made any other discoveries in the text.

Always eager to talk about the diary which seemed to personify my own quest, I launched into the story about Emily's deed to the farm.

That is a story I could tell for hours.

I do not know what makes a writer,
but it probably isn't happiness.
~ William Saroyan

Chapter Twenty-Two

~∞~

August 17th - *So, a trip to Chicago should be fun, right? I haven't been out in ages...*

Not long after Dan had gone home, I got a call from Charlie, telling me her trip would have to be cut short. "It's a work emergency. I'm so sorry! I can still meet you in Chicago, but I'm not going to be able to come out to the farm after. Are you horribly upset?"

I was disappointed, of course, but the most important thing was being able to spend the time with Charlie. Did it matter where it happened?

"No, it's fine, really! Chicago will be fun, and I'll take however much time you can spare me. I have so much to tell you."

"Well, I'm going to work on finagling an extra day for Chicago—or at least flying in early and flying out late. Since it's a work thing, they'll take care of changing my ticket. I'll let you know tonight what I come up with. But whatever happens, I'll see you in Chicago day after tomorrow. Ok?"

"I'll be there. Don't you worry."

***

There was no more need for meal planning, grocery lists, or taking on any more cleaning projects. So with those out of the way, I spent the next two days happily ensconced in Emily's diary instead. With the question of her wedding now settled, it was time to take more of a look at her marriage. I'd skimmed enough of the diary to know that things had soured between the two, in spite of Emily's early attempts to convince herself of the contrary. It seemed she believed she could have made things better if only she had behaved as she should.

But over time, the Emily's unhappiness seemed to boil down to just two things—James' anger over what he saw as her refusal to help him with his work on the farm, and her possession of the deed to their farm.

It was her story of the deed that I wanted to hear.

As I had before, I allowed Emily to speak for herself. With her diary opened before me, I closed my eyes a moment and imagined...

Emily

Sunday, 4 January, 1874 - I look for the first time at my New Years Present, it proved to be just what I surmised it was—a Deed—yes, James gave me a Deed of his farm.

I could hardly believe my eyes. Giving me the deed seemed such an honor, a demonstration of his complete trust in me. Yet, I was uneasy, too, despite what appeared to be such a generous gift. For several days the sense of disquiet ate away at me, until James finally assured me that his motive for the gift was pure—in case he should die first he wanted to make certain there would be no trouble about it being divided. He also desired that I would keep it free from encumbrance, so it could not be lost to debt collection. In spite of my recollection that James' father had done the same with his mother—giving the deed to protect the farm from creditors—I chose to believe James' motives were true, and be happy in the gift. The farm was now in my hands—or, at least, its deed.

The Panic of 1873—setting off a failure of countless railroads and banks—had financially devastated the entire country. Over the years which followed, economic hardship haunted many of our neighbors. Some families lost their farms to bill collectors or banks, while others were left destitute when husbands abandoned wives and children to seek employment elsewhere—like my own sister, Harriet. Many of those husbands never returned.

There were others who faced the loss of a farm with suicide—again leaving their families dependent on the charity of neighbors.

Glancing back through the pages of my diary, I see my own accounts of wives who, because of overwork and overworry, ended up in an Insane Asylum. Beggars stopped by my back door daily, desperate for something to eat. Yet in spite of all the hardships around us, our farm was surviving, even prospering to some extent, and I was doing all I could to assure it remained so—raising turkeys, churning and selling butter, and making all our family's clothing. However, I often wondered what would become of us. James was constantly borrowing and lending money—and yes, I resented it. How could our little family endure if he gave away all we had?

James continued suffering bouts with "the blues," just as he had before our marriage, but over the years those episodes grew increasingly worse. He was often uncommunicative or complaining that I did nothing to help him with the work. He argued to keep the children out of school to help with the work—but I fought back to make sure they gained a good education.

Once killing a newborn calf with no explanation of why he did it, James was particularly harsh with the horses, to the point several went lame. My favorite—Beauty—was terrified after he took a pitchfork to her as she was pulling the wagon. She became quite uncontrollable after that, and I could not continue to have to break her over every time I drive her. Yet since I rarely left the house anymore, it was not so necessary as it once was.

29 March, 1883 - I sometimes think tis a real disease that some people have to have a time every so often. They seem to get so full of some undefinable thing they must explode...

I had no name for what ailed James, but I wished so many times I had known the sadness which overtook him even during our courtship and early marriage would not only persist, but grow so much worse over time—and it all seemed to center itself on the idea I was out to steal his farm. He was also convinced I did nothing to help him with his work, and I was out to take all his money—although I

163

often wondered what money that was, since a large portion of our income came through my efforts.

As I grew older and became so ill that I was often unable to do the housework—obliged, on one occasion, to crawl on hands and knees to feed my turkeys because of his refusal to help—his claims of my abuses toward him grew worse. He would tell anyone who would listen that I forced him to do all the work on the farm and never lifted a finger to help—and they believed him. My neighbors would snub me if we crossed paths, and my own sister wrote letters to family and friends detailing my "sins" as they were itemized to her by James.

And then, in addition to James' mental—and sometimes physical—cruelties to myself and the children, he began to demand I give him back the deed for the farm.

1 June, 1883 - It is indeed trying to my nerves to live as I have had to for years. I am sorry tis so but I think something will have to be done...I dare not give him the deed of the farm, but want to do right.

The last few days had been terrible. James is convinced I will turn him out of our home or that he will somehow lose everything, yet I think I had not best give him the deed. I want it so we will all have a home while together, and that it will belong equally to Henry and Sarah if they outlive us.

Things have gotten so bad between James and me that he is no longer speaking to me—refusing to answer when I speak—for days on end. I have not dared to go to sleep many a night for fear of what he might do, and it wears me out. I have grown so nervous that I once dropped a boiling tea-kettle and burned the mutton I was cooking for dinner.

***

Nearly a year went by, but things did not improve. Except for the days when James would refuse to speak, the angry comments directed at me and the children continued, and he harped on me constantly about the deed.

164

One night, on our way home in silence after settling the calf-keeping account with Mr. Richmond, James abruptly broke the stillness.

"Emily, I believe you mean to kill me sometime. I want you to tell me if you do. I want to meet my God prepared."

I was horrorstruck at his words, and was afraid he might attempt something wrong. Yet in my defense, I said only, "You have no reason for such unjust talk."

James laughed—such a bitter sound. "I have many reasons," he said.

Yet when I asked him to name them, he would not say. It seemed like riding with a maniac in a dark night alone. After that, I grew afraid to be left alone with him.

One day James said to me, "Give me what you have of mine and you may have the rest."

Knowing he was undoubtedly speaking of the deed he had given me all those years ago, I still said, "I do not consider I have anything of yours."

No good could possibly come of giving it to him. I was sure James would simply turn the children and me out of the house, and we would be left with nothing. Our lovely home—and our security—would be lost to us forever.

He grew red in the face at my refusal to comply, and I was afraid of what he might do. Finally he spoke, almost spitting his words at me. "You don't, eh? Then you and I are done forever on earth."

He continued to drive home, but spoke not another word the rest of the way. I could hear him breathing hard, the anger radiating off him in waves. He whipped the horses much more than was necessary in his efforts to go as swiftly as possible. I wondered for a moment if he was trying to wreck us.

I sometimes hardly know what I should do. My health has suffered greatly from the pressure his anger puts on me, and I know the children are suffering as well. My head feels literally to have been smashed to pieces, it hurts so badly it affects my eyes so as to make an appearance of stars among waves, so I can hardly write, and then the worst makes me dizzy. I almost feel as if drunk when I walk, as if I would pitch over. I have also been sickened with dropsy, my hands and feet often going numb, making it difficult to do my work.

17 December, 1884 - James commenced his talk the first thing, said there was one thing troubled him a great deal, that he wanted to divide up & have what belonged to him. I told him very well...

I am growing more nervous all the time, what with James badgering me to give him the deed, and now saying that he wants a divorce. I do not want to see a lawyer and make known the reason why I keep the deed of our place, nor can I endure much longer to be tormented about it.

I asked him his reason for doing as he does and what I had done that was wrong, and he turned on me in a moment, speaking with such bitterness in his voice "You are entirely disinterested in my business, and unfaithful to me. You ask me to do things that are not my business to do--but you care nothing for anything to do with me."

What things are you talking about?" I asked him.

"One is filling the stove reservoir and keeping the fire going," he said. "And you don't have any thought for the calves or anything."

"Well," I said "there is no use for me to do any of those things. You have told me time and again you wanted me to mind my own affairs. Have you changed your mind?" I asked him. "Do you now want me to feed the calves, pigs and take care of the horses?"

Staring him down, hoping to convince him I was not afraid of him, I waited for an answer. Yet he only turned and slammed out the door, muttering under his breath all the while.

Ah me, there is no reason in him. It seems no matter what I say or do, he will not be happy. It is only handing over the deed that will please him.

2 April, 1885 - I gave James a deed of the farm. Indeed I felt as though I was signing myself out of a home. I said to Mr. Bronson

166

"It seemed pretty bad to be compelled to do such a thing as this, that I should never have done it had I not have been obliged to." He said a deed was good for nothing if one was compelled to give it...

It had been just over eleven years since James gave me the deed to the house—a New Year's gift, he called it. But even then, in spite of trying so hard for all these years to convince myself of the purity of his motives, I knew that he had only offered it in an attempt to keep it from his creditors. My holding it had long protected my home, keeping it safe for the children and me, but now I have been forced to give it up.

I have tried so hard to keep secret the sickness that James suffers and the abuse that he has heaped on all our heads. But all was for naught. James himself spread falsehoods among our neighbors and family, making me out as a villain to any who would listen. Harriet even came over one day, shortly before I handed the deed to James and told me that she didn't blame James at all.

"He has been a perfect slave to the children and you— everybody knows it. You ought to help him milk, but you won't." Narrowing her eyes, she said, "You think you are too good to work... but you are not. Yet you *will* not."

I was shattered. My own sister had heeded James' lies about me and turned against me. But indeed, why not? Every time she wanted to borrow from us, James would give it, no matter whether our family needed it or not.

All I ever wanted was to be sure that my little family had a home—but now? I do not know how much longer it will be until James finally turns us out.

Reading a book is like re-writing it for yourself. You bring to a novel, anything you read, all your experience of the world. You bring your history and you read it in your own terms.

~Angela Carter

Chapter Twenty-Three

~∞~

August 17th - *How is it possible that words on a page can hold such heartache?*

Once again, all I could do was address Emily directly. The bond between us seemed so strong I could easily believe she was just on the other side of the page, reading my thoughts. Hearing my voice as I could now hear hers.

With my own journal open before me, I began once more to write...

Oh Emily, you've painted such dreadful pictures with your words... I hardly know how to interpret them. I am forced to wonder time and again—if James was so awful, and you had proved yourself so competent through raising your turkeys and your valuable skills with a needle and thread—why didn't you just leave him? You and your children were clearly suffering from the stresses of living in such a situation. Surely any life away from him would have been better than your life with him...

I couldn't help but notice, though, that over the years Emily's writing about James changed. In the first year of their marriage, she once noted she "cried because James did not want to go to the Nelson's," but she also said it was "foolish to cry, for James is too kind to have his feelings hurt by my silliness of crying." Her desire for peace in her home—whether because of her own need for it, or because of society's mandate that the emotional state of a home was a wifely responsibility to maintain—was greater than her desire to do the things, like visiting with neighbors, which clearly meant so much to her.

But by the time twenty years had passed, the conversations Emily recalled seemed little more than a mutual exchange of name-calling.

"You are the biggest fool of a woman I ever knew," James said.

To which Emily replied, "It is nice to be a man if one is a man..."

It was hard sometimes to believe the same woman who wrote with such optimism in the early pages of the diary ended her life in such pain. Yet, it was an entry Emily wrote less than a year before her death that wrenched my heart most of all. In it, I believe she came closest to laying out the misgivings she had before her marriage—all seen through the lens of her daughter Sarah's relationship with one of her would-be suitors:

13 June, 1887 - Sarah looked for Frank Mead last evening to take her to her school, and he was to visit in the afternoon. He did not come. Were I to have known of the hypocrisy of which people were possessed, and the cunning used to dupe one's reason until they get one lured from happiness to the cares and sorrows of married life, I most surely would never again be more than once disappointed by a young man's not being more punctual to meet their promises, for they grow worse and worse, and worse, until all confidence is lost, heartbroken & despair. Ah Sarah, Frank is too much like Pa about some things. Had any one brave advised me to beware of where I was going to seal my future life before it was too late. All those seemingly good excuses would be but idle talk...

If there was even one place in the diary where Emily was obviously speaking intentionally to an audience, surely this was the one. Not only were Emily's words directed in warning to Sarah, but she also seemed intent on molding an image of herself as a sort of

169

"suffering saint" for anyone who might read the text she was leaving behind.

The ability to create such images with words is a gift—but I was still left wondering what the other side of the page might contain. If only I could see the story that James might have told.

In every story, there is always another side...

***

I was coming close to the end of Emily's diary. I had skimmed through quickly in an effort to reach the end—just like I used to do when I was younger. Reading enough to get the gist of a story, then skipping ahead to find out what how it all turns out.

But I always returned to the book once my curiosity was satisfied. Only then could I relax and enjoy the journey of the tale.

I knew I'd be doing this with Emily's diary for a long time to come, going back to learn more about her children, what happened with her parents and siblings—maybe even finding a clues that could lead me to discover my own great, great, great grandmother Harriet. But then, I would be content with just finding the end of Emily's story.

It was time for me to return to it now.

***

By November of 1887, Emily and her children—now ages 24 and 22—had moved into a rented house in Manchester, and because of her deteriorating health, Sarah took over not only Emily's care, but also the transcription of many of her final diary entries. She wrote that James came by occasionally to saw wood or to bring food. Just over a month before Emily's death, while she was nearly paralyzed and suffering with bedsores, she recorded—in her own hand this time:

19 February, 1888 - James was here every day this week...he went back home very much offended that we do not want to go back there. He says "he can not earn anything alone, that I must come and help him. That it is ended with him if I do not, that he will support me no longer, and if I have anything I must get it myself. He takes laudanum. I hope he may not, but fear he might...

I may not know what is wrong with James, but I know what laudanum is.

Oh Emily, are you worried that he is using it, and maybe that is what has been causing his paranoid behaviors?

Such a titillating little nugget Emily left hanging there, but I'm left with more questions than answers as I read on.

2 March, 1888 - James says he has rented our place to James Hutchinson. He intends to work for Uncle. How I wish he was so we might all live together. I have not been very well the last two weeks. A Blue Bird has come to visit and cheer me. She roosts scarce six feet away on a grape vine near my window...

I was surprised James gave up his farm to someone else—in spite of his earlier demands that Emily must return to help him with it—a notion which surely seems to contradict his story that she was doing none of the work. If she hadn't been helping with the work before, how would her return to the farm make any difference?

But I was most taken aback at that last little line, recalling my first day in the farmhouse, just weeks ago, wandering the rooms upstairs and finding the bird nesting on the window sill. She is gone now, her babies fledged. All that remains is the nest tangled in a vine which creeps up the side of the house.

Yet, I can't help wonder for a moment if your blue bird was ancestor to mine, whether generations of blue birds have somehow sought out that spot to roost—returning home, just as I did.

Is that nest is simply one more link between Emily and I?

There is one thing I know for certain—your diary has thoroughly captured my imagination. Silly as it probably sounds, I feel as if it was written entirely for me—to find, to read, to...

To what?

I think it's to share.

We may look old and wise to the outside world. But to each other, we are still in junior school.
~Charlotte Gray

Chapter Twenty-Four

~∞~

August 19th - *Gawking from the sidewalk, I could almost hear Judy Garland singing "How ya gonna keep 'em down on the farm...*

I left early to make the drive into the city, and was still about twenty miles outside Chicago when I realized Charlie's 11 am flight would be landing any minute. We'd decided to meet at the hotel rather than fighting the arriving hordes at O'Hare—and it was a good thing we did. There was more traffic on the freeway into town than I'd seen in years, certainly more than anywhere in Iowa, and I was beginning to doubt the wisdom of driving rather than flying in. If there were so many people there on the outskirts of the city, I didn't even want to think about how bad the traffic downtown was going to be.

I'll bet she beats me to the hotel.

Charlie booked us into *The Langham* for the next two days. It's a gorgeous hotel, overlooking the Chicago River, she said, and even had an in-house spa.

"Just what you need. I'm booking us a package. And I've got a fabulous restaurant in mind, too. Maggie recommended it. This is going to be so much fun."

Yeah... if I ever get there.

An hour later, just as I pulled up in front of the hotel, I got a text from Charlie, along with what appeared to be an aerial photo of the city, saying:

Room 1214. Come on up. The weather's fine.

Feeling just a bit giddy that I'd finally made it, I texted back:

I'm here!!!

A valet came for my car and the bellman whisked away my bags, and before I knew it I was being ushered through the hotel lobby toward an elevator bound for the 12th floor. The hotel lobby—the little I saw of it during my hurried transit through the space—was spectacular. All glass and mirrors, the cream and grey upholstery on the sofas and chairs that flanked the window-walls of the space softened and expanded the two-story reception area. I could hardly wait to see our room.

Once in the elevator, I texted again to tell Charlie I was on my way up. I could hardly wait to see her. Our plans to spend some time together over Spring Break had fallen through as she had a last-minute deadline thrown at her, so although we spoke almost weekly, I hadn't seen her since Christmas. As wonderful as the next two days were likely to be (*I do love a day at the spa*), I was most excited about the chance to spend some time with my little sister. It had been much too long.

Rounding the corner from the elevator, I could see Charlie waiting for me at the end of the hall. Shrieking like a couple of schoolgirls, we ran at each other as if decades, not mere months, had passed since we'd last seen each other. The bellman may have smirked at our enthusiasm, but he didn't say a word. He simply slipped past the two of us now bouncing up and down in the hall, setting my bags on a bench at the end of one of the beds.

Charlie finally turned and acknowledged him with one of her sweetest smiles, assuring him we'd let him know if we needed anything, tipped him and practically pushed him out the door.

Whirling back to me, she threw out her arms and said, "Isn't this place amazing? Maggie arranged it for us. It's her favorite hotel in Chicago—and our stay is on the company's dime. I agreed to meet with one of our clients tomorrow morning, since I was going to be here anyway, so they booked me in here. My meeting is early so you can sleep in—then we have the whole rest of the day to go sightseeing or shopping, or whatever your little heart desires. After that, we'll head out for dinner at this incredible restaurant Maggie recommended.

Meanwhile, take a look around and get settled. We have an appointment at the spa right after lunch."

I tried to pay attention, but I was utterly captivated by the view around me. Maggie arranged a river-view suite for us—and what a view it was. A wall of windows faced the river, offering views stretching all the way to Lake Michigan. As astounding as the sight was at noon, I was sure it would be breathtaking at night. The room was wonderful as well. All creams and tans, splashed with plum accents, it boasted not one but two bathrooms, one with a sunken marble tub and a walk-in shower.

How on earth is the spa going to beat this?

Charlie refused to let me just stand there gawking, though, telling me I had fifteen minutes to change or she'd drag me out in my denim shorts.

"Time's a wasting, sis! Let's get moving."

***

Lunch was two plates of Mediterranean chickpea tacos--with tabouli and hummus—at *Elle on the River*, an outdoor café situated along the Riverwalk, right outside the door of the hotel. Our server, Andy, did his best to talk us into the Orange Creamsicle dessert, but with the spa visit just half an hour ahead, we both refused to succumb to temptation (*that one definitely gets filed under unfinished business*). Sitting under an umbrella, enjoying the somewhat sticky breeze off the river and sipping a mineral water, I had never felt so decadent in my life—at least not until we reached the spa.

My darling sister made reservations at the in-house *Chuan Spa*—hot stone massage, facials, and foot treatments. The spa itself was visually stunning, with floor to ceiling windows, glass chandeliers and silvered lattice work separating the reception desk from the waiting area. White marble floors in the entry contrasted with the dark wood accents and marble walls in the lounge. The treatment rooms, with the same mix of warm browns and creams, simply pleaded with patrons to relax. And the treatments themselves? Well, I just wasn't ever going to leave, that's all there was to say.

Charlie had requested a couple's package so we could chat, but honestly, it wasn't too long before we were both so "blissed out," I doubt we said more than a dozen words to each other anyway. Tranquility reigned between all the way back to our room—where I headed to the bedroom for a nap and Charlie made a few calls to confirm her morning meeting and talk to her boss.

Drowsy and relaxed, I lay on the bed, gazing at the view outside the window and thinking how different this trip must be from the one which brought Emily to this same city a century and a half ago. This hotel had not existed then, but I remembered she had written of climbing eighty feet to the top of the courthouse observatory to a spot where she could see all the ships sailing on Lake Michigan—just as I could see them from my window. She also spoke of the depot, calling it "a beautiful building," as she passed through it on her way back to the train for an overnight trip to Dubuque, then another four hour train ride to Manchester after crossing the Mississippi by boat. I smiled as I closed my eyes, so thankful my trip had taken only four and a half hours, door to door.

Modern technology is a wonderful thing.

I fell asleep wondering what Emily would have thought of the spa.

***

Awaking to a twilight sky reminiscent of the 'Evening in Paris' perfume bottle which once graced my mother's dressing table, I felt dazed by the memory. After all these years, it was hard to believe I could still be surprised by my mother's absence—the pain as corporal as the day I lost her—simply through a chance sight or scent. I stood at the window for a moment, remembering. The twinkle in her eye, her infectious laugh, her hands soft on my face. Allowing the ache to wash through me, I hung on until it once more ebbed away. I remembered a beautiful line I once read, an essay claiming that those we love never leave—they simply become a part of us. The blood in our veins. The spark between synapses. That sweet ache of nostalgia is simply a sign that they are still alive within us.

Truer words...

Tucking my hair behind my ears, I took a deep breath to clear my head and wandered out into the sitting room of the suite just as Charlie was picking up the phone to order room service. Just looking at her, I could see my mother in her eyes. Charlie was so like her— alive and always present in the moment. I might have lived happily within my own thoughts forever, but the two of them found their energy in the people and things which surrounded them.

We were so very different.

"There you are," she said. "I was beginning to wonder if you were going to sleep all the way through 'til morning. Are you hungry? There are some yummy-looking sandwiches here."

She slid the room service menu across the table toward me, saying "See if anything looks good."

We both chose the tomato and mozzarella Panini with spinach salad, and after ordering our meal, Charlie filled me in on the next day's plans. Once she'd returned from her meeting, we'd head downtown for some shopping.

"We're going out to find something fabulous and fancy for a night on the town," she said. "First, we've got dinner reservations at a place called *Vermilion*, an Indian-Latin fusion restaurant Maggie recommended. She says it's amazing. When I told her how much you like Indian food, she promised you'd love it."

I did love Indian food, but Jack had detested it.

"Too spicy," he claimed every time I brought up the possibility of going out for Indian food. A meat and potatoes guy, Jack's taste buds were not exactly what I'd call adventurous. We rarely went anywhere where the menu didn't revolve around steak or pasta, so I was always thrilled at the chance to try something new.

"Do they do vegetarian dishes, do you know?"

On the rare occasions I'd eaten out in Iowa, I was always forced to choose between either pasta or grilled cheese sandwiches— and it was a good guess an Indian restaurant was likely to have neither.

"I hope there'll be something I can eat other than veggies and rice."

"Yes, Miss Worrywart, they have vegetarian dishes. I checked. I promise you won't starve tomorrow night." For all her big city ways and sylph-like figure, Charlie swore she could never become a vegetarian; she loved barbecued anything way too much.

"Well, then I'm in. But you mentioned a night out...what else do you have planned?"

Watching her waggling her eyebrows and grinning at me, I knew she was up to something.

"Ah, now that's a surprise. Maggie is working on something for me—and you, my dear sister, are just going to have to wait and see."

"Now," she said, deftly changing the subject. "Tell me all about Emily and her diary..."

She didn't need to ask twice.

Of two sisters one is always the watcher,
one the dancer.
~Louise Glück

Chapter Twenty-Five

~∞~

August 20th- *It was an amazing day, but couldn't help the way I felt...*

Morning arrived early. Way too early, if you asked me. Although Charlie tried to be quiet, I could hear her rummaging around in the bathroom, getting ready for her meeting. We'd stayed up late talking—mostly about Charlie's very active social life—so I hoped to sleep in a bit. Apparently, that was not going to happen. So while she dressed, I threw on a robe, and surveyed the intricacies of the elaborate coffee machine.

Mmmmm... not bad, but what I wouldn't give for a soy cappuccino right now.

Tossing a scarf around her neck and tugging her bag over her shoulder, Charlie said, "I'll be back no later than ten. Be sure you're ready to go by then. We've got a full day ahead of us."

Waving her phone in my direction, she called out, "I'll text when I'm on my way back. Be ready to go." With that, she pulled open the door and disappeared down the hall.

I sat for a while, enjoying the coffee and the quiet of the morning, watching boats on the lake and remembering our conversation after last night's dinner. Charlie told me about someone she went out with a few times ("It's nothing serious—yet—but he's the first guy I've dated more than once since Richard."), and interrogated me over why I wasn't dating yet ("It's been over two years, Lizzie. It's not good for you to be alone so much"). I told her I wasn't interested, that I'd start to date eventually, but she wouldn't let it go.

"I know you, Liz. You can't move on because you haven't really let go of Jack. I know you think you're not ready, but you're just scared."

I had been pretty mad at her then, but in the clear light of day, I knew she was right. I was scared. Just as with my writing, I was afraid to try to do life without Jack. It was just easier to continue doing nothing.

But for the day, I just didn't want to think about it.

***

Charlie arrived back at the suite about three hours later. She'd texted to let me know she was on her way so I would be ready to go. Her meeting went well, she said, sounding relieved it was over. On the way back she'd talked to Maggie, filling her in on all the particulars of the conference and finalizing the details of our evening out.

"I'll tell you all about it, I promise. Just not yet," she said. "But don't just sit there, let's get going. We've got some shopping to do!"

The Magnificent Mile—Chicago's answer to Paris' Champs-Elysees--rolled out practically outside the hotel's front door. Knowing we'd probably end up throwing our exhausted selves into a taxi on the way back, we decided to walk the few blocks over this morning, just to get a closer look at the city. The Trump Tower was right across the street, and the historic Wrigley Building, which I'd seen through the hotel widow last night, its gleaming white façade lit from below, stood at the end of Michigan Avenue. Having seen photographs of it for years, I couldn't help but consider it a familiar face in a sea of strangers. We hadn't even hit the stores yet, but I was awestruck by the city.

I couldn't help but think again about Emily and her travels through Chicago on her way to Manchester. Chicago was a much smaller city then, but for a farm girl like Emily its size must have been overwhelming. Clearly, she was awed by the sights—over 100,000 people lived there in 1860—but none of what she saw on her trip likely existed anymore. The fire that devastated Chicago in 1871, and the several which followed, completely changed the face of the city. I wondered if there was anything left, other than the railroads, that Emily would even recognize.

Even coming from the 'Emerald City' of Seattle, I had to admit Chicago was amazing. Michigan Avenue truly did remind me of the illustrious roadway through Paris, stretching from The Louvre to the Arc de Triomphe. Wide avenues and sidewalks, trees and flowers everywhere. It was a beautiful sight, but Charlie wasn't about to let me stand there gawking. Before I knew it, she was dragging me from one store to the next looking for the "perfect outfit for tonight." When I threatened non-compliance due to a lack of information, she agreed to tell me about my surprise over lunch.

"But in the meantime," she said, a stern voice contradicting the sparkle in her eye. "I expect some serious shopping cooperation on your part." Waving her forefinger at me, she gave one last warning.

"No more dawdling!"

Leaving *Ann Taylor* a short while later, I dug in my heels, insisting I wouldn't take another step without food. A few doors down was the *Grand Lux Café,* whose menu promised both salmon and veggie burgers, so we decided it was the perfect spot for lunch. Incredibly, we didn't have to wait long for a table, and after giving the server our order, I told Charlie it was time to confess what she was up to.

"Ah, wouldn't you like to know, dear sister?"

Making the same face she used to make as a kid when she knew something I didn't—all 'I've got a secret' smiles—she taunted me a while, then finally gave in.

"Ok, I promised. I'll tell."

Clearing her throat as if she was about to make an auspicious announcement, I worried for a moment she was going to climb up on the chair as she did when I was in seventh grade and she decided to announce to Mom and Dad the existence of my secret boyfriend.

I am still trying to forgive her.

"Ok, are you ready?" She paused, trying—I knew—for dramatic effect. "Well, Maggie managed to snag us theater tickets for...are you sure you're ready for this?"

I glared at her across my burger, making sure she realized I had enough of her delay tactics. Finally, with a huge smile lighting her face, she burst out with, "We've got tickets to see *Coraline* at the City Lit Theater."

My mouth dropped open, speechless for a moment. I loved children's literature, and Neil Gaiman's little book was one of my favorites.

"Coraline? Really? I love that book! I can't believe you got tickets on such short notice."

"Well, Maggie is something of a miracle worker," Charlie smirked. "But actually, she has a cousin in the cast. She made a call and someone found a couple of good seats which might otherwise have gone to waste. Anyway, they're ours now!"

"So when do we need to head back to the hotel?"

Charlie just laughed. "Whoa, girl! We've got plenty of time. And we haven't even found shoes yet! Eat your veggie burger like a good girl, and then we'll go looking for some fancy footwear."

***

Schlepping our shopping bags out of the taxi and into the hotel elevator, I was ready to collapse. Both Charlie and I found fabulous shoes to go with equally fabulous dresses for our night on the town, we decided to do dinner after the theater, so we had a little time to relax before rushing out the door again. While Charlie called to change our reservations to a later time, I kicked off my shoes, made myself another cappuccino and sat down with my feet up.

Reservations made—for both dinner and a cab to take us to the theater—Charlie came in and flung herself across the bed.

"I can't believe how much my feet hurt! You'd think I don't walk all over a big city every day."

I just laughed at her, and with my best 'I-told-you-so' face, reminded her that I'd suggested she wear comfortable shoes if we

181

were going to do that much walking. But considering how sore my own feet were, I doubted it would have made much difference—not that I was going to admit it to Charlie.

I think a good foot soak is in order—after I finish my coffee.

***

The play was marvelous. I always loved Neil Gaiman's little book about the girl who learned to 'be careful what you wish for.' A little creepy—even on the printed page—the black button eyes of the villains' costumes were so well executed, and the cast and crew did an extraordinary job with the fantasy story that unfolds in a world discovered behind a bricked up wall. But it was Coraline's realization that being brave isn't the same as not being afraid which rang in my ears as we headed off to dinner.

Why do I have the feeling the whole world is trying to tell me something?

Speaking of dinner...*Vermilion*, the restaurant Maggie recommended, served an Indian-Latin fusion menu that was, quite simply, beyond incredible. The decor—a stunning mix of off-white walls and furnishings, light and dark wood accents, with black and white photographs gracing the walls—was no match for the atmosphere. The second I walked through the door, scent memory transported me to a spice market I wandered in Marrakesh oh-so-many years ago on a trip with Jack. The fragrance in the air was positively intoxicating.

And the food?

Indisputably mouthwatering. I had the Vermilion Thali with coconut rice and my carnivorous sister devoured the Tandoori Skirt Steak with pico de gallo. As odd as the combination might sound at first, the Latin and Indian influences were well-matched and scrumptious beyond words. For a moment, I considered the possibility of moving to Chicago just so I could have the opportunity to eat my way through the entire Vermilion menu.

After dinner, we wandered into the lounge to listen to the music—an amalgamation of Indian, Latin and more typical lounge fare. Charlie—ever the social butterfly—was on the dance floor before we'd even been seated. Although her partner's friend asked me to dance as well, I declined and sat at our table alone, watching my sister and relishing the rhythms. When Charlie finally rejoined me, she was exhilarated—and more than a little ticked off at me.

"Lizzie, what on earth are you doing here all by yourself?" With a scowl that could have burned through metal, she added, "Why aren't you dancing? You love this music."

I was just about to offer my aching feet as an excuse, when—brow furrowed and frowning just like when she was five years old and incensed over some imagined slight—she slid into the booth and cut me off.

"You are beyond ridiculous, you know that? One dance is not a lifetime commitment."

I could tell she was getting wound up when—still glaring at me—she started flinging her hands around, as if trying to punctuate her point.

"Your husband is dead, you know. You aren't being unfaithful if you enjoy yourself... I'm starting to think you want to be miserable and alone!"

Irritation etched her face, and folding her arms across her chest, she added one last shot in my direction.

"What are you so afraid of?"

I wish I knew.

Don't try to figure out what other people want to hear from you; figure out what you have to say. It's the one and only thing you have to offer.

~ Barbara Kingsolver

Chapter Twenty-Six

~∞~

August 21st – *Endings and new beginnings. Sometimes, when they travel together, it's hard to tell one from the other...*

In the taxi on the way back to the hotel, Charlie apologized for her earlier outburst, but her question had truly hit home.

What am I so afraid of?

As exhausted as I was, I was up half the night thinking about her question. I was a woman whose husband was never coming back, no matter how much I might wish it. I was a writer who hadn't been able to write for over two years, and even though I was trying, I didn't have any faith left in my ability to pull it off. And apparently, on top of it all, I was also a huge disappointment to my sister.

My sister...

Nothing ever simmered below the surface with Charlie. Whatever her mood—joy or sorrow, or anger—she was always at a full rolling boil. Still, in spite of her current aggravation with me, I was secure in her constant support. Charlie would never turn her back on me.

Wide awake at three in the morning, I couldn't help comparing my relationship with Charlie to Emily's with her sister Harriet—my own long-distant grandmother. Harriet, according to Emily, stood with James against her, even calling James "a perfect slave to the children and you," claiming that "he has done everything there was to be done," and she did nothing—a story that Harriet and James told to anyone who would listen.

Near the end of Emily's life when she was ill and unable to walk, Harriet had stolen away a precious memento left to Emily by their mother—after claiming it did not belong to Emily at all in spite of their mother's stated wishes. What a betrayal that must have seemed in Emily's eyes. I couldn't imagine the pain I would feel if Charlie ever did such a thing to me.

Her transparent anger was much easier to bear.

***

By four a.m. I was finally drowsy enough to nod off for a few hours. When I finally woke up, Charlie was again waiting for room service. But she was clearly waiting for me—I scarcely sat down when she began to speak.

"I know you weren't trying to be difficult Lizzie, and I'm sorry I went off on you like that. Really, I am." She paused for a moment, before asking the same question I spent half the night considering.

"Don't you ever get tired of avoiding life?"

She looked me in the eye and said, "Jack would hate this life you aren't living. He would never have been happy to see you turn your back on all the things you love."

I knew she was right. But how does one just stop being afraid?

We had a lovely morning together—at least once the air between us cleared a bit—but by noon my sister said her effusive goodbyes and was in a cab on her way to the airport, as I was waiting for the valet to return my car. Charlie was still hoping she might get a chance to come out to the farm for a few days, but I had so little time left before I had to return home, I told her not to worry about it. I did have her promise, though, she'd spend Christmas in Seattle with the girls and me.

***

Like a skipping record, Charlie's comment about the life I wasn't living had etched a groove in my mind. Arguing with myself on the way home, I reminded myself that I had a life. I was teaching again. I made this trip halfway across the country to revisit the farm. I was trying to write a book...

185

"What more does everyone want from me?"

Alone in the car, I couldn't help feeling irritated—and just a bit guilty. Smacking the steering wheel with one hand, I wailed aloud.

"It's my life, isn't it? Why does everyone think they get to have an opinion on how I'm living it?"

Deep inside, though, I knew I was not living the life I wanted. There was little I loved more than writing, but when Jack died my inspiration fled and I just let it go. I loved to travel, but I wasn't doing that either. One of the things I yearned for—number three on my life list—was crossing the country by train. But since Jack died, the thought of making such a trip absolutely terrified me. I may still long to sit and watch the prairies speed past my window, rocked by the rhythms of the train hurtling down the tracks, sleeping like a baby in the solitude of a sleeper car, but... how would I ever overcome the fear that kept me from doing those things I loved?

I wasn't sure they were even possible anymore.

***

Just over four hours after I left The Langham, I turned into my driveway. Considering all the traffic I hit heading into Chicago, the drive home was surprisingly easy, and the roads—at least outside the greater city limits—relatively uncluttered. Obviously leaving town in the middle of the day is the only way to go.

Checking my phone, I found a text from Charlie, telling me she'd made it home with no airline glitches, and had even been bumped to first class for the flight home.

That's my sister!

***

Dinner and dishes dispensed with and a load of laundry tumbling in the dryer, I had just picked another volume of Emily's diary when the phone rang. It was Daisy, ostensibly to hear all about my trip to Chicago, but I could hear in her voice she was bursting with news of her own.

"We had a great time, honey. Shopping, dinner, theater, the greatest hotel ever, and an afternoon at the spa. Your Aunt Charlie truly outdid herself this time! But tell me about you. How is the job going? Has it been as good an experience as you hoped?"

"Oh Mom, the internship has been amazing. I've learned so much, and my boss has been so supportive—of everything." There was a long pause, and I could tell she was working up the nerve to tell me something. It couldn't be bad news. She sounded too happy. But whatever it was...

"Mom, Justin asked me to marry him last night." I could hear her, practically holding her breath on the other end of the line, waiting for my reaction. I wasn't sure what she was worried about, though. I liked Justin—very much—and she knew it. When she brought him home to meet me in April, I could see things were getting serious between them. This engagement was definitely no surprise to me, but clearly she was concerned about what I'd say. I figured I'd better put her out of her misery quickly or she'd pass out from anxiety, still clutching the phone.

"Daisy...that is such wonderful news. Congratulations to you both. Is Justin there? Can I talk to him?" I wanted to assure her I was happy for them, that she had nothing to worry about from me.

"No, he's gone out to pick up some dinner. He wanted to give me a chance to speak to you alone. But I know he'll want to talk to you soon..."

She sounded relieved that I was pleased, but I could tell there was still something on her mind.

"Daisy? Is there something else, honey?"

She could be such a worrier at times.

I wanted to do what I could to assure her I was happy. That I would be fine when she got married.

"You know I like Justin, and I'm happy for you, don't you? I could see immediately how much you two love each other."

I stopped for a moment, waiting for her to continue.

"Mom, we want to get married here in New York. And we don't want a big wedding. Just family and a few friends." Again, she paused as if waiting for my response.

187

"That's fine honey, whatever you want is ok with me. I promise I am not one of those mothers who freaks out when their daughters want to skip the whole big white wedding, so if that's what you're worried about..."

But before I could finish my sentence, she interrupted.

"We're getting married in three weeks."

Ok... how was I supposed to respond to that? She grew up hearing the story of how her dad and I announced our plans to get married with barely a month's notice, so any objection I might make would only bring on cries of "but Mom, you did it"—or at least it would if this was Alice I was talking to.

Alice...

"But honey, if you get married so soon, Alice won't be able to be there. Is there a reason you don't want to wait until she gets home?"

Although I was doing my best to sound calm, my mind was racing. "Daisy... are you pregnant, honey?" I asked gently. "Because if you are..."

"Mom, no! I am not pregnant!"

I had to smile at that. She sounded positively indignant I would even think such a thing. I wanted to ask her what the hurry was, but before I could open my mouth, she finally came out with it.

"Mom, Justin just got this great job—his dream job, as a matter of fact—in Australia. He leaves in three weeks, and I'm going to go with him. My boss is even going to give me a recommendation for a job in Sydney—with a publisher who specializes in children's books. And I'll be able to get a Master of Publishing at the University of Sydney, too. We'll have lots of opportunities to see Alice while she's there, too. I've already talked to her about it, and she completely understands about the wedding. We even figured out we can Skype the whole thing, so she can sort of be there, anyway."

Well, it seemed that everything had been worked out without any input from me.

Apparently all I have to do is show up.

"So, three weeks, huh? Is there anything I can help with?"

"Well, you can call Aunt Charlie and Uncle Will, to give them the news. We want them both to be there if it's at all possible. And... you can walk me down the aisle—if you will?"

There was nothing left to do but cry.

***

I promised to arrive a few days before the wedding—surely there would be something I could do to help at that point. Daisy would call again in a couple of days, once they'd settled everything, to let me in on the details.

"Meanwhile, just figure the wedding will be September 6th—and let me know as soon as you've made reservations. I love you, Mom. Thanks for being so understanding!"

Once I'd called Charlie and Will and secured their promises to be there for the wedding, I plopped myself down on the living room couch and considered all I needed to do in the next two weeks to be ready to leave for New York. I'd be heading back to Seattle from there right after the wedding, and return to my classroom just a few days later.

My low-key summer just picked up speed—way too fast.

I also thought about Jack, and how he had looked forward to walking Daisy and Alice down the aisle, ever since their births. My eyes filled with tears, but I didn't want to give way to them, not then anyway. With too many plans to make—and a list to write assuring everything got done in time—I got up off the couch, and walked over to the trunk reaching for a tissue from the box sitting on top. Standing there wiping my eyes, I had an epiphany. Like me, Daisy was a sentimental soul and would be thrilled with a wedding gift which once belonged to a long-lost relative like Emily. With her upcoming move to the other side of the planet, though, wedding gifts needed to be small and portable—like cash—but I wanted to give her something unique. A one-of-a-kind object that would remind her of family ties, no matter where in the world she lived.

There were some lovely things in the trunk—beautiful old books and pottery—or maybe that cut glass vase. How perfect would that be? Excited by the thought of a treasure hunt, I figured now was as good a time as any to search for the perfect gift for my daughter.

True stories can't be told forward, only backward. We invent them from the vantage point of an ever-changing present and tell ourselves how they unfolded.

~ Siri Hustvedt

Chapter Twenty-Seven

~∞~

August 22nd - *As it finally gave way, goosebumps rose on my arms, and I caught myself holding my breath...*

Opening the trunk, I picked up the quilt, carefully arranged right where I first found it. That would definitely come home with me, to hang on a wall somewhere in the house where it could be seen and appreciated, not folded away and forgotten. Setting it on the chair, I turned back to grab the books stacked up under it. Pulling them out one by one, I considered them, wondering if one of them could be the perfect gift for Daisy and Justin—seed for a library of their own someday.

Unpacking all the smaller items under the quilt, I reminisced about the day, just weeks ago, when I'd opened the trunk for the first time—finding Emily's diary, opening the drawers and unpacking their contents...

Wait a minute! I'd never gotten that second drawer open. How could I have forgotten? I'd been so distracted by the diary, I'd never even tried a second time to unjam it.

Maybe I can open it now.

Tugging on the handle, I could see it was still jammed—a wad of paper in the drawer runner seemed to be holding it closed. Wondering if a knife might be able to reach inside and dislodge it, I ran to the kitchen and snatched one from the dishwasher.

It took a bit of finagling, but I managed to jimmy the drawer open just enough to pull the papers jamming it up out of the way. After that, it pulled open easily—so easily, I decided the paper must have been put there to keep the drawer closed and in its place inside the trunk. Since it was now so loose, I simply removed the drawer so I could look over its contents.

Brimming with a few loose papers covered with algebra problems, it also held several small booklets that appeared to be sewn together by hand, and one volume with a label inside the front cover proclaiming that it came from Congar's in Manchester. Each booklet was filled with writing—and appeared to be written by the same hand which transcribed the volumes of Emily's diary.

Were these earlier diary volumes, maybe from Emily's childhood?

Cautiously, I picked the hand-bound up pamphlets one-by-one. Aged and fragile, with no protective cover, several had pages that were difficult to read due to faded ink or tattered pages. Still, I looked them over carefully, examining them for dates or anything else offering clues as to what they were. Nearly every booklet began with a date, just as the diary volumes had, so I sorted them into chronological order, leaving aside for the moment the drawings and poems. Leafing through them, I noticed there was something familiar about several of the dates. It seemed to me that many of the months and days on these pages were the same as those in some of the books I'd already read.

I hurried into the kitchen where I'd carried the diary while I was working on the short stories. Taking the earliest volume from the stack, I opened it to the first page and found the first date—March 29, 1858. Returning to the living room—diary in hand—and the mound of booklets on the floor next to the trunk, I picked up the first in the stack. It began with the same date.

I've got goosebumps...

What was this? Were these copies of the larger diary volumes—or could they be original writings? Had Emmie begun her diary in these handmade books, only to later copy them into a format more likely to last?

It certainly made sense.

What an amazing find these were. If these were indeed earlier texts, I was curious to see whether there were differences between these and the later copies. From my own experience as a teenage diarist, I remembered vehemently scribbling out embarrassing lines when I reread some entries months or years later. Once or twice I'd even torn out a few pages, my then-present self embarrassed at what I viewed as childish declarations of undying devotion to someone whose name I barely even recognized any longer. I had occasionally "made a good story better," recording things as I wished they'd been, not as they actually happened. As an adult, I knew that I had not always written the whole truth of a situation, because it was simply too hard to face—even in a book I kept only for myself. Even a diarist always chooses what she will write.

Could Emily have taken some artistic license with her words, altering her narrative in some way—maybe to ignore things she considered distressing, or to portray herself as she wanted to be seen? I knew she had never spoken the tale of the neighborhood gossip that dogged her for over a year. Could there be other things she had glossed over or altered?

How would I ever know for sure?

I needed to begin at the beginning. With the first volume and the booklet beginning with the same date open in my lap, I began again with the first entries to see how they compared.

March 29, 1858 was the first date in both versions. The fragile foolscap paper was hard to read in places, but except for what appeared to be a few inconsequential grammatical changes—cleaned up syntax and spelling—they were pretty much the same. But if I was going to recopy my diary fifteen years later, I'd correct my grammar, too.

The second entries in both copies held a few more differences, with more detailed descriptions of her day's activities in the bound volume version than in the paper booklet. There were also a few variations in who she spent her time with on her visits. The booklet had her having dinner with "Uncle Horace Garlick"...then calling on

Ann Salsbury. The bound version found her calling on "Mrs. Green," then staying "with Lucy Ann to dinner. At two p.m. started to go to Uncle Marcus'...arriving at four o'clock. Tired." Small changes, and likely unimportant, but she'd clearly done a little editing in one version or the other.

The two versions continued on this way, with mostly tiny differences between them, until an entry in April. The foolscap version read as follows:

Tuesday, 20 April - Did not rise very early this morning. Emma Culver came after some flower roots. Harriet went home with her, got some flower seeds, and Hattie Hall. While we were eating dinner it rained. Hattie got up from the table and ran all the way home because she was afraid of the rain. Got as wet as a drowned rat. After tea, Fanny Brower came to go home with her mother. Done a little of everything. It is quite lonely now that Pa and Edna are both gone. At home.

It read like a pretty ordinary day—just a list of things she did. It was odd to read that Hattie ran all the way home in the rain because she was afraid of it, but sometimes people are funny (or maybe Hattie was only ten years old; that could explain a lot). When I turned to the bound copy of the diary for its version of the day's events, though, part of it was like reading about another day altogether.

After beginning the entry as she had the other, somewhere in the middle the tale took a sharp turn, becoming another story altogether—one I had come to know pretty well:

Last Christmas & New Years I attended Cotillion parties at Canandaigua with Sylvenus Hamlin. Lizzie wants him pretty badly...

My breath caught in my throat...

Emily apparently added this little plot point about Venus and Libbie to her diary at some point. But the real question was, since both entries carried the same date, which was the original? Could she have made one version to share with her sisters or friends, perhaps—and another for only herself?

So... which one is true?

I spent the rest of the night reading through the booklets, comparing them with the bound volumes—but too caught up in Emily's revisions to do much more than scribble notes while I read. Luckily, they covered only about eight months in 1858 or I might have been on this mission for weeks. With a growing list of differences I discovered stacking up in the journal Will sent, I was left with the feeling my treasure hunt had just evolved into an examination of the evidence in a mystery novel.

Just as the horizon was beginning to lighten, I opened the last book I'd found in the drawer, a store-bought accounts book from Congar's. Written across the top of the first page was a single word, References, followed by a note from Emily herself, no doubt a reminder to herself or any future reader exactly what her purpose was in this book:

To day is the sixth of May 1873. I have my diary written in small books & commence to copy it in this book. It almost causes a tear to start to when I look back to the commencement of my keeping a history of my life. Aye, 15 years ago. I only regret that I did not commence as early as when I was a merry school-girl of fifteen.

My heart began to race...

Here, written in Emily's own hand was the answer to the question I asked when I first discovered the alternate version of her diary: had Emily rewritten her story in some way? Up until this moment, it certainly appeared so, but I couldn't say for sure. How would I ever know which version came first, or why the various volumes didn't match up? Yet here, Emily herself had supplied the answer.

She *had* rewritten her life.

Oh not in every detail, but in those which for some reason mattered to her, even fifteen years after the fact. But that still left me with one question, perhaps the most important one of all.

But, why?

Unexpectedly the dream I had after writing the account of Emily's train trip from Michigan to Iowa came roaring back. How angry she'd been with me, accusing me of revising her life to suit my purposes. It made me laugh now, realizing what her dream self had accused me of was exactly what Emily herself had done.

Yet it also made me wish I could talk to her, to ask her why and to hear her answers face to face. I'd been reading and writing my responses to her diary for weeks, my thoughts consumed with hers. But now I wanted more.

I want the answers only she can give me.

With the story she laid out in her diary, I could imagine she'd wanted to leave a different image of herself for her children, for posterity. Her life had not turned out the way she hoped, that much was clear. Her long hoped-for loving marriage turned eventually to a nightmare. The things she was raised to believe were a woman's greatest honor became ashes in her mouth, souring her on everything to do with her husband. Yet those values still fought for preeminence in her identity.

Still, this was all simply conjecture on my part. I could only speculate on why she felt the need to polish the image she painted within the pages of her diary—I would never know.

Abruptly, in the midst of all my suppositions, I had an idea.

A conversation.

Why couldn't I have one...with Emily? In my dream, she spoke her piece, begging me to listen without judgment or embellishment as she told her story. Maybe now it was time for us to talk to each other.

But... how?

In the space of a single heartbeat, it all became crystal clear.

As a fiction writer, the tools of my trade dovetail gracefully with my imagination. Asking "what if...?" Creating events that didn't happen—even those which cannot happen—and helping a reader believe in them, even if just for a little while.

So, snatching up a pen and the diary Will sent, I flipped to the next blank page and smiled to myself.

I knew exactly how to begin. How to get to the truth—*the veritas*—at the base of Emily's story. If I could write a conversation, maybe I could discover what she wanted to say. To find what I needed to hear. To understand.

For Emily, for myself—and maybe even for a reader still to come.

*It is ... through the world of the imagination
which takes us beyond the restrictions of
provable fact, that we touch the hem of truth.*
~ Madeleine L'Engle

Chapter Twenty-Eight

~∞~

'Life in Continuous Present'
Introduction

Twice upon a time, there lived a woman named Emily. Born on a farm, Emily had her eyes fixed on a wider world than the one she knew. As she came of age and contemplated a life outside her father's home, she also began to keep a diary, recording in its pages the events of her days and the yearnings of her heart. Now, Emily was a nineteenth-century girl, raised on the romantic novels of her day, like those written by the Brontë sisters or Jane Austen. Tales filled with women who yearned for love, and men who pleaded for a beloved's heart and hand. And there was nothing Emily wanted more than a life and home filled with love.

Yet Emily also had another vision. She dreamt of accomplishment and self-fulfillment. Along with her beloved novels, she also devoured the writings of women like Mary Wollstonecraft and Judith Sargent Murray, women who believed they and their daughters should have the same rights for independence and opportunity granted to men. But in the distant time and place where Emily lived, such things were difficult for a young girl to come by.

Young Emily was not prepared to give up her hopes so easily, however. No matter how challenging it might be, she was determined that the life she lived would fit both the design she found in her books and the loftier notions of the more thoughtful women of her day. And after a time, when she realized her reality wasn't matching her dreams, she chose to rewrite the chronicle of her life—creating, in essence, the story of a second self.

This is a story—but not the only possible story—of why.

***

This tale I offer begins with our first Emily. The one who hoped and dreamed, and then mislaid the dream somewhere in the midst of the sameness and drudgery—and disappointment—of her days. Yet the story continues with a second version of Emily, who also hoped and dreamed, but made a way to fashion her past--and even her name—into a story she hoped to leave behind for all who would follow. It is this second life story which first drew the attention of another woman, right there on the farm which brought them together.

Emily was born on the edge of the American frontier, in the newly-birthed state of Michigan. She grew up on a small farm, the oldest of four children—talented, curious, and determined. She went to school and excelled, particularly in math. She wrote poetry, presented essays at the local Lyceum, and taught school at the age of 16. Emily wanted to be a writer and later an artist, but her society affirmed a woman's value only through obedience to its archetypes of womanhood—marriage, home and family. She wanted to spread her wings, but was declared "the angel of her home" instead. She may not have always been pleased with it, but to the best of her ability, she did as she was told.

Emily's society envisioned the perfect woman as pious, pure, submissive, and above all, domestic. Anything outside this frame would lead to the loss of woman's virtue and the collapse of culture itself. How heavy was the weight of responsibility that Emily carried, yet she bore it for the promise that if she did her part, her virtue could transform her world—no matter how wrong that world might go.

So Emily took on the tasks she'd been raised for, regardless of the leanings of her own heart. She married, had children, and prayed she would always do right and never offend. That she might continue to polish an image of virtue which would elevate her husband and children. She worked hard to make a happy home, but she wanted...more. She cared about the world around her, the suffering of wives whose husbands were given to drink, their voicelessness in the face of their wounds, and the opportunities denied them simply because of their gender. These two sides of her nature often warred within her, with the conflict often spilling across the pages of her diary.

Ah, the diary...

The words she'd someday leave behind her, offering a glimpse of the person she'd been. She may not have been able to make her life what she'd been led to believe it would be, but she could still tell her story as she chose.

Thus, Emily began to inscribe her transformation into Emmie. Where romance was lacking, she wrote it into her story. She supplied the details which caused it to sing within her own memory. No longer was she simply a household drudge who'd settled. She was a woman who yearned—and was yearned after. As her life went on and motherhood became its beating heart, she wrote a tale of sacrifice, surrendering all for her children's well-being, counting their virtues and successes as her own. Yet she also chronicled an account of the longsuffering wife, hiding her husband's failings from the world at the expense of her own reputation—and finally her health.

She reinvented herself the heroine of her own story.

This Emmie then took the tale she wrote and buried it. Hiding it in the deepest recesses of her house, awaiting the day it might be found by someone who would read it and attend to her heart.

And when that day came, it was Lizzie who found it.

It was Lizzie who unlocked the door to the house, and discovered the story's furtive hiding place. Lizzie who opened the covers and read. Lizzie who listened—at last—to the harmony of Emily's two hearts. The duet had become a trio.

Lizzie was a twentieth-century girl, yet she was also raised on the novels of Emily's day—as well as those which followed after. Born 130 years after Emily, Lizzie also arrived in the world a talented and curious soul, full of dreams and promise. Like Emily, she grew and considered a life outside her father's home.

Yet she was the more fortunate of the two. Lizzie's dreams featured love and self-fulfillment, too, but most of her dreams came true.

In the nearer time where Lizzie lived, such a life was easier to find.

In time, though, as they too often do, Lizzie's dreams began to fade in the face of loss—and those losses, piling up one by one, brought her to a place where she no longer believed in the identity she'd created for herself. She wondered how to go on when she no longer knew who she was.

Emily and Lizzie grew up miles and centuries apart, but one day a farm drew them together. And on the farm belonging to both of them, they encountered each other

...and this is where their story truly begins.

We're constantly changing facts, rewriting history to make things easier, to make them fit in with our preferred version of events. We do it automatically. We invent memories. Without thinking. If we tell ourselves something happened often enough we start to believe it, and then we can actually remember it.

~ S.J. Watson

Chapter Twenty-Nine

~∞~

'Life in Continuous Present':

Beginnings

Seated in the kitchen with Emily's diary in her hands, Lizzie puzzles over an enigma of time and space. When she was young, she loved to read books about time travel, imagining what it might be like to visit another era, or talk with someone who might one day appear unannounced on a city street, somehow transported from her past or future. And during those years, there was no movie she had loved more than the original version of H.G. Wells' *The Time Machine*.

"The book was better," she'd always say when asked, but there was a scene in the film offering a visual image the book could never mirror quite so well, proof that a picture can indeed be worth a thousand words. She remembers it so well, that now, though years have passed since she'd last seen the film, it unspools easily past her mind's eye.

The Time Traveler seats himself in the time machine and begins his exploratory trek through time. Hours, and then days, shift slowly forward at first. But as he continues his watch, the dress on the mannequin in the shop window across the street begins to change over and over, even as he inches the lever ever farther forward. Becoming more confident in his experiment, he pushes the device closer to its limits, and sunrise and sunset begin to click by in almost a single instant, like the ticking of a clock. He travels farther and faster, while the windows of his home are shattered and shuttered in rapid succession. Walls come down as new buildings are erected around him. Homes evaporate into open fields. Factories spring up, then collapse. Time moves ever more swiftly. The transformations around him now so rapid he can no longer even see the changes. Until at last the machine spins to a halt, throwing him off into a place—and time—he could never have imagined. Yet, he's never left his home.

Gazing around her, Lizzie remembers this same room was once Emily's kitchen. She would have spent hours here every day. Baking, cooking, and cleaning. Teaching her children to read.

On this same date 140 years in the past, Emily might have been sitting here in this same spot. If she had a time machine, she could pay her a visit—right here in this room.

What would Emily think of all that happened here? Several generations of children have been fed, bathed and taught here—her own father and grandfather included. Emily might not be a direct ancestor, but now that Lizzie understands their connection, she finds it doesn't matter anymore. They are still two people who share the same space—in a continuous present of time.

Allowing her imagination its liberty, Lizzie turns in her chair until she is facing the doorway to the dining room. In a twinkle of whimsy, she calls out, "Are you here, Emily?"

She chuckles at the eccentricity of her thoughts, but in a moment the hairs on the back of her neck prickle to attention as an unfamiliar voice answers back from the next room.

"Lizzie? Is that you?"

Images from television and movies surge through her mind. Elizabeth Bennett blundering into Amanda Price's bathroom in *Lost in Austen*. The frenetic fifth season of *LOST*, its cast careening through time before finally skidding to a stop in the 1970s. Marty McFly, nearly dating his own mother in *Back to the Future*.

But those things only happen in the movies. Emily can't really be here...can she?

Does it matter?

A woman appears in the doorway. Dark hair and eyes, antiquated attire—undeniably the same woman who'd haunted Lizzie's dreams on a not-too-long-ago night.

"There you are. I wondered where you'd gone."

She enters the room, smiles, and holds out her hand. "Hello, I'm Emily. How do you do?" she says. "Am I in time for tea?"

Once decided that if this is foolishness, she is fine with it, Lizzie welcomes her warmly, shaking her hand and drawing her into the room. Once Emily is seated, Lizzie moves to fill the kettle.

"I'm so happy you're here. Do you like Earl Grey?"

***

Thirty minutes later, they sit companionably in the kitchen--a place now become, to Lizzie's somewhat muddled mind, not unlike the 'wood between the worlds' in C.S. Lewis' tale, *The Magician's Nephew*. A place that Lewis' child hero described as "rich as plumcake." The world has quieted around them, its edges blurred as if there nothing exists outside this farm and the two women seated at the table. Tea has been steeped and poured. The initial sense of absurdity at their meeting has passed, and the two—each from a different time and place—begin to speak of those things which drew them together.

"You found it. I knew you would." Emily smiles knowingly at Lizzie. "It was waiting for you after all. But we can talk about that later. You have questions, do you not?"

"The diary? You did mean for me to find it... I knew it."

"I have been waiting for you a long time, you know." Emily regards her earnestly, as if willing her to believe and understand. "When you were a young girl daydreaming on the porch, I knew that you were the only one who could write my story as it should be written. You are, perhaps, the only one who can understand why I needed to do it."

"But I don't understand, Emily."

"We should start with the simple things, then. You'll want to know why...why I was so angry with you before."

Emily smiles at Lizzie's surprise, nodding her head. "Yes, that was me. I know you thought you were dreaming, but I've been here all the time. Just waiting until you were ready to speak with me."

So much made sense now. Lizzie's sense that someone had been looking over her shoulder from the moment she decided to come to Iowa—and maybe even before—directing her every step, and moving her toward the trunk in the attic when the time was right to find it. Guiding her reading to just the right passages in the diary, and helping her to understand Emily's world. Even down to the timing of finding the original version of the diary. Emily had orchestrated the whole thing.

Pausing as if to emphasize her words, Emily begins again.

"I was angry because you'd caught me at my own game. Yes, you made more of my story than I had. Taking my simple tale about a train trip to Iowa, and making it into a youthful romance—and one with a handsome southern sympathizer at that. You struck at my vanity I suppose, making me out to be someone I did not think I was. Still, I expect I was also dismayed I had not thought to do it myself. You caught me in my reinvention—and you did not even realize it. At least not yet."

"But why, Emily?" Lizzie asks. "Why did you write all those things—changing the truth of what happened to something else? The diary I found first...or the one stuck in the drawer—which one was real?"

"Does it truly matter? And is either less real than the other?" Emily says. "Both accounts involved my choice of what should be written."

Eyeing at her intently, Emily continues, "When you write one of your books or even your diary, are you making a list of every little thing which happens over the course of a day, or are you choosing which events to tell? Of course you select which things will comprise your account—everyone does. The author did not chronicle every moment of Cinderella's misery. Charlotte Brontë did not include in her tale the moment of Jane Eyre's birth. Not including those things is not telling a falsehood. The authors simply decided those details were not so important as the rest.

"Each of us sees things differently. The stories I wrote about James would not be the same as the stories James might have written of himself. The stories he told of me to any who would listen did not seem true in my eyes. And any story I might write about you would likely not seem truth to you—but it would be my truth. My version of life as I see it."

Irritated at what appears to be little more than an attempt on Emily's part at dodging her question, Lizzie opens her mouth to speak when Emily continues with a query of her own. Asking about her conversation with Jack on the side of the freeway just a few short weeks ago, Emily reminds Lizzie of Jack's observations that she is always creating an image of herself and her life through both her characters and her writing.

"What was it he said to you?" Emily asked. "Oh yes, I remember. He asked, 'Aren't you showing your readers the world you want them to see? Rewriting history as you think it should have been, not as it really was?'"

The two sit facing each other across the table, the silence around them, absorbing like cotton wool the last drops of Lizzie's irritation. She recalls telling Jack this amending is just "what writers do." But she also realizes what Emily is asking is how what she did in revising the diary is any different.

Lizzie ponders the question, before finally turning to Emily to ask, "But I call it fiction... do you?"

Emily smiled. "How did I begin my diary? That 'pretentious banner,' as you called it?"

Reaching for the first volume, Emily opened it and read aloud, "Diary—which may compose reminiscences of the life, from day to day of Miss Emmie E. Hawley."

She closed the book and looked deep into Lizzie's eyes. "Reminiscences... written by one woman about another who truly no longer existed. The girl who was Emmie had, in my mind, replaced the Emily—wife and mother, careworn woman—whose life was not turning out as she'd been led to believe it would. What I wrote—or maybe invented—was the biography of someone who no longer existed. Someone who never quite existed. Yet, Emmie was the woman I wanted my daughter to know, to remember. Idealistic and imaginative. Untouched by heartache. Emmie was the woman I had wanted to be. If I got a little carried away in creating my identity...well, you did as well."

Seconds tick by on Lizzie's great-grandmother's clock, like the pendulum on a metronome.

Like the only sound in the world.

Perhaps all anxiety might derive from a fixation on
moments —an inability to accept life as ongoing.
~Sarah Manguso

Chapter Thirty

~∞~

'Life in Continuous Present':

A Moment in Time

Outside, the farm is quiet. From far away the rumblings of a twilight train wander wide across the cornfields. Walking back up the path from the barn, the two women stop at the edge of the drive, watching the colors of evening fade into black.

"Tell me of your daughters, Lizzie. Daisy and Alice, correct?"

Lizzie, pours out her story of maternal pride and love, telling of accomplishments and dreams for the future—and even dreams dashed with Jack's death. "They miss him so. Daisy just became engaged, but it breaks her heart her father will never meet her fiancé. Never walk her down the aisle. Never see his grandchildren."

She quiets for a moment, observing the silence. "My mother never met her grandchildren either... She never met Jack."

Silent tears slip down Lizzie's cheek.

"I missed my mother so when I moved from Michigan," Emily says, wrapping her arm around Lizzie's shoulders. Pulling her close, offering comfort.

"After I left home, I saw her again only twice—and then she died. I was not so young as you, but I thought my heart would break with her loss. I was unable even to be there to lay her to rest."

The evening sky now a velvet black, stars have winked into view, one by one. A full moon hangs low in the west. Another hour or so and it will rest for the night.

Pulling her thoughts back to the present, Lizzie recalls the meteors that will soon be visible, "Over there, I think. The Perseids.

Jack and I used to stay up late or get up before dawn to watch them, every year."

In the face of swelling memory, she continues. "We'd swaddle up in blankets and lay on deck chairs in the backyard to watch it. Sometimes the girls would join us." Heaving a sigh, she adds, "We missed them that last summer. Jack was at a conference in DC..."

Silence falls again. But in this place between places, on a small farm in Iowa, disparate times seem to have compressed and converged. In this moment, this heartbeat, the nocturnal remembrances of both women splash across the sky, as if the very air drips with them. In the northeastern sky, dozens of meteors begin to stream from the stars, a constant radiance coursing outward from Perseus. Not far away, a brilliant comet gleams low in the northern sky; two large tails streaming behind it.

Like the dress of the mannequin in *The Time Machine*, the image has altered; but here in this place, she is garbed in the mode of two eras at the same time.

The sight of it is a bit unsettling.

As the night grows deeper and the air cools, the women huddle closer, each gaining comfort in the presence of the other. Shrouded in memories—of the past, the future, the present…a continuous present in which all points touch and balance—they breathe as one.

Emily speaks at last, turning to point toward the widow's walk. "It was such an extravagance. James called it showy and told me I was vain to insist on it. He was right, of course, but I so loved to see the sky from there."

"One night—right there on the roof—I watched for hours. The children were asleep, but James refused to come out. The stars were so bright. It was breathtaking."

Never turning her eyes from the sight before her, Lizzie asked, "and you saw the comet, too?"

"You read the diary, did you not? It was dazzling. Just like that," she says, her eyes fixed on the smudgy light in the sky. "Yet it was not the first comet I'd seen." Emily recalls, reciting as if from memory...

"I remember seeing a brilliant Comet in the year 1858. Mother was afraid it was going to hit the earth and destroy it..." She turns and faces Lizzie as she continues, "How strange it is that many people are so ignorant about the works of Nature."

Smiling now, Emily says, "Fear can be a terrible thing, can it not?"

Lizzie knows she is no longer speaking of the comet, or people's dread of an environment they do not fully understand. Emily was identifying her own surrender to fear.

"In the same year I saw Coggia's Comet, one of my neighbors hanged himself. James Van Alstine told his wife he was too much trouble to her and began to cry...then he went outside to the barn. Hours later she found him there. His fear of losing his farm to creditors drove him to abandon everyone and everything he loved. He could no longer face his troubles."

"You think I might kill myself?"

"On no, Lizzie, I have no fear of that. However, there is more than one way to avoid facing difficult things." Hugging her arms as if to ward off a chill, Emily took a few steps before continuing. "You believe you cannot write since your husband's death. Is that the truth—or merely the story you've written for yourself? It is a question you must answer. Do you truly wish to be remembered as the woman who gave up the things she loved simply because she was afraid to do them?"

Lizzie is quiet, taking in Emily's words. "Jack said the same thing." Looking up, she watches as the meteors continue their dash through the stars. "But I've been writing. I want to write your story, but I don't know if I can tell it well enough that anyone would ever want to publish it. What more can I do?"

Emily turns toward her, and says, "You and I are both storytellers. I think it is how we best understand the world. Now, may I tell you a story, Lizzie?"

Not waiting for an answer, Emily returns her gaze to the stars and begins to speak.

As Einstein himself pointed out...we're like people in a boat without oars drifting along a winding river. Around us we see only the present. We can't see the past, back in the bends and curves behind us. But it's there.

~Jack Finney

Chapter Thirty-One

~∞~

'Life in Continuous Present':
Emily's Story

"It was a very long time ago when I lived in this house, and the world was a different place from the one you inhabit. In that long ago day, girls were raised to believe they had an almost sacred duty to marry and raise a family. To desire anything else was unthinkable— considered by some a rebellion against God and man. And once a girl was married, the purpose of her existence was simply to make a happy home. She alone was held responsible for the contentment and spiritual condition of her family, to the point that if her husband abandoned her, or drank and abused her or her children, she was considered somehow at fault.

"Although I wanted more from my life than to live in this state, in the end I did as I knew I must.

"It was with this belief in duty and destiny I married James. If harsh words came between us, I desired only that I might be a better wife to him. That we might never dispute or disagree. Time and again, after arguments or misunderstandings, I recorded in my diary "my prayer that I may never speak an unkind word to him that God has seen fit to give me," noting "how foolish to cry, for James is too kind to have his feelings hurt by my silliness of crying." As I had been taught, I believed his discontent somehow grew from my own error.

Yet time passed, and I began to recognize there was more happening with James than simply my failure to uphold the trust of "true womanhood" that my society required of me. No matter how I prayed or held my tongue, his unpleasantness grew. I worked hard every day, earning extra money to send our children to school so they could gain a good education—but James resented it. He wanted them to stay home and work. He would refuse to speak to us, or disappear without a word for days on end. He began to have violent spells where he would grow so angry he would abuse our animals—and even our son Henry and me. He threatened to take his own life on more than one occasion. I knew not what to do for him."

Taking a deep breath after such a long speech, Emily begins to pace the length of the porch, gathering her courage to continue.

"I grew nervous and fearful, afraid to be left alone with him while the children were at school. I wondered many times if there was anything I could do, should do. But I did nothing, told no one. I couldn't bear that any of my neighbors might think ill of me, still believing his behavior must somehow be my responsibility.

"One night I wrote in my diary, penning words which still trouble me at times:

The heart sometimes is broken by trouble and its possessor dies a martyr. I tried so hard to live through it without it being known by the outside world, suffered untold sorrow by hearing his abusive language, yet I did not dare to displease him. I have written many things in my journal, but the worst is a secret to be burried when I shall cease to be. God alone knows I have prayed every day that I might have wisdom, that I might know the right way, and do right in all my words and doings. I can say with all my heart my conscience is clear.

"I poured my heart out on those pages, but even there I could not speak the whole truth of my life. I had drawn an image of myself and my family, and I could not speak against it. I played the part I was given before the audience of my society, and my fears of their displeasure kept me standing on that stage."

Turning to face her, Emily readies herself to end her discourse. To drive home her point—hoping Lizzie is prepared to hear.

"Fear can lead us to do terrible things, Lizzie—or sometimes, to do nothing at all. In that long ago day, I had only two choices. I could stay—or I could leave. If I left James, I would be spurned by my neighbors for abandoning my husband. I would have no home, no money. I would be alone, save for my children—who would also suffer for my choice. I could not take the risk. So for a long time I stayed and accepted my lot. Near the end, when my worries had already destroyed my health, I did move into town, leaving James alone on the farm. But it was too little, too late.

"In the end, fear stole away my very life."

Her words hang in the air, expanding to fill the spaces between and around them until they seem to reverberate through the whole of the world. Taking Lizzie's hands in her own, Emily offers one last plea.

"Please don't let your fears do the same to you."

If a story is not about the hearer he [or she] will not listen .
. . A great lasting story is about everyone or it will not last.
The strange and foreign is not interesting—only the deeply
personal and familiar.
~ John Steinbeck

Chapter Thirty-Two

~∞~

'Life in Continuous Present':
Lizzie's Story

They sit silently, two women watching the stars sweep across the face of the sky. There is much left to say, yet it does not seem a time for words—at least not yet. Alone in her thoughts, Lizzie begins to consider her fears. Listening as Emily recounts the story of her life and her marriage, Lizzie is speechless before the hardships she had faced, but she also realizes every story has at least two sides. What was it Emily had said earlier? That the stories she told were her version of "life as I see it."

The only stories we can tell are our own.

It is nearly silent as the eastern horizon begins to lighten; little can be heard but the faint whisper of the chairs rocking gently on the porch. Both women are lost in thought. The night spray of meteors has disappeared, and the comet is fading from sight as well. All that remains is the brilliance of Venus—known by the Babylonians as the bright queen of the heavens. Observing its continued glow against the looming light of day, Lizzie remembers the myths she discovered long ago, research she'd done for a book about Irish astronomer Annie Scott Dill Mauder, who in 1906 became the first woman elected to the Royal Astronomical Society. Lizzie's first novel, *Her Eye on the Heavens*, lies tucked away in a drawer—unpublished still—yet she'd learned so much about astronomy in the process of its creation.

Somehow that made the time it took to write it feel like less of a waste.

Turning to Emily, Lizzie's voice intrudes on the stillness. "Do you see that bright star over there?" She points toward the lightening horizon. "Right above the tree? It's actually not a star at all. That's Venus, the planet nearest our own in both distance and size. Next to the moon, it is one of the brightest objects in the night sky. It's so reflective that nearly three quarters of the sunlight which falls on it is mirrored back into space. When we look at it, it is the sun's rays we see."

Sensing that Lizzie is following a train of thought, not simply reciting her research, Emily responds to keep her talking. "It is beautiful," she says. "I saw it many mornings, hanging low in the sky as I pumped water before breakfast."

Still gazing at the dazzling point in the sky, Lizzie continues. "Did you know the astronomical symbol for Venus is the same as the symbol for female? A circle with a small cross beneath it? It represents a hand mirror of the Roman goddess. I never knew that. Venus was recognized even by ancient Rome for its reflective properties."

She pauses a moment, considering. "I guess women were seen like that, too. But as reflectors of what? Man's glory? The world around them? A mirror holds no light of its own... it merely imitates whatever is shone on it."

As the edge of the sky grows ever lighter, and Venus begins to fade, a rosy glow washes over the smattering of clouds now rising with the sun. A new day is nearly upon them. Although the night has been virtually soundless, the bustle of day begins. A breeze rustles the cornfields, birds trill in the trees. The distant horn of a train can be heard. Along the horizon, a tiny sliver of gold breaks just at the edge of the distant tree line. At last the light of Venus flickers out. Both women understand their time together is almost at an end. But Lizzie isn't finished yet. She's just beginning to understand Emily's purpose. What Emily's story means—to her.

Speaking more quickly now, Lizzie is anxious to find her way to her answer. "You saw yourself as a mirror for James. It was the only work your society gave you to do. Allowing him to see himself in you, and to expose an image of the person he—and they—thought you should be.

"But a mirror is more just than a reflection. It is also a way to know yourself. The glass can become a portal of self-discovery."

With more conviction in her voice than has been there in a long time, Lizzie stands and steps to the edge of the porch, still watching the spot where Venus has vanished from sight.

"I don't want to see myself as merely a reflection anymore. Not of Jack. Not of anyone. I don't want to be afraid of seeing myself for who I am."

Emily stands as well, breathing in the genesis of the day.

"It will be fully light soon," she says. "It is almost time for me to go. But before I do, there is one more thing I must say."

She turns back to face Lizzie, her eyes searching. "You have nothing to be afraid of, Lizzie. You can write—if you choose—any story you wish to tell. You can travel where you will. Go to New York, learn to paint, take a train. Whatever you desire, you can do."

Emily walks toward the front door. But before she enters, her hand now resting on the doorknob, she looks back over her shoulder at Lizzie.

"I did not have the freedom to make those choices...but you do. Don't be afraid to make them."

With one last smile in her direction, Emily nods her farewell, opens the door and disappears inside.

We may say that the characters in fairytales are 'good to think with'... the job of the fairytale is to show that Why? questions cannot be answered except in one way: by telling the stories. The story does not contain the answer, it is the answer.

~ Brian Wicker

Chapter Thirty-Three

~∞~

'Life in Continuous Present':
The Story is the Answer

Once upon a time, two women met on an Iowa farm and shared the stories of their lives across time and space. Through the telling, they grew to understand each other—but more importantly, they came to comprehend themselves.

It was through those tales that one of them—the only one who still could—learned to face her fears, and become the person she had always longed to be. The stories helped to heal her heart, give her courage, and renew her faith—in herself, in her dreams, and in her future.

Lizzie recognized she could write again—it was time. A story had presented itself to her, but it was hers to choose. The future ahead—as far as it is possible for anyone—was hers to create. The composition of her life was in her hands.

She needed only to address a new audience.

With Jack's death, she had lost not merely her purpose in writing, but the one person for whom she had always written. To continue to write without him—or so she had thought—would have been to deny his importance. To create something in which he would play no part. It would be turning her back on the past.

Yet, she now understood things differently. She saw that her best audience had always been herself.

She was really the only one who mattered.

The text created in a continuous presence but now fixed in time, must be recreated by a reader in a new, continuous present.

~Margo Culley

Chapter Thirty-Four

~∞~

August 27th - *I knew it would work. In the writing, I had uncovered my answer...*

I laid down my pen, closed the journal, and pushed back from the table, stretching my arms to the ceiling. I could never explain how good it felt to write like that again. Allowing my imagination free reign, birthing a story which seemed to spring from someplace deep inside me...

It had been such a long time.

I knew it would need work, but I had written my way to a certain level of clarity—at least about my own life. My stylized conversation with Emily had done its work. Emily, Charlie—even Jack—had all tried to help me understand that what was holding me back was my own fear of letting go of the past. But I couldn't move forward unless I stopped looking back.

I didn't have to give up my memories, but I did have to leave the past where it belonged—in the past. It hadn't been so much that I was afraid to write as it was I was afraid to write without Jack. Afraid to begin something which he had no part in. To see only myself in the writing. It had been easier to do nothing than to face myself.

So, nothing... is exactly what I did.

Emily's story made me see things differently, though. Although she had begun her marriage with high hopes, things did not turn out as she planned. Without her voice spilled across the pages of her diary, I could never have imagined the pain of her life. Different than my own, but pain, nonetheless. And I—like Emily—allowed my pain to grow into fear, a fear which held me captive for far too long

But what was it Coraline said in the play? When she saw her fears reflected in the mirror? "When you're scared, but you still do it anyway, that's brave." It was time for me to be brave—not once I'd vanquished my fears, but in the face of them.

Like Coraline, I wanted to be able to say, "I will be brave...No, I *am* brave."

I didn't choose to lose my husband—or anyone else—but I still had a choice about what to make of my life. A decision I made every morning—whether to give into fear or face it. Choosing to act in spite of it. And from this moment on, I knew what I would do.

I was choosing to write. Emily's story convinced me that moving on was the only way to truly live.

Thinking back on the way I had written my conversation with Emily, I couldn't help but wonder, "Would Emily have told her story this way? Would she actually have been so comforting—or so wise?" And I had to admit, I didn't know—and it really didn't matter. Reading a book is always as much about the reader's story as it is the writer's. Emily's life story, once filtered through my own, took on a life she may never have intended—just as the book I hope to write with it may someday do the same for yet another reader.

That is the way it is with stories...

***

On his way back from town, Alex stopped by the house to fill me in on some of the neighborhood goings-on while I'd been away.

"You remember the Fosters up the road? One of their cows got out on Saturday. We found her a few hours later, though—wandering out behind your barn. No harm done, though, and she's safely back home." With a twinkle in his eye, he added, "I guess even cows like a little adventure now and again—just like the rest of us!"

After thanking him for keeping his eye on things while I was gone, and especially for keeping my barn safe from the marauding cow, he asked about my trip and whether Charlie was still planning to visit. When I told him she wasn't going to be able to make it after all, but I'd be seeing her in New York in three weeks for my daughter's wedding, he was a bit disappointed.

"Now that's too bad. I'd have liked to meet her," he said. "But congratulations to you and your daughter. Weddings are pretty exciting, aren't they? We've got one coming up, too. But, before I forget, I did want to ask about your plans to write your book about an Amish. Did you ever find one to write about?"

I completely forgot about the Amish!

"Actually, I've decided I'm going to write about Emily...you know, the woman who wrote the diary? She lived here in this house, and I have the story of her life right in my hands. How could I possibly write about anything else?"

"That's a fantastic idea! If there's anything I can do... I know folks around here would love to read a book like that." Alex face lit up, and laughing, he turned to face me and asked, with a twinkle in his eye, "When it's finished, can I get an autographed copy?"

Now it was my turn to laugh.

"Not only can you have an autographed copy, Alex, but I promise to let you know as soon as I get an acceptance letter!"

***

I had been talking about writing again for months, playing with the idea of writing Emily's story, and even "tried out" a few possible story lines from Emily's life, I never truly felt the importance of telling her story until that moment. I knew now no matter what—whether anyone was ever interested in publishing it or not—that I would finish it. I had been led to the diary, and I was meant to write her story. If she'd been here, my mother would have assured me that writing Emily's story was clearly my destiny.

One grain of sand at a time…

Storytelling wasn't about making things up. It was more like inviting the stories to come through her, let themselves be told.

~Jennifer McMahon

Chapter Thirty-Five

~∞~

August 29th - *Things always seem to work out in the end…just as they should.*

Although I wanted nothing more than to spend every waking moment working out the details of my novel, there were practical things to be considered now. I'd have to head back home to Seattle right after Daisy's wedding, but still had no plan for what to do with the farm. I certainly couldn't live here, but I wasn't ready to give it up, either.

If I didn't sell, what would I do with it?

I should have known it would be Alex who offered me the perfect solution. He had been there all summer with just the right amount of help every time I needed it—from moving the trunk to finding Emily's grave, to corralling that wayward cow before she could kick down my barn door. One afternoon about a week before I was planning to leave for New York, he stopped by to say hello and to ask how much longer I'd be in town. While we stood in the driveway chatting, he asked if I'd come to any conclusions about the house.

"I don't know what to do, Alex. I don't want to sell it—at least not yet. But I don't think it's a good idea to leave it standing empty either. The property manager hasn't been able to find me a renter, so I'm feeling a bit stuck."

In his typical thoughtful way, Alex pursed up his lips and thought for a moment before speaking. "Would you consider renting it out?"

"Renting it would be ideal, but the property manager hasn't been able to find anyone who wants it."

"What if I had someone for you?" He peered at me from under the hand shielding his face, his eyes crinkling with delight. "I just might know someone who's interested."

"Really?" I said. "You do? Can I ask who?"

"You remember my grandson Matt? Dan's oldest boy? He came along to help us move the trunk...

"Matt? Sure I remember him."

"Well, Matt's getting married in about a week. They got an apartment in town, but they'd rather be out here on a farm... just can't afford it yet. He works with me, so it would be good if they were closer—and your place is right next door. I haven't mentioned it to him yet. Didn't want to say anything until I talked with you."

I could see the enthusiasm in his eyes. He dearly loved his family, and I knew he liked having them close. "So... what do you think?"

What do I think? It's perfect!

"Are you kidding?" I said. "It's just what I was hoping for. I wanted to find someone who would take care of the place. It's important to me that it's in good hands. But, are you sure he'll be interested in just renting--and with such short notice?"

"Don't you worry about that. I know he'll be interested. Otherwise they'll end up living in a little apartment.... No, thank you!" Alex was clearly not pleased at the thought of Matt and Stacy stuck in a little apartment.

"And if you ever do decide to sell," he added, "I bet he'll want to be first in line."

With such a short time left before I had to leave for New York, I had pretty much given up on finding someone to live here. I could hardly believe the answer had just driven up to my front door. I asked Alex to talk to Matt and Stacy about it and let me know if they were interested. I'd be thrilled to have someone I knew in here.

"Just one more thing, Alex. Do you think you could finagle me an invitation to the wedding?"

***

Things worked out better than I could have hoped. Matt and Stacy were thrilled over the idea of moving to the farm. Matt even decided he'd be able to start building his own herd—since he'd have a place to put them—so there would be cows in the barn again. Silly as it might sound, I can't tell you how excited that made me. It would be a real working farm again. Uncle Dean would be pleased.

I think Emily would be, too.

Since I had renters, I could leave all of the furniture behind, and that made Matt and Stacy pretty happy, too—knowing the house would not be empty when they arrived at their new home. I gave them permission to paint or redecorate in any way they chose, remembering how important it is for newlyweds to feel a house is really theirs. I did decide to take a few things with me though. I wanted Emily's trunk (including all of its contents) and the mantle clock which once belonged to my great-great-grandmother, and arranged to have them—and everything else I didn't want to carry to New York with me—shipped home, to arrive there a few days after I did.

Memory is never a precise duplicate of the original... it is a continuing act of creation.

~Robert Cartwright

Chapter Thirty-Six

~∞~

August 31st - *This summer has certainly flown by. Didn't I just get here?*

The last few days flew so fast it seemed mere moments before I found myself seated at a table by the edge of a lake, watching Matt and Stacy dancing for the first time as husband and wife. The wedding was beautiful, yards of white lace and ribbons, and lots of happy tears all around. The newlyweds looked so blissful, spinning there on a dance floor surrounded with flowers and twinkle lights. They would soon be joined by family and friends, but this moment belonged to the two of them alone. I couldn't help but remember my own wedding, dancing with Jack, almost dizzy with my own happiness—but I couldn't help looking ahead either. Six days from now, Daisy would be marrying the man of her choice, and another page would be added to the journal of my life. Why was it in moments like these time seemed to almost stand still? A measure of minutes, separated in time and yet somehow held together in space.

It's that Time Machine mannequin all over again...

The sun would be setting in another half hour or so, but the party seemed to be just winding up. The dance floor was growing crowded, with even the smallest of Alex' grandchildren—or great-grandchildren—joining in. Alex' family had gone out of their way to welcome me as one of their own, making sure I was introduced all around and enjoyed myself. And really, how could you not have a good time at a wedding? I had just scraped the last of the pale pink frosting off my fork and washed it down with some sort of fizzy pink punch, when Alex walked up and sat down beside me. "Beautiful wedding, huh? I can't believe how fast they've grown up, but I'm so proud of Matt. Of both those two kids."

I smiled and nodded in agreement, and said, "And it's my turn next. My little girl is getting married in less than a week. In New York City of all places!" Sighing a little as I watched the dancers, I added, "Daisy would love this. I hope wherever their ceremony is, it's as lovely as this place."

"Yeah, it is awful nice out here," he said, admiring the view around us, "...and a great place to play on a summer afternoon. We spent a lot of time out here as kids—your dad and uncle, too, swimming in the lake and fishing back there in the crick." He paused as if he was watching the scene play out in his head. "Lots of wildlife out here, too. Yesterday, I saw a bunch a wild turkeys out there in the fields while they were setting up for the wedding. Seeing them scramble to get out of the way of the trucks, flying over the road—that was a kick."

My mind's eye filled with a parade of turkeys tossing themselves across the road like beanbags and I couldn't help but laugh.

"You know Alex, sometimes—especially when you're telling me one of your stories—it feels like the past is just peering around the corner. Out of sight, maybe, but never completely out of reach."

I used to think—probably due to my sci-fi fixation—that I might someday open a door and find the past being lived out behind it. Here in Manchester, I had never been surer such thing could actually happen.

Alex chuckled a bit before countering in a sing-song cadence, "Oh, it is, my dear Liz. It sure is..."

The sun was sinking fast and vivid colors began to stain the clouds hovering along the horizon, adding to the beauty of the evening. Standing and turning toward me, Alex tipped his head in my direction and extended his hand, asking, "Excuse me, ma'am, but can I talk you into taking a turn around the dance floor with an old codger like me?"

His invitation took me back for a moment. I hadn't planned on dancing, but after Charlie's lecture at the restaurant in Chicago, reminding me that a dance was not a lifetime commitment, I knew it was time to take another small step toward leaving behind all my fears. And dancing with Alex would be an easy one—almost like dancing with my father.

"Oh Alex, I'd love it. Thank you for asking!"

I stood and he took my hand, tucking it into the crook of his elbow, leading me across the crowded dance floor. My dance skills barely extended to a waltz, but Alex? In spite of his age, he was one terrific dancer. He had my head spinning before long, and in more ways than one I felt lighter than I had in years. But I was so focused on trying to stay on my feet, I didn't even notice Dan's approach until the song ended and he asked if I'd honor him with the next dance. Alex gallantly bowed in my direction, and walked over toward a cousin who was seated in one of the chairs ringing the dance floor—he wasn't about to sit this one out. But before I could process what was happening, I came face to face with Dan's brilliant blue eyes.

Like dancing with my father? No, not so much...

The world around me seemed to skid to a stop, and in that moment I was right back in Vermilion, hearing Charlie's angry words ringing in my ears, 'What are you so afraid of?' My fear of moving forward without Jack kept me from living my life, but I didn't want to live that way anymore. It was time for me to let the past be the past—and dancing with Dan was a small step in the right direction.

Just smile and say yes, Liz. This is definitely not going to kill you.

Worried he'd noticed my hesitation, I smiled as brightly as I could and held out my hand.

"Thanks, I'd love to."

Not only can I do this, but I think it just might be fun...

***

Hours later, the stars sparkled like diamonds scattered across a velvet sky as wedding guests began trickling home, one carload at a time. I was still on the dance floor—although by then I was seated in a chair at its edge, rubbing my aching feet. I don't think I danced so much since high school but now that I'd found my feet again—so to speak—they didn't seem to want to stop. Dan was as good a dancer as his father (*not to mention, pretty darn handsome*), and I greatly enjoyed his company. Spinning around the floor, we compared notes about watching our children grow up, courses we took in college, and I told him all about the plans for my book. Over the course of the evening, I think I took a turn around the floor with nearly every male Hikler relative—including a few under the age of ten—but I somehow always seemed to circle back to Dan. I hadn't had so much fun in years.

Aside from the bride and groom still swaying on the dance floor, gazing adoringly in each other's eyes, there were a few stragglers enjoying the music. I could see the DJ starting to pack things up, though, while relatives and friends were starting to wrap up leftover cake and food, shoving paper plates and forks into garbage bags.

I looked over at Dan, sitting in the chair next to me, and said "This has been a wonderful evening, but I think it's about time for me to head home. I need to get an early start tomorrow morning."

Helping me to my feet, he looped my arm through his and walked with me as I searched for Alex, wanting to say good-bye before I headed out. As soon as we found him, Dan took my hand in his and wished me luck with Daisy's wedding, as well as completing my book project.

"All of Manchester will be waiting to see how it turns out," he said, with a chuckle. "But... no pressure!"

We all laughed at that, but it was true. It seemed every time I ran into another of my neighbors, whether shopping in town or driving by the farm, they'd stop to chat, mentioning either that Alex told them about my finding the diary, or wondering if I had any plans to write about it. Never had any group of people been so enthusiastic about a book which hadn't even been written yet.

I thanked Dan for a being such a tolerant dance partner, and for an unforgettable evening.

"It was a beautiful wedding. I can only hope Daisy's is half so lovely."

I also promised to let them all know when the book was finished, adding with a laugh, "Maybe I can bring the book tour to Manchester when it's published."

Dan was definitely enthusiastic about the idea, and Alex assured me that the local bookstore would be "thrilled to have a real live author come to town."

"Well then, I'd better get to work, hadn't I?"

As Alex started chatting about book tours and suggesting the possibility of holding a signing party at the farm, one of the ladies on the cleanup crew called for Dan, asking what to do with all the food. "Well, I better get back there and help with the mess. That's what the parents are here for, right? That...and paying the bills."

Dan, taking my hand once again, leaned in and kissed me on the cheek. "Goodnight, Liz. It's been a pleasure getting to know you," he said.

Heading back toward the reception, he turned back and smiled at me before grabbing up two trash bags and swinging them into the bed of a nearby pickup.

Nope, not an evening I'll soon forget.

"I can't believe you're leaving us already," Alex said. "It feels like you just got here." For a brief moment, I was surprised to hear him speak. Watching Dan walk away, I almost forgot Alex was there.

Pulling myself back from thoughts that felt like a tangled string of "what ifs..." I turned toward Alex and said, "Yeah, it seems like that to me, too."

I'd been here in Manchester for just over two months, but time had just flown by. I'd gotten to see the farm again, met some wonderful people, discovered Emily's diary, had a fabulous—and in some ways, life changing—couple of days in Chicago with Charlie, and even started a new book. None of which was what I truly expected when I made an impulsive decision to come to Iowa to see Uncle Dean's farm one more time.

And you danced. Don't forget the dancing...

"Well Alex, my boarding pass reads 2:45 p.m." I said. "And I still have to make the drive into Chicago in the morning. I've got a daughter getting married in a few days, and from the nervous phone calls I keep getting, I'm sure there's plenty left to do yet."

Alex chuckled, agreeing that weddings did seem to bring out all kinds of anxiety in people. He took my hand and tucked it into the crook of his arm as we walked the short distance to my car. Overhead, the stars sparkled as gravel crunched beneath my feet. With a slight nip in the air that hadn't been there even a week ago, I could tell the turn of the seasons was fast approaching. It was time for me to go; my future was waiting.

Once we reached my car, Alex turned and said, "Now don't forget, you promised me a copy of that book of yours. I'll be waiting for it."

"I won't forget, Alex. When it's finished, the first copy is yours. I promise!" I reached my hand out to take his, and he carried it to his lips.

With a little wink, he smiled and said, "It's been a pleasure having you here, ma'am. Now that you know where we are, don't be a stranger—to any of us." He opened the car door for me, so I could slide inside. "Come and see us again—real soon."

Alex, are you playing matchmaker here?

Promising I'd come back to visit as soon as I could, I waved once more as I drove out toward the highway and back to the farm. Such a lovely man—a true gentleman. I wondered what I would have done this summer without him.

Another meeting that was clearly meant to be.

It was such a lovely evening. A slight breeze ruffled the leaves in the trees, and the light in the window seemed to be welcoming me back. Yes, the farm had become home to me. It was hard to think about leaving it. Yet at the same time I had such a sense of ... what?

Anticipation? Hope? Let's just say I knew the moments were once again been piling up, and soon my life would once more change "all of a sudden." Like the late-summer crispness in the evening air, I could feel the changes coming.

Far away across the fields, a train whistled—and I couldn't help but smile.

There is more to your life than you ever thought.
There is more to your story than what you have read.

~Max Lucado

Chapter Thirty-Seven

~∞~

September 1st - *It is so hard to leave the farm behind. So much in my life is changing—again...*

After loading my bags into the trunk the next morning, I walked back into the house for one last look around. I wandered rooms one by one, calling up not only childhood memories now, but new ones as well. It was so hard to leave.

Finally, I entered the kitchen. Inspecting the contents of the refrigerator to be sure I'd emptied it of anything which might spoil before Matt and Stacy returned from their honeymoon, I turned back toward the middle of the room and did something I'd wanted to do ever since I'd written the conversation between Emily and me. I spoke to her—out loud.

"Emily, are you here?"

Feeling just a little bit silly, I wondered for a moment what I'd do if she actually answered. It didn't matter though, I had a few things to say to her and whether I looked ridiculous or not, I was going to say them.

"Thank you, Em. Thank you for everything. For choosing me. For leading me to your diary. For sharing your story and your life with me. It means so much more than I could ever say."

I picked up my purse and keys from the table and walked out to the dining room, drinking in my final view of this house that always seemed the very embodiment of my childhood.

"You may not have written for me, but you allowed me to become your audience for just a little while—and in doing so, you helped me see myself in your diary. Your story changed my life. It changed *me*.

"I can never thank you enough."

Still meandering, I turned to the fireplace and ran my hand over the hand-hewn mantle. I wondered if Emily's James built it, or whether my own great-grandfather added it after he bought the farm some fifty years later. I remembered the clock which stood sentinel here during my childhood, its ticking filling the early morning silence of the room, counting off the moments of life for at least four generations. It was now carefully packed inside Emily's trunk, heading across the country to its new home on the mantle in my library, to continue its measure of moments for me on the other side of the country. It would also to act as a reminder of my connection to this farm—and my past.

"I'm going to finish writing your story, Em, and I'm going to get it published. If Avalon won't take it, I'll find someone who will. I promise you that."

I glanced at my watch. I had to get moving if I was going to have enough time to return the rental car. Checking my phone one last time to be sure my boarding pass was handy, I turned toward the front door. Stopping in the entry, I spoke one last time.

"This isn't really a good-bye, Emily. You and your story are going with me—and not just in your diary. I'll be carrying it in my soul, as well.

"No more excuses. I'm choosing to live my life. I promise you that, too..."

***

I jumped into the shuttle and hoped I'd make it in time. Traffic had been horrendous and the drive into Chicago took nearly thirty minutes longer than I expected. Pulling up to the curb, I thanked the driver, and jumped out with my bag. I hurried past the lines at the ticket counter, suitcase bumping across the tile floor, and hoped I wouldn't be too late. Heading straight through the building, I pulled out my phone, brought up my boarding pass, and joined the line.

Mere moments later, ready to board, I felt the inevitable butterflies, but for once they seemed to be fluttering with excitement rather than fear. I'd longed to make this trip my entire adult life—and there I was, finally about to embark on the journey of my dreams. Just like Emily had hopped on a train all those years ago, waiting for it to carry her away to a brand new life, I was headed to New York to watch my daughter do the same. The Amtrak Cardinal would be pulling out of Union Station any minute, carrying me toward my daughter's wedding, yes, but toward the first great adventure of my brand-new life, as well—a train journey through the colors of the Blue Ridge and Allegheny Mountains, along the Ohio River and all the way to New York's Penn Station.

I was beyond excited.

Adjusting the bag on my shoulder, I considered Emily's diary now nestled within it. Over the next two days on the train, I'd map out my ideas for the book inspired by her diary, and work on a synopsis to send off to Kylie over at Avalon—and maybe even to Maggie, if Avalon wasn't interested. I was hopeful this time they'd appreciate what I was hoping to do with the book. Still anxious about their reactions, I had no illusions that my every fear would wisp away as easily as the smoke now rising from the engine. But I knew now that courage would come through my actions, not my feelings—and it was time to act. Just like making reservations to travel to Daisy's wedding on a train, fulfilling my life-long dream, it was time for me to take the first step toward keeping my promise to Emily. To tell her story.

The moment has arrived.

"All aboard!"

A book is a heart that only beats in the chest of another.

~Rebecca Solnit

Epilogue

~∞~

"Where on earth are those keys?"

Fishing around in the bottom of my purse for the third time, I hear a familiar jingle, finally locating the keys in the deepest recesses of the front pocket.

I need to head out soon if I'm going to make it to the airport on time.

Daisy and Alice are flying in from Sydney this morning, with Justin arriving Christmas Eve morning. I haven't seen Daisy and Justin since their New York City wedding in September. And Alice? Not since last March when she was home for Spring Break. I can hardly wait to have them both back home with me again.

Will and Charlie will be arriving later this afternoon after meeting up at the airport in Denver and flying the last leg of the trip together. The two of them are planning to rent a car just so I won't have to make another trip to the airport today. I can't tell you how thankful I was to hear that.

My whole family together for Christmas? It doesn't get much better than this!

The last three months have been so hectic. I only taught two classes at the high school this quarter, and my last day on staff was last Friday. After spending summer on the farm and finally beginning to write again, I realized my heart just wasn't in teaching. Writing is the only thing I ever wanted to do.

With my smaller workload this fall, I was able to devote more time to writing Emily's story, and just three weeks ago sent off my manuscript to Avalon. I got a call from Kylie about a week later, wanting to tell me how much she personally enjoyed Emily's story.

However, although it just didn't seem to be a good fit for Avalon, she did wish me luck in finding another publisher. "It's a story that should be heard," she said. We discussed several other book ideas I'd been mulling over now that I was finished with this one, and she expressed interest in a few of those. I promised to get back to her once I'd fleshed the ideas out a little more.

I had to admit I was a little disappointed when Avalon said no, but I had known all along they weren't likely to be interested—and that left me free to send it out to a few other people on Amy's list.

Speaking of Amy, she called a few days ago, just to let me know she'd heard from another of the publishers we sent the manuscript off to. It was another "thanks, but no thanks," but she reminded me once more not to be discouraged.

"Don't worry, Liz. You've got something good here. We just needed to keep looking until we find the right fit."

Purse and keys now sitting on the table by the door, I only need to pull on my boots and a jacket and I'm ready to go. It's not raining at the moment, but I've seen today's forecast (and the sky)— it's only a matter of time before the downpour begins.

As I pull my jacket from the hanger, the doorbell rings. Opening the door, I find the mailman waiting on the porch with a certified letter. After signing for it and noting that it's from another of the publishing companies I sent Emily's story to, I look at my watch to decide if I have time to open it now or to just drop it in my purse to read while I wait in the cell phone lot. There are still a few minutes to spare, so I tear open the envelope, unfold the letter, and begin to read:

> Dear Liz:
>
> My staff has completed our review of your novel "A Continuous Present." I am pleased to inform you that we think your work would make an excellent addition to our list of titles. Flora Campo, our Senior Publishing Services consultant will be contacting you shortly...

"Woohoo! They like it! They really like it!"

With the letter clutched tight in my hands, I dance around the entry, jumping up and down and squealing at the top of my voice.

But unexpectedly, everything inside me quiets, and I stop—still and silent—as if straining to hear a faraway sound. It feels like he's here. As if Jack is standing beside me, his voice falling soft on my ear, "I knew you could do it... and I am so proud of you."

I close my eyes and drink in the moment, before speaking aloud.

"You told me I could—and you were right. Thank you for believing in me, Jack. I love you—for always."

As swiftly as the feeling rose, it is gone. I have a future ahead of me, but he will not be part of its creation. I know that now and I am as ready for it as I'll ever be. Although he will always be a part of me, it's time to let him go.

It's time to move ahead with my life.

I can't wait to share my good news about the book with the girls, but I think I'll wait until Will and Charlie arrive so I can tell everyone at once—if I can manage to keep my secret that long.

I can't wait to see their faces.

Wishing I could tell Emily her story is about to be published, I want nothing more right now than to be standing in the farmhouse, speaking face-to-face with her as did my counterpart in the novel. Instead, I give voice to my thoughts right here in my Seattle home.

"We did it, Emily. We told your story. Our story. Before you know it, it will be out there where hundreds—maybe even thousands—of people can read it....They'll hear your words again, almost as if you were still here."

My mind floods with words Emily penned one November evening in 1885, just two years before her death. I can hear them now, loud and strong, as if she is standing—smiling—in this very room...

"Oh how grand it would be if one could live two hundred years, live to see the wonders wrought, to see the progress in art & science. Not for mere life alone. It almost enraptures us in reverie of thought to even have an idea of such a life..."

Now it's my turn to smile.

"Maybe you will live two hundred years, Emily... maybe we both will."

It has all come together—just as it was meant to. Those little grains of sand piling up. Changing the course of my life, one day at a time.

A trip, a trunk, and a diary—all now transformed into the book I've been waiting all my life to write.

It's nearly time to go, but before I head out the door, I remember a call I need to make—to the one person I'd promised to tell as soon as something happened with the book. Pulling my phone from my purse, I tap out a few numbers and wait for an answer.

"Hello, Alex? It's Liz."

His deep voice rumbles through the phone, and I answer, "Merry Christmas to you, too! It has been awhile."

Almost giddy with my news, I pause and take a deep breath, hoping to quiet my thundering heart.

"Hey, do you still want that copy of my book? Well, I just got a very exciting letter from a publisher, and I think I'll be able to arrange it for you before too much longer."

And with a certain pair of bright blue eyes dancing through my mind, I add one final thought.

"I might even be able to deliver it in person..."

Acknowledgements

In spite of all the hours spent alone, huddled over notebook or keyboard, no writer works in a vacuum—and believe me, I am no different. There are so many people who had a hand (or at least a finger or two) in the creation of this novel, I'm not sure how to begin to thank them all, but I'll do my best.

My humblest and happiest thanks to—

My thesis committee—Michael Kula, Judy Temple, Andrea Modarres, and Nicole Blair—for working with me on this project and helping me turn my story from something only I could love into a book worth reading. Thank you all—*so very much!*

My writing group—Kari, Tom and Peter. Thank you for reading countless drafts, listening to me talk (*and talk and talk...*) about diaries, stories, trips to Iowa—and Emily. You guys rock!

My "outside" readers—Patty, Sandi, Linda, Katy, and Cindy. Thank you for the suggestions, corrections, finding all my typos and plot holes—and for all your generous words of encouragement. You truly gave me the inspiration to get this book done.

My sister Kathie, who accompanied me on my research trip to Iowa. Thank you for playing assistant and spending your vacation pursuing *my* dreams—poring over Emily's diaries, poetry, sketches, and knick-knacks; tromping through fields and barns; chasing down Amish buggies with a camera (ok, that was all you!); putting up with mosquitos while we watched for fireflies and visited Emily's grave, and showing an amazing amount of enthusiasm over my project. I love you, and I'm still sorry we didn't make it to Wisconsin.

Wilbur Kehrli, for playing host at Emily's farm—allowing me to photograph nearly every inch of his home—showing us around Manchester, and then becoming our tour guide through the better part of NE Iowa, all the way to the Mississippi River. Wilbur, you were an invaluable source of information and inspiration, a charming host, and even inspired a key player in the novel, helping Lizzie to find her story—and herself. Thank you!

The wonderful people at the State Historical Society of Iowa Archives in Iowa City—Mary Bennett, Charles Scott, and Paula Smith. You had boxes full of Emily's papers waiting for me when I arrived, taught me to use a microfilm machine, and allowed me to dig through anything with Emily's name on it—taking pictures to my heart's content (wearing the appropriate gloves, of course)—to excavate items that had once belonged to Emily and her family, many of which found their way into the trunk Lizzie finds in the attic. You were all amazing, and I can never thank you enough for your help.

The Golden Key International Honour Society for the generous research grant. Without it, I would never have been able to make the trip to Iowa—and my novel would be a much sadder thing.

Anna Salyer and UW Tacoma's amazing troupe of librarians who walked with me every step of the research path.

Amy and Kylie—"I count myself in nothing else so happy..." as in your friendship (with additional thanks to our old friend, Will S).

My family—sons Eric and Ryan, daughter-in-law Naomi, and grandchildren (Keegan, Sage, Elijah, Cedar, Legacy, Harmony, Mason, Scout, Felíz, and Ransom)—who encouraged me to write this book and are undoubtedly thrilled I actually finished.

My parents—who always cheered my successes. (I miss you Mom!)

My wonderful and one-of-kind husband, Ralph, who took over hearth and home (and laundry) to allow me to follow my dreams—wherever they led. You are my rock, and I literally could not have done *any* of this without you. I love you, forever!

And last—but definitely not least—Emily herself, for considering her life worth remembering, for being a cooperative subject, and for acting as my muse throughout the entire project.

To each and every one of you, I am eternally grateful!

Biography

"Life in Continuous Present" may be Margaret Lundberg's first novel, but it is not her first book. At the tender age of ten, she wrote a memoir detailing her life thus far—four years of adventure found in the company of her sister and two best friends. Although that first book remains unpublished, Lundberg never gave up on the dream that one day she would become a "real" writer.

Fast forward a few decades—following a twenty year career as a decorative artist—Lundberg returned to college in 2009 to finish the degree she left behind in marrying and raising her two sons. Focusing on writing in both her undergraduate and graduate years, she had several non-fiction pieces and research articles published, whetting her appetite for even more types of writing. As the culmination of nearly six years spent earning two degrees, Lundberg penned this novel as the quintessence of her MA thesis research involving 19th century diarists and their creation of identity through audience awareness. Finding Emily Gillespie's diary—almost by accident— sent her on a journey through time and across the country, from Washington state to her own mother's birthplace of Iowa, in search of the woman behind Gillespie's words.

Lundberg is currently in the early stages of writing her second novel, and admits that although her "Life in Continuous Present" protagonist's life is almost nothing like her own, she does share her fascination with time travel.

Lundberg currently works for the School of Interdisciplinary Arts and Sciences at the University of Washington Tacoma. When she isn't writing, she indulges her love for Bollywood movies, and books about…well, pretty much anything. Lundberg lives in University Place, WA with her handsome, blue-eyed husband, Ralph—and is the proud grandmother of ten exceptional grandchildren.

Made in the USA
Las Vegas, NV
15 December 2020